Maybe Next Time

Also by Cesca Major

Writing as C.D. Major

The Silent Hours

The Last Night

The Other Girl

The Thin Place

Writing as Rosie Blake

How to Get a (Love) Life

How to Stuff Up Christmas

How to Find Your (First) Husband

The Hygge Holiday

The Gin O'Clock Club

Writing as Ruby Hummingbird

The Wish List of Albie Young

The Garden of Lost Memories

Maybe Next Time

A Novel

Cesca Major

wm
WILLIAM MORROW
An Imprint of HarperCollins*Publishers*

This is a work of fiction. Names, characters, places, and incidents are products of the author's imagination or are used fictitiously and are not to be construed as real. Any resemblance to actual events, locales, organizations, or persons, living or dead, is entirely coincidental.

HarperCollins books may be purchased for educational, business, or sales promotional use. For information, please email the Special Markets Department at SPsales@harpercollins.com.

FIRST US EDITION

Library of Congress Cataloging-in-Publication Data has been applied for.

ISBN 978-0-06-323992-0

23 24 25 26 27 LBC 6 5 4 3 2

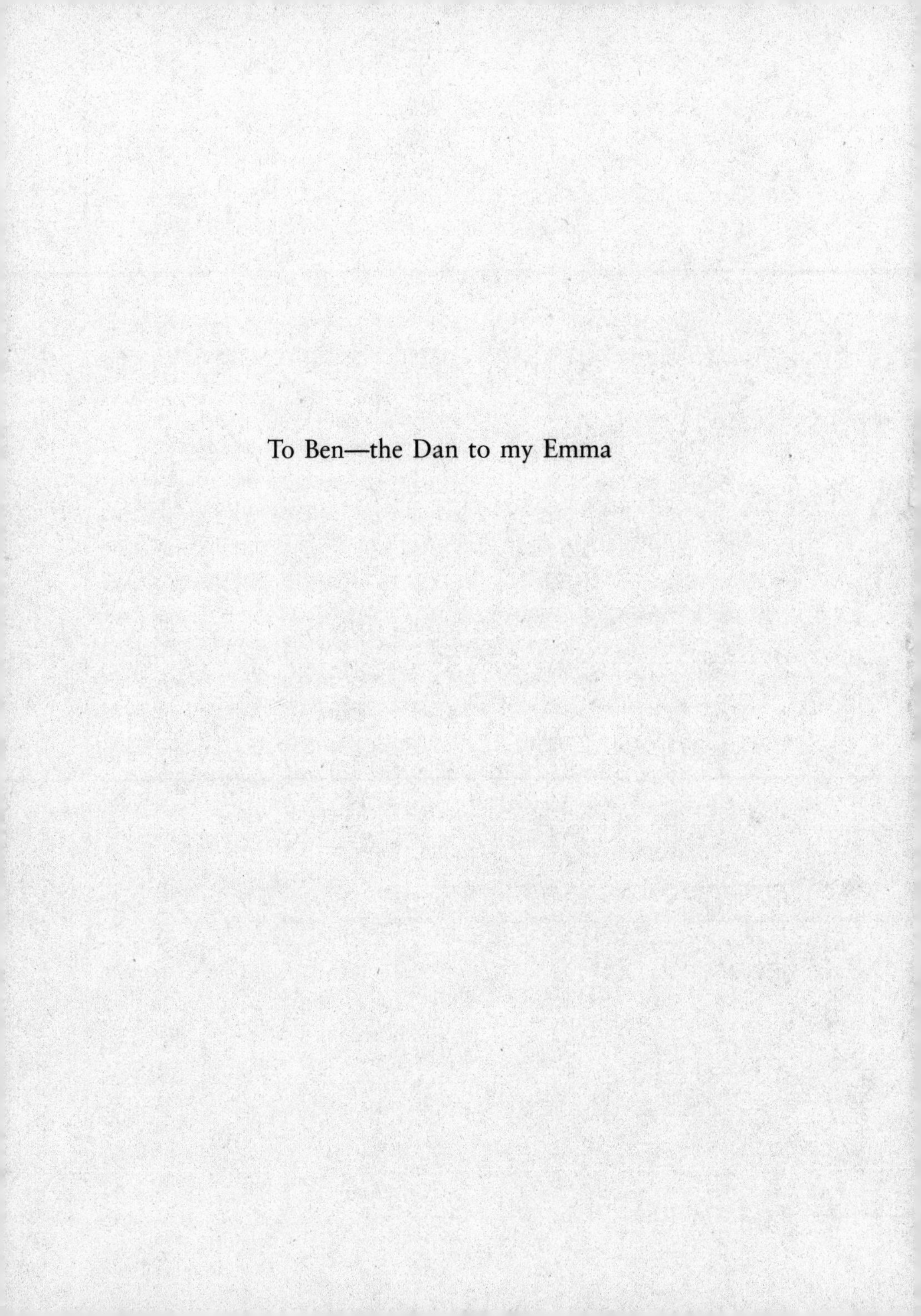

To Ben—the Dan to my Emma

Be where you are; otherwise you will miss your life.

Buddha

PART 1

1

3rd December 2007

Dear Emma,
If it were up to me we'd celebrate our anniversary on the day of our first date. But of course, you want to mark it today. You love telling people this story.

Did you know I actually spotted you first on that crammed tube? I remember seeing you in your black turtleneck, the now-familiar red lipstick, your raven hair tied up into that twisty thing you do. But I glanced away because a) I didn't want to be Creepy Tube Guy and b) I was dressed as an extra in The Sound of Music.

I was so aware of you as the tube rumbled on. Jules said something funny and you did this incredible soft laugh. I couldn't help peeking up again. When you met my look, I remember the shock of feeling that ran down my spine.

I tried to concentrate on something else, cursing work's Fancy Dress Friday and feeling so wrong-footed in my lederhosen and Tyrolean hat. Not that I'd have been brave enough to do anything. And anyway I was sure you'd be with someone already. A man equally chic—who'd wear perfectly cut suits, speak three languages, be great with kids, love animals, and have a massive knob.

But fate intervened when the train jerked and I stumbled, missing the pole with my hand. My Tyrolean hat fell off and rolled to a stop by your shiny, brown laced boots. I was gushing sorry and kneeling in front of you in lederhosen with Jules laughing and saying, "Guten tag," *when you gave me that first smile: pity obviously, because I was a man who couldn't even stand normally in a tube. Your boyfriend would stand really straight and still in a tube.*

"It's a nice hat." The first words you said to me. Your voice was confident, smooth, and I found myself worrying if my hair was flat as I placed it back on my head. I'd never worried if my hair was flat before. Speak, man, I thought. Speak. I wished I'd plumped for something other than "Thanks".

I remember feeling sad I'd missed my chance, that my exit was two stops away and now I would leave and you'd disappear on the Central Line out of my life. I'd never know what you were like, whether this electric feeling I had was a real one. But then you looked across at me and asked if I knew any good German markets. If I could write one down. The woman two seats down from you smiled into her book.

And I thought YES—I think this intriguing woman wants my number (or she thinks I'm actually German and genuinely wants to know about German markets). I felt flustered as I patted my pockets for my pen and my A6 notebook (and, no, I don't think it's that weird a thing to carry around—but I do wish Hattie hadn't told you I used to record bird species in it. Thanks for that, sis). But I didn't have it, only a pen, a 50p piece, a crumpled receipt, and my house keys.

I smoothed out the back of the receipt from Boots and quickly scrawled my number. Then I went over it twice which I worried made me look a bit psycho but I thought I'd made the seven look like a one.

The row of pastel-colored terraced houses that signaled we'd soon be slowing to a stop at my station flashed past the window behind you. I went a fraction too early, clumsily thrusting the Boots receipt in front of you. "If you want to go to a market," I said. Your mouth broke into a smile and I felt a glow in my chest. I was about to return the smile when I froze, suddenly remembering the last time I'd been to Boots.

But it was too late. You'd taken it. It was now in your hand. You were still smiling like it was a Good Thing. Jules was smiling like it was a Good Thing. The woman two seats down was smiling like it was a Good Thing.

Holy shit.

I wanted to snatch it straight back. Your purple nail varnish swam in front of me as I panicked. My mum had asked me to pick up some more Anusol for her piles. Oh my God. I'd written my number on the back of a receipt for Anusol.

Numbness spread down my body as I wondered whether to say something about the Anusol, that it wasn't for me.

I was frantically casting about for something to say, anything to distract. Your boots. I'd liked your lace-up boots. THAT WAS WHAT I WANTED TO SAY, *your* BOOTS. I OBVIOUSLY DIDN'T MEAN TO SAY ALOUD "I LIKE YOUR BOOBS."

Oh God, the sheer fucking horror of that moment.

The little widening of your eyes before I started stammering "YOUR BOOTS, YOUR BOOTS," like I had shoe-based Tourette's. I'd never blushed in my life but I could feel my face burning up like I had LAVA inside of me. And you were amazing when you laughed and tried to defuse my embarrassment.

BUT OF COURSE the tube decided THAT was the moment to squeal to a random halt. I could literally SEE the end of the platform out of the window. Freedom from this nightmare I was stuck in.

"My stop," I squeaked. An actual squeak. A sound I wasn't even sure I could make. "Home," I said. Because apparently I didn't talk in sentences anymore. Maybe I could smash my way out with the little hammer?

Jules and the woman two seats down were openly laughing at me.

My face reflected in the glass was a wide-eyed ghost even as you were thanking me for the receipt.

I just nodded, so grateful to you for trying to be nice, trying to be normal: it made me like you even more. Not that I said that because I was mute now: it was unlikely I would ever be able to speak to a woman again.

The tube juddered and the next moment it had stopped at the platform, the doors slid open, and I practically dived through them.

As the carriage moved away, I glanced back and, just before you were lost to my sight, you craned your neck round and grinned at me.

God, I remember that whole evening being torturous, pretending to Dave I was cool if you didn't call but constantly checking my phone like I was fourteen years old again, checking my pager. That smile, that amused sparkle in your eyes. And you did message me, late, just before bed, the screen lighting up my bedroom, hope a shade of ghostly blue.

"How normal are you compared to today? 1 being completely normal, BORINGLY so; 10 being, well, like you were today?"

I laughed, and we swapped messages and, when you'd established I might not want to pickle you and keep you in a jar, we arranged to meet and God you were sensational and I literally haven't looked back.

It's completely typical of you that you want to force me to remember that day. Hattie said she peed herself a little when you recounted it to her a few months later.

So, despite regular winking and sheep-throwing on Facebook, you wanted us to be romantic and the idea for these letters was born. I can't wait to read yours.

Right, what has been awesome about the year and being with you?

Our nights out in Camden, obviously—comedy nights, plays, dancing, sawdust, sweat, red wine.

The way you continue to thrust books on me because you don't trust people that don't read.

The way my friends love you too (and my parents—although my mum told me after you'd first met that she liked you more than me which is Too Far).

The surprise Eurostar picnic.

That Suffolk coastal walk in torrential rain (we were so brave).

I keep waiting for it to go wrong. For you to expose yourself as a closet racist or a hoarder of weird junk. But, although you surprise me all the time (who knew you loved darts and collected shitloads of shells?), I'm always hit over the head again by my sheer luck in meeting you.

You said I love you on 17th August (See? We could make THAT our Dateversary) and I still attest I said it first and you didn't hear me. Your hearing is actually one of the things I'd criticize about you. Sometimes it's like you're dragging yourself back from another place entirely.

I do love you though, Emma, you're amazing. I've never been more glad of a decision in my whole life, horrifying though the memory is. Thank God for that Boots receipt.

Here's to one year together.

Dan x x

P.S. OK, this was a really cool idea.

2

Monday, 3rd December 2021—10 p.m.

Dan noticed it immediately. "That was *not* there before."

"Hmm . . . ?"

Dan pointed at the folded piece of paper on the kitchen countertop, his name hastily printed on the front. Without a word he crossed the room, put on his reading glasses, and unfolded the sheet. Not a flicker on his face betrayed his emotions as he scanned it. He lowered his hand slowly. "You just wrote this when you went to the loo."

I put a hand to my chest. "I can't believe you'd say that!" (OK, I had, I totally had.)

"Admit it!"

"I had it in my bag all day. So, I just *put* it there while you were gone."

"I don't believe you, Emma."

"I'm your wife, Daniel," I said, which didn't really make sense and I'd only added his name because he'd added mine.

He waved the paper. "You misspelled affection."

"It's a tricky word," I stuttered.

"And it's three lines long."

I scoffed, "I don't always have to write really *long* letters. I thought this year I'd—"

"Emma." He cut me off, his voice stern; Dan rarely sounded stern. If it had been a lighter moment I might have commented that it was quite sexy. "Just admit it, you forgot . . . again."

Oh God. I licked my lips, wanting to buy myself time. Last year he'd been so gutted. And it had shocked me into action. I had promised—*promised*—I'd do better. It had been my idea all those years ago and my early letters had often been six pages long, "front *and* back" as he used to tease. Why hadn't I put a reminder in my phone? Or asked Hattie to remind me? Or one of the kids? Or just remembered like a nice, decent, thoughtful human? Like Dan had . . .

His brown eyes were sad: magnified by the new reading glasses he loathed ("Reading glasses! I'm forty-two, Emma!"): he was hurt. Again.

I wasn't sure why I chose to go on the attack instead. "Why are you making such a big deal about this?"

He curled his fists, crumpling the hastily written note in his hand. "Because it *is* a big deal. Or . . ." he paused. "I thought it was. Maybe you don't . . ." He raised his head and I was shocked to see tears film his eyes.

"Dan, don't be like that."

"I'm not being like anything. I'm allowed to be bloody sad."

"Mum? Dad?" A small voice from the top of the stairs. Both of us swiveling toward the sound.

"God, you've woken the kids." Guilt made me lash out. I moved to the kitchen door, saw Miles at the top, clutching his favorite Tigger to his chest—even at eight years old he couldn't really sleep without him. "Hi darling, go back to bed. I'll pop up and tuck you in in a minute."

"Were you fighting?"

I shook my head, pain stabbing my chest. Memories of my own childhood fears when I'd heard the regular rows between my parents late at night floored me for a moment. "No, darling," I choked and forced a smile. "It was the telly. Night, night . . ."

I returned to find Dan in his coat and shoes, forcing a leash on a reluctant, whining Gus.

"He's been a bit off," I said, hoping to divert from the row.

"Come on, Gus," Dan snapped, standing up.

Definitely still angry. Normally he would have asked what Miles wanted, offered to pop up and see him, but instead he couldn't meet my eye, had wrapped the leash around his fist, knuckles white.

It felt strange. Dan never got angry. *I* got angry, I was the one to swear when I scalded myself or flew off the handle over the fact I'd forgotten recycling day or some company had put me on hold, or when my parents made another excuse as to why they couldn't visit. Dan was a pretty placid guy but tonight his jaw was rigid, his muscles tense as if he was about to explode.

Gus, crouched low, his nose almost touching the floor, resisted Dan's tug on the leash with a whimper.

"Don't pull on him like that . . ."

"I'm not pulling on him. Gus, come on."

Dan scooped up a barking Gus and carried him out of the house anyway. The door slammed.

Cradling my head in my hands, I stood there. Christ. This was all my fault. I should have just apologized.

I needed to fix this.

"Mum," Miles's sleepy voice called from the landing.

Shit.

"Hey darling," I half-whispered. "Sorry, Dad went out with Gus, I'll come up and tuck you in, in a sec."

He returned to his room.

I looked around the kitchen at the detritus of our meal. Dan had cooked chicken thighs in tarragon sauce, the envelope that had started this whole thing was by my place setting—my name written in black ink, a little heart just above the "a." I was nervous of that letter too. Dan's could be funny, loving, but they were always honest. And this year I was scared of honest. I was about to go upstairs when I heard it.

My skin broke into goosebumps as my head turned toward the door.

What *was* that?

Oh my God.

3

15 hours earlier . . .

I was on my side, facing the window.

The sound of a bicycle bell.

I opened my eyes and winced. A slight crack in the curtains, a shaft of sunlight crossing my face.

I turned over.

"Hey," he said.

I was about to smile, about to say "hey" back. But the digital clock blinked behind him and I sat up so suddenly I felt dizzy.

"Shit."

Dan sat up too. "What?"

"Hold on," I said. "Headrush. I thought I set an alarm for earlier."

Dan scooched back down, watching me as I crossed the room, "Come back to bed, Emma. The kids aren't even up yet."

"I can't."

Something unreadable crossed Dan's face as I glanced over at him. "You've got time."

"I really don—Ow." My hip knocked into the post of our bed.

"Are you all right?" Dan reached for me.

"I'm fine." Rubbing my hip, I moved across to our chest of drawers to unplug my mobile from its charge. I was already scrolling as I stepped inside our en suite.

"Oh for . . ."

"What is it?" Dan called.

"No loo roll."

He didn't reply. I rolled my eyes and stood up, turning on the shower. Placing my mobile on the side of the sink, I frowned at the dusting of orange in the basin. What was that from? I peered closer, brushing at the tiny dots with a hand.

A Facebook message pinged. I groaned inwardly as I saw the name. A woman who was meant to be picking up my practically unused fold-up bike—a fortieth birthday present I'd used about once in two years—wanted to rearrange the time of pickup. Again. This woman had canceled on me almost every day for what felt like my whole life. The entire family had been squeezing past it in the hall for the last two weeks. I wondered if it was all worth the £50 I'd sold it for on the local Facebook mums' group. I sent a thumbs-up back.

The mirror was steaming up by the time I put down the mobile and pulled off my pajamas. I needed to book another hair appointment; as I tied my shoulder-length hair back, fine gray hairs emerged among the black, and it was less than a month since I'd last dyed it. Catching sight of my face before it disappeared in the fog, I frowned—was that a new line? Did I need Botox? My client, Scarlet, had told me about a Viscoderm filler that was better. And what was the vitamin that was good for skin? D? B? Was B the one for hair?

"Ow," I twisted and turned down the shower. Oh my God, why did Dan have to scald himself every time he washed?

Moments later I emerged, the sound of a child thundering past our bedroom door. It had to be Miles—eight years old but already the same size as Poppy. Rifling through the pile of clothes on a chair I pulled out a rumpled white shirt and burgundy corduroy high-waisted skirt. But who had time to iron? Boots? Heels? I sat on the edge of the bed, rolling up tights, leaning back to glimpse the weather out of the window. No rain, so I reached for the heels.

Some weird music, a few words, were coming from Poppy's bedroom and I glanced up, about to call to her. She needed to eat breakfast before school. Beach photos on Instagram pulled my eyes back to the screen—God, wasn't Amelia's book due tomorrow? This week certainly. There she was in a hammock with a bright red cocktail, then jumping in the air on a white sand shore. Hashtag blessed.

I switched to Twitter—zipping down the endless angry political tweets to see if there was any book news. Christ, the Arthur tweet was up to over 1.2k likes and 391 retweets. My insides lurched in panic; what would this mean for today?

I drifted to the door, still scrolling. An editor I knew was moving publishing houses; I should take her for lunch and see what she might be looking for.

"Poppy," I shouted, voice half-hearted as my eyes froze on an article from *The Bookseller*. An announcement about a new book from a big-name author that sounded scarily like something I'd been excited about last week in my submission pile.

Clattering into the kitchen I opened the fridge, glancing down at Gus who was lying in his fleece bed. "All right for some," I said. He didn't raise his head of springy curls, his bowl of food untouched at his head.

A cough at the table and I noticed Miles in his school uniform staring at a dry bowl of cornflakes. "You all right?"

"Dad left for milk."

The door opened as he spoke and Dan emerged, unshaven, cheeks flushed, thick brown hair sticking up at every angle, holding a carrier bag. "Here you go," he slid the milk bottle over to Miles who barely smiled in acknowledgment.

My phone pinged again before I could finish my thought. "Oh my God, did I tell you that bike woman has canceled again?"

Dan slid a hand around my waist, his chin brushing the side of my head as he handed me a brown paper bag. "Cinnamon swirl."

"Thanks . . . and the Arthur stuff has got worse overnight. Some big-name authors in the US have been retweeting it. Christ. Oh, and also Amelia is in the Maldives, look." I twisted, waving the phone in his face. "Some resort where dolphins bring you breakfast or something," the screen was a flash of turquoise. Dan quite enjoyed my Amelia stories—a celebrity from a popular show about London socialites—she had over a million followers and the publisher who'd bought her vegan cookbook was waiting on her first novel. "I hope Claire doesn't see this; she's already given her two extensions."

Momentarily wondering why Dan seemed so quiet, I turned to Miles. "Oh, and Miles . . . TEDDIES."

Both Dan and Miles jumped.

"Sorry," I adjusted the volume, my brain flying off in five different directions. "Have you got any old soft toys for the Teddy Bear Raffle? Dan—did we put them all in the loft or chuck them?"

Where I would hoard, Dan would organize. He had box files in assorted colors, used those tiny sticky circles so that paper never ripped. I mean, the man had a special box for missing buttons and a laminated dumpster permit.

Dan slumped into a kitchen chair opposite Miles. "Why are you organizing that again? They left playgroup years ago."

"I know but, well, I've promised now." I glanced down, the playgroup thread on WhatsApp already had thirty-seven notifications. Dan was right, of course, I'd told him I would step down, but no one had offered to take my place. It had been such a lifeline for me in those crazy early years. Respite from the chucking meals on the floor, endless night-time visits for a pacifier/bad dream/water/cuddle/pee, Peppa Pig on a hideous loop so you found yourself humming the theme tune at any given moment. It was about the only affordable option in our area with flexible hours: they needed volunteers.

I avoided his eye and collected up my things for work, not forgetting the vital papers printed off late last night. My stomach rolled as I thought of the morning ahead. I looked at my mobile again, still no text from the taxi company. I saw another message though, "Oh, you remember Jacob, Miles? He went to playgroup with you. His mum says they're moving to Surrey. I said we should have them over before they go."

Miles lifted dull eyes to me.

"Are you feeling all right, buddy?" Dan asked, reaching across the table to place a hand on his forehead. Miles shrugged him off with a huff. I met Dan's eyes; Miles was never irritable. It was bad enough having one child who seemed to already be acting like a teen despite being a few months off turning eleven.

Dan bent down to pat Gus as I grabbed at my wallet, checked my handbag. "You all right, boy? Off your food?"

"Oh for . . ." Checking the clock as I picked up my keys, I

moaned, "I have to go to the office before the meeting. Poppy needs to get down here or she won't have time to eat."

Dan straightened. "I'll sort them, you can go. I'm starting later this morning, remember? I've just got to be in by eleven for that meeting with the new client." He paused after he said it, as if he was leaving a gap for something.

"Great." I blew him a kiss, his expression strange as he sat back down. I reached down to ruffle Miles's mop of hair.

"Love you both," I called from the hallway. "Ask Poppy about the teddies, OK?" I heard her thundering down the stairs, "POPPY," I yelled, "ASK DAD TO TALK TO YOU ABOUT TEDDIES, OK . . ."

Poppy appeared on the landing above me, long hair uncombed, white shirt loose, skinny legs in a tartan school skirt. "Where's my blazer?" she asked.

"Hey, ask Dad," I called, stretching to get my coat from its hook; the handlebars of my bike dug into my side. "For fuc—" God, why didn't that woman pick it up already? I could put it back in the loft, or do that Freecycle thing. "DAN. Poppy needs her blazer, and I'll text you later about food for the kids' tea, all right? I could make toad-in-the-hole?" I shouted, already opening the door to the street, mobile stuffed into my coat pocket, mind already on the commute. I could read that submission I'd started yesterday on the tube.

A voice called back, "You forgot your cinnam—" but I'd already slammed the door.

Denise @CommitteeChat 6:30pm tonight. Please don't be late.

Catrin @Emma Denise is totally referencing you.

Denise @CommitteeChat The rota states that Emma will be taking the minutes this evening.

Catrin @Emma God forbid you fuck up the rota. Lol.

AuthorLou @Emma Sorry it's early. And you so don't need to reply quickly. I don't want to be *that* author. I've just been on Amazon and I've got 2 new reviews today! But one of them was a 1 star that said the binding is loose and I was wondering if I need to ask Amazon to take it down?

AuthorLou @Emma Sorry! Should have added it to my last message. So I've just been on Goodreads and someone has 1 starred it saying that they think Carl is a bit rapey. Do you think I should mark their review as offensive?

AuthorLou @Emma He's not rapey is he?

AuthorLou @Emma Sorry! Last one I promise! Should I worry that I've got no reviews yet on the Waterstones site? I've checked other authors who had books out in the same week as me and some have got over three so far. Does it matter?

Jas @Emma Gah have you seen Amelia's Instagram? I want to be her.

Hattie @Emma Time for a catch-up at lunch?

Poppy @Mum Dad says he doesn't know where my blazer is.

4

The moment I left the house I thought of thirty things I needed to tell Dan and texted him as I walked.

"I think her blazer might be on the hook in the downstairs loo."

"Tell Miles to remember his homework!"

"He might need gloves too."

"Can you defrost some sausages?"

Normally he'd reply with a teasing emoji or a *"Yes your majesty"* but today I got a terse *"OK."* Frowning, I looked at the two letters. What was up with him?

Christ, had I remembered the papers I'd printed off for the meeting? Had the taxi sent a confirmation? Oh, did I make toad-in-the-hole on Saturday too?

The tube was just over the road and I stepped off the pavement. The sound of a bell, a shout and I lurched backward as a cyclist swerved round me. My heel caught in the drain and I panicked as I reached to free it.

"For fuck . . ." The cyclist glared over his shoulder.

Heart pounding, I put my phone away, pausing to calm my breathing and take extra care to look right then left before crossing.

As I pushed through the turnstile the back of my left heel was rubbing against the stiff leather. Why hadn't I worn the boots?

Standing on the escalator, the smell of onions and damp around me, I stared at the other commuters in a range of different coats, clutching bags, zipping up rucksacks. Another Monday, another ordinary day. How many of these faces had I unwittingly stared at on other Mondays? I pulled out my phone once more, a window of time to draft some replies to things.

Forty-two Committee notifications now, two more WhatsApp messages from Lou, whose first novel had been out for two weeks. Why didn't I have a specific work phone? She loved a panicked WhatsApp message. And an email. And a phone call. I started to type.

The tube spat me out as I tapped and I moved in the flow of commuters up and out, blinking at the shock of the milky blue sky. Walking quickly toward the agency, I stopped at the small café on the corner, realizing I hadn't even had a coffee or anything to eat yet. That cinnamon swirl must still be in its bag on the kitchen counter. Oh, maybe that was why Dan was cross with me?

"Hazelnut latte, please," I said distractedly to the barista with the tattoo on his neck, a twisted symbol in black. I'd never asked what it was despite visiting the café almost every weekday.

He smiled at me, a gap between his two front teeth which always reminded me of Poppy, "And a blueberry muffin?"

"All right," I mumbled, realizing how often I ordered the two things, a creature of habit. God, when had I become that? "Thanks . . ." I trailed off, realizing I should really ask his name. Would it be too embarrassing though? To ask now after he must be handing me about my thousandth muffin? I pulled out my mobile again.

"Oh, skimmed milk," I added quickly, looking back up, remembering Amelia star-jumping on the beach that morning. Like skimmed milk would combat the hazelnut syrup hit. I really needed to lose the half stone, fine, stone, I'd put on in the last couple of years since turning forty. But who has the time to sign up for a gym? Or go running? Or just fit in exercise in the endless list of things to do in the day.

I saw a message from Hattie about lunch and bit my lip. I'd *love* to see Hattie for lunch but could I really take an hour for it? This meeting from hell was lined up and Linda had insisted we meet at the office first, which just added more time. And I was always making Hattie head to Hammersmith so that I could nip out of the office when she worked from home in Wimbledon. She said she didn't mind, the tech company she worked for in Silicon Valley were chill and she tended to work later in the day so her mornings were less full, but it wasn't fair on her. I left the message unopened so Hattie wouldn't see I'd read it. When had I even last seen her? It'd been ages for us, way too long and I missed her: I'd definitely reply when I knew what my day looked like.

Christ, I had twenty-seven emails already and I'd only checked them last night before bed. My chest squeezed a little. Grabbing my bag and coffee, I headed out of the café with a shouted thanks.

Sneaking quietly into our office, a peeling white building sandwiched between two larger, glass-fronted offices, I glanced at the coat rack, relieved to see it empty. Dread pitted in my stomach at the thought of the morning ahead. Would the stuff I'd put together be enough?

I squeezed down the hallway still in my coat, my bag brushing the books stacked in precarious towers that lined the walls.

I'd only answered three emails—two of them rejections for Scarlet's latest book, currently out on submission—before getting interrupted by the buzzer.

Scarlet had been my first signing. In among being a mum to two teens and supporting her ill husband with teaching work, she still produced wonderful novels; she could plumb the depths of emotion like no one else. I knew I needed to phone her, to update her. A new book deal would restore her faltering confidence. I would check in later; reassure her we still had options.

The buzzer went again and the car purring in the narrow one-way street was the taxi I'd booked. Grabbing my bag and slamming the front door behind me, I wondered how I could delay him. As I was lifting my mobile to my ear to phone Linda I saw them, walking along the pavement, arms linked as if they were a retired couple out for a stroll, not a worry in the world.

Arthur Chumley, startling in red corduroy trousers and an unironed rust jersey, long graying gray hair curling at the collar, Linda in her favorite fur coat (mink, "vicious little things, Emma"), her hair a cloud of stiff bottle-blonde curls, lips stained red, she drew from her cigarette.

"Gemma," Arthur said, lifting my right hand to his dry lips.

"The taxi's here," I said, pointing at the waiting vehicle with my left, another car stopping just behind it.

"We had to go out for coffee—Jasmina offered Arthur instant," Linda said with an eye roll, lipstick on her front tooth. "Imagine! He can't abide granules."

"We really do need to get on . . ." I said, quickly extracting my hand from our most successful client's clutches. The hand that pretty much paid all our wages. Ten million copies worldwide, a successful nineties TV series, creator of the world's most famous one-armed alcoholic detective. He'd been one of Linda's first acquisitions when she started the agency forty years ago, and even though I was no longer her assistant, I was still called on for all matters relating to his publishing. It felt like both Linda and Arthur wanted a subordinate, solidifying their own opinion that he was the most important author out there. It was a role I'd tried, and failed, to get out of playing.

"Do we have to go?" Arthur pouted. "I'd much rather take you beautiful ladies out to lunch."

"Oh Arthur," Linda pealed, stubbing her cigarette out on the pavement. "So naughty," she said. "It *is* an absolute bore. But Emma here has *assured* me she's got it all under control."

I couldn't help the panicked glance in her direction. Under control? I'd spent every second since her phone call that had blown up my weekend worrying what might happen in the next couple of hours. This meeting could change everything: for the agency, for Arthur, for her, for me.

"All you need to focus on is writing us more of your wonderful books," Linda continued, oblivious to the three cars now paused in the street, the taxi driver lifting both hands in exasperation as honking filled the air.

"We really need to get on," I said, over the noise, moving toward the taxi.

"To our chariot," Arthur announced as if he was escorting us to the Oscars and not to our professional deaths.

I thought of Scarlet's rejections as I settled into the taxi, watching Arthur, who smelled of sour milk, bang his meaty thigh as he lamented the takeover of young female crime writers in the industry—"They're everywhere now"—Linda soothing him from her seat. What was I doing?

Denise @Committee Can we please acknowledge this reminder. Emma will be taking minutes. The meeting begins at 6:30pm. Carriages 8pm.

Catrin @Emma Naughty Emma. And wtf are "carriages'?

Jas @Emma Wanted to be there but got sent away in disgrace over coffee. Hope meeting goes OK and we still have jobs. See you back in the office later 😬 X X

AuthorLou @Emma Thanks for the replies. I soooo didn't think he was rapey either. Just passionate! Did you see that article this morning in The Bookseller? Apparently Mumnoir which was all the rage is now totally saturated. Agh. Do you think my book has missed the boat?

AuthorLou @Emma I just read another article in the Guardian about Mumnoir being a new thing so maybe it will be fine. Ha! Maybe I'll email Jane about it. She still hasn't replied to my email last week though about that other author's cover. Do YOU think readers will get them confused—I do think the image is really similar? Maybe we could all discuss it? I'm around loads today! Or tomorrow. Or later this week.

AuthorLou @Emma OK so on the cover thing I showed my friend this other author's cover and she thinks they're really similar too.

AuthorLou @Emma Although she did say she liked the apple on mine, the way it was rotting. Am around loads! No rush! Speak soon!

Claire @Emma Is Amelia on track to deliver? I need to brief the marketing team on this.

Hattie @Emma Lunch?

5

3rd December 2008

Dear Emma,
Two whole years. You've upgraded us from "Friends" to "In a Relationship" on Facebook so I know we're pretty serious! And I see so much more of you since Dave moved out and Hattie moved in. I thought he was cool about it but you're right, that snakeskin in my bed was probably no accident. I just couldn't let Hattie keep living with our parents—she was getting way too into jigsaws and whist.

Maybe I should be a bit jealous of your closeness to her but I like it, I know how much you miss Jules now she's in Oz. I see a different side to you when you're with Hattie—I like busting in on you both when you're "working from home" together—onesies and face masks on, laptops on standby as you make each other peal with laughter.

I'm also relieved you seem OK with the weird siblingness of us—the bickering and stories (yes, we did take Stone Club seriously, members only admitted if they could produce an unusual-looking stone). I catch you watching us sometimes with a wistful expression on your face that always makes me want to hold your hand.

You hint at the different childhoods we had. You say things casually sometimes, like the Christmas holiday you spent with Jules's family because your parents booked to go to Antigua for six weeks without you, and I'm sorry if my appalled looks derail you. But I think these stories are your way of explaining why you work through things on your own sometimes. Why you forget that you're meant to tell your boyfriend where you're going to that evening, or that weekend. I hate when you just announce plans, relief overwhelming me when I realize I'm in them too.

I know Hattie always wished I was a girl growing up. It's why I know an uncomfortable amount about women's fashion (a straight man should not know what culottes are). So it was always going to be the case that she would adopt you. She bloody loves you. She loves you for your spontaneity (that mid-week trip to Brighton, the unicycle lesson) and your kindness (picking her up from Herefordshire at 3 a.m. when Ian refused to drive her back, making her fondue when she got that HR job she so wanted).

You're nice to everyone you meet—you're always telling me about their one redeemable quality even when I think they're being a prick. "Maybe we caught them off-guard." "Maybe someone hurt them once." It's a pretty awesome trait and, of course, means that everyone you meet seems to like you. It does mean it's hard sometimes to know who you're really close to—you're still a bit of an enigma. But you look for Hattie right after you tell me news, you race to her room after work to show her an article you read that she'd love (apparently no one can know too much about

Ryan Reynolds). And I love that you want to join our strange gang—it was a good day when you became a paid-up member of Stone Club (that rose quartz in the shape of a cloud was inspired).

I know you love me. You tell me in quiet moments, you tell me casually, you tell me often. You wrote it at the end of last year's awesome letter. I sometimes read those words when I want an ego boost (Should I admit that? Is that weird?) and so I hope this letter might make you feel loved too. So here goes . . .

You make my insides go haywire when you look at me a certain way.

You fit in with my family like you were meant to be part of it. I know we can be a bit much as a foursome but my parents both adore you. Mum hasn't stopped going on about the necklace clip thing you gave her when she'd told you she struggled with losing her glasses. And if your parents don't want to spend time with us then that is their loss. Maybe it'll be easier when they're in Spain permanently, it seems to hurt you more that they are less than an hour away and might as well be on another planet.

You give me space and time when I need it. I knew I had to leave that job. I was burning out and uninspired. Strategy consultancy—not a barrel of laughs—who knew?! But leaving it was shit, and scary, and you were amazing at letting me bore on to you about whether I'd made the right decision, whether I'd ever get work again, etc., etc. AND you let me stay in my pajamas playing Xbox with (barely any) judgment. No lectures or stress or questions. Just your head on my shoulder, a hand on my leg. And saying I should shower or you wouldn't have sex with me was fair—it had been eight days.

You make me braver. I can't believe I'm writing this from an airplane. You're right though, why not? It gives us both a chance to think about what we want to do long-term while also surfing. We've been flying for five hours and I already feel I've left my worries behind. And Hattie has promised she'll keep the stone collection safe and won't sublet the flat or invite Snakey Dave back, which helps.

In less than a day it's going to be Summer in Sydney, a quick stopover with Jules, and then sixteen whole weeks of JUST US. You're currently next to me, sleeping with one of those cushy eye masks over your face, your mouth a tiny bit open and a little blow-up pillow around your neck. You look ridiculous and I am totally in love with you.

Here's to an amazing third year together.

Dan x

6

The well-lit, high-ceilinged lobby of the publishers was a relief after the taxi ride. Arthur now sat on a purple sofa directly beneath a large poster of his latest bestseller, bemoaning cancel culture and the extinction of the white male. Linda perched beside him, head nodding like the Churchill dog.

The editor who met us, Hayley, a friend who'd acquired one of my first authors, wouldn't meet my eye, which I read as a Bad Sign, even in the lift when it was clear someone had farted. No one acknowledged the rancid stench, and as we stood in that tiny steel space I knew that scent was the smell of impending doom.

I licked my dry lips, trying to order my thoughts. The agency needed Arthur's income. This meeting had to go well. If it didn't then I knew my plans for later that week would be up in smoke. And I owed it to Linda, to the agency. She'd given me my first break almost eight years ago, I needed to help her now.

Ding.

The meeting room was intimidatingly spacious. Two women were sitting at the large oval table, their grim expressions reflected in the glass top. I pulled out a chair only to realize Arthur had walked over to the floor-to-ceiling window and was gazing out at the sparkling Thames that snaked past the building. "When a man is tired of London, he is tired of life," he said, as if he was at a dinner party holding a prawn vol-au-vent. "Samuel Johnson," he finished.

Stony looks met the words and my palms dampened.

"Mr. Chumley," Melissa, CEO of Charter Publishing, eyes enlarged behind purple frames. "Thank you for coming in to see us this morning. Obviously, we would like to address the quite serious situation that arose this weekend."

"Ah, the Wokerati wanting my scalp, you mean!" Arthur pulled out a chair with a flourish. "People love to be offended these days."

"Your words *were* offensive," Melissa stated, eyes narrowed. "You wrote," she said, reading loudly from a piece of paper in front of her, "'I would much rather be stuck in bed with her, not her book. There'd be more action.'"

"I was speaking privately to another writer."

"Twitter is not private," Melissa snapped, her mouth set in a hard line.

"I realize that now," Arthur said pompously.

Linda leaned across the table. "Arthur here is obviously very sorry people could not see the joke," she said, barely containing her eye roll at him. "He has deleted the tweet that caused such a ridiculous uproar."

"Deleting it doesn't actually make it go away. It was screen-shotted hundreds of times, it's still out there," Melissa said.

"Screenshotted or not," Linda waved a hand. "Arthur sold almost a million books for you last year. What's one little chirp?"

"Tweet," I corrected in a whisper.

Linda glared at me. I knew I needed to fly to Arthur's defense too—I had the sales figures, a prepared statement to issue online, both in my bag, but I found my throat closing up.

"In the future my tweets will stick to the prospects of Leeds United and vintage cars," Arthur chuckled.

Melissa's reply was icy. "The thing is, these things are important, important to us as a company, to the author who was on the receiving end of an entirely unwarranted, disparaging remark from an established author." Her hand curled into a fist on the glass, "And it has only been ten months since the bullying allegation . . ."

"Well, if you will employ oversensitive twenty-year-olds . . ." Arthur murmured, his hand clenched around his water.

"If we don't believe you're taking these things seriously," Melissa's voice rose, "I'm afraid Charter Publishing would need to think long and hard about our current contract renewal."

I winced. If Charter pulled out now, it would leave a huge hole in the agency's finances, not to mention that after a few years of declining sales, solidified by a global pandemic, Arthur's books weren't quite the jewels they used to be. Would we be able to find him another publishing house willing to pay as much? Particularly as everyone in the industry would know Charter had dropped him and why. He'd get offers, of course, but I think both Linda and Arthur might be surprised by how much less publishers were willing to pay for someone incendiary, with falling sales and no loyalty to his fellow authors. I cleared my throat.

"Arthur knows how badly he got it wrong," I piped up. "In fact," I added, straightening my shoulders, "just on the way over, he mentioned how refreshing it was to see so many young female writers in the crime world. Didn't you, Arthur?"

A fraction of a pause, the slightest nod of his head.

"And he was telling me about a bursary scheme he'd heard of that encourages more diverse voices into the crime community."

Melissa's expression lightened, and I heard a small, sharp inhale from Linda.

"With a big name supporting it, and a generous contribution to the scheme, well . . . it seems to me an excellent way to drive forward the change he wants to see."

Melissa glanced at her two colleagues, her fist unfurling. "That is comforting to hear. Involvement in this scheme might go some way to rectifying some of the damage done."

"We could prepare a short statement to that effect," I went on, gaze steady, voice confident. "Alongside the apology, of course. And then I'm sure we will all be relieved to put this sorry business behind us."

I sat on my hands, hoping I would not be smote down by my lies. To my left, I could sense Arthur bristling but he seemed to have the good sense to stay quiet.

"Well," the pause dragged on as Melissa's colleagues stared at her, "I have to admit this is a relief." She suddenly looked a little more friendly. "We obviously want to continue this successful partnership," she said, enunciating each word carefully, "but we are also extremely aware of today's climate and do not want to be seen to not act when one of our authors so flagrantly goes against the principles we try to uphold as a company."

Arthur was getting away with it; I could feel my shoulders dropping a couple of inches.

Shame filled me as I realized my part in helping him. I thought of his words this morning, his tweet, the lack of respect, the bullying incident—a young editorial assistant who hadn't been seen since. I blinked. Was this really what I wanted?

"Well," I said, pushing back my chair, "we should probably

get on and work out the details." I wanted to get out of this room before the bubble burst. "Linda?" I turned brightly.

Linda stood, her expression stony.

Arthur glanced across at her. And then, when she said nothing and followed me to the door, his back stiffened, a vein going in his neck as he stalked out.

Me @Dan Have we got any zucchini? The kids are really bored of peas.

Me @Dan Meeting was fine though, thanks for asking.

Me @Dan Dan . . . ?

7

Arthur was livid, sulking all the way down in the lift and refusing to share a taxi back to the office with me. "Promising my own money. Muzzling me. Women everywhere in publishing. They won't be satisfied till we're all out."

Linda was glaring at me as she followed him into the taxi. "I'll take Arthur back alone."

I wilted on the pavement. Did they have no idea what might have happened? Did she really not understand what I'd potentially stopped?

"Emma has somewhere else to be," Linda said pointedly.

I opened my mouth to fight back but the words were lost as Linda closed the door of the taxi. Sometimes I still felt like the grateful assistant she'd first hired. *Find your backbone, Emma.*

Setting off for the tube station, the rub from my heel shooting pain up my leg, I pulled my mobile from my bag out of habit. I had two missed calls and a voicemail from Hattie.

"Just calling about lunch? Or just a coffee if you can grab some time?"

Guiltily I stared at her name. What I wouldn't give to see her face. I knew how lucky I was that my sister-in-law also happened to be my favorite friend. If I rang her now and told her about my heel no doubt she'd appear with a pack of Band-Aids. She didn't normally chase me like this. It really had been too long.

Ping ping ping.

"*I'm sorry*," I typed, watching my emails rise, my messages ignite. And then there was the Arthur statement to sort. "*Busy workday. Soon though, I miss you*," I added.

Her reply was almost immediate. "*How about this evening?*"

"*Committee meeting, sorry,*" I typed.

"*OK. Tomorrow?*"

"*Sure.*"

Staring at the reply, I bit my lip. I should phone her. Now that I thought about it I hadn't seen Hattie in weeks, not since that tense Sunday lunch at their house. I really needed to help smooth things over with Dan and Ed. Ed had only been making a joke about Hattie getting under his feet and Hattie had laughed. I don't know why Dan had to make it so awkward. I didn't see Ed's expression but Dan might have misread the look; he can be a bit paranoid when it comes to Ed, I think.

My WhatsApps drew my attention away.

"Oh for . . ."

"Hi, Emu I've been soooooo busy I'm not sure I'm going to be able to send it this week. Could you let them know? I just need a little bit more time. Thanks so much. Kisses. Amelia."

Now I had to mollify her editor. Great. I stuffed my mobile back and plunged back into the tube station, already drafting a reply in my head.

Small relief on opening the office to discover an empty coat hook: Linda would have swept Arthur off for a liquid lunch.

I headed down the dark hallway to the small bathroom under the stairs. It happened so quickly. I opened the door, reached for the light just as I saw the figure lurking in the darkness. I screamed, the figure screamed, there was a flash of light—

"EMMA."

"FUCK."

The figure was clutching a mobile phone; the figure was my colleague Jas who was inexplicably standing in the dark in the bathroom. As I looked down I saw letters and books on the closed lid of the loo.

"Jas," I said, hand on my heaving chest, "what the actual . . . What are you doing?"

"I was hiding," Jas said. "I heard them upstairs—quite ranty—and they called out so I hid—you know she only uses the bathroom on the first floor—and then I thought they'd gone but I wasn't absolutely sure and then I got obsessed with this submission on my phone. It's YA—witches but like, so not cliché, and I think it might be really good or the worst thing ever but I want to read on which is good, right? You always say if you want to turn the page then that's good. The protagonist though, gah, she is making some pooooor decisions and . . ."

"Oh my God, Jas, shut up. I really need the loo." I hopped on the spot.

"Ha." Jas bent to scoop up the letters and the books before squeezing past me, her mustard-yellow chunky knit sweater catching on the handle. "Sorry."

I locked the door, lifted the lid, and sat down.

"I'll make you a coffee," she shouted from next door. "I got new pods because apparently Arthur can't abide granules."

"That's a terrible impression of her," I said as I stepped out of the loo. "It's more nasally. Abiiiide. Listen . . . abide."

Jas started laughing as she ripped open a box of capsules.

"So, how did the meeting go? Have you seen Twitter? People are still retweeting it. He is the actual worst." She shivered with her whole body.

I leaned in the doorway of the kitchen. "It was . . . well, they still want to publish him so I take it as a massive win as we still have our jobs."

"Hurrah," Jas said, pressing down on the machine. "I mean, morally yikes but hurrah for employment."

"I suggested he contribute to the scheme you were telling me about last week actually, for underrepresented female crime writers."

"Oh cool—thank you," she beamed. "Oh, I bought you an apple turnover. It's in that bag," she pointed.

"You are the second person today to buy me a baked item," I said, gratefully picking it up and peering inside. "Thank you."

"Who else?"

"Dan," I said through my first mouthful.

"Awwwww." She often made that sound when I told her anything nice that Dan did. "He's the best."

"You're biased because he brought you a new 'J' mug when you told him yours had smashed."

"But that was basically the nicest thing a human man had ever done for me ergo I will wuv him forever."

"That is very sad, Jas. You need to hang out with nicer human men."

"There aren't any. I have scoured the whole of South London and have come up with nothing, nada, nil. Maybe when I am old I can find my own Dan."

"Yes, maybe when you are as ancient as I . . . He is pretty great," I admitted, thinking back to the cinnamon swirl at home, guilt stinging me. Had I even thanked him?

Jas handed me my coffee, the scent filling the small galley

kitchen. "I'm chasing up those audiobook contracts today by the way. You'll need to sign them when they send them across. I was also thinking we should amend the client contract to include those rights; the old one doesn't mention them."

"Check you, bossing admin on a Monday."

Twenty-four with brilliant taste in books, Jas was fantastic. She was great with writers, reassuring, encouraging but firm. I knew I needed to persuade Linda to give her more freedom to start her own list, or we'd lose her. She was ready to go out with her own authors. After Friday maybe that would happen. I didn't want to let her down. Friday was as much about me as Jas.

"We don't say bossing it anymore, Emma," Jas said solemnly. "Us Gen Z say, I'm the CEO of admin."

"Gotcha."

Jas laughed as she followed me through to our shared office. She reveled in our age gap. To her *The Crown* was a history documentary; she'd marvel at my memories of things in the year she was born. "Did everyone fancy Tony Blair when he became PM?" "Was Princess Diana as amazing as she seems?" "Did people really not have mobiles? What happened when you were running late? Did you just . . . have to wait?"

She was very handy when it came to my own parenting. She explained the latest websites, apps, appropriate age for devices, and more. She thought it was cute I was worried about Facebook. "They're not on Facebook, Emma." After my session with Jas, Poppy had been shocked to discover I knew that TikTok wasn't a chocolate bar (as Dan had guessed). Maybe by the time Poppy was old enough to have an account on it another app would have replaced it. Navigating that stuff felt exhausting but Jas had genuinely helped me try to relax and trust my kids to tell me if things were going wrong.

Back at my desk I was balking at the new emails that had popped up since I'd last checked.

"Oh by the way," Jas said, taking her place in a swivel seat on the other side of the room, her woolen teal coat draped over its back, "Ernestina sent me the latest draft of her book which I read over the weekend and like, I am obsessed with it. I really want to show you the start, see what you think, see whether you think it's ready to be submitted?"

"Oh, I . . ." I frowned at an email from our film and TV scout wanting an update on the latest Scarlet submission. I didn't want him to lose heart, I must try to place that novel. Her last book had been optioned but it had all fallen through. I had a call about pitching it to America later with our US agent. That could turn things around. And I should read her idea for her fourth book. I'd been meaning to for ages.

"Only if you've got time, obviously, but I really think she's onto something . . . it feels really current."

Jas's voice had faded as I clocked the date in the bottom right of the screen.

Oh God.

How had I not realized its significance until now?

Suddenly Dan's disappointed face in bed that morning made total sense, his strange quiet, and of course the relevance of the cinnamon swirl I'd casually forgotten on the side.

"Bugger," I whispered.

Jasmina swiveled round, frowned. "You all right?"

Oh . . . bugger.

Me @Dan Don't worry about the sausages! I'll shop! I'll get the zucchinis too!

Me @Dan And I'll cook for us tonight.

Me @Dan Hope you're having a good day. See you later 😊

8

The day was already darkening when I turned into our road, jostling with the shopping I'd just bought and trying to read my phone which had pinged with a message from Linda.

Arthur would not be making any commitment to any "woke scheme."

"Oh for . . ." I squeezed past the bloody bike in the hall staring at the words—just as my heel slid out from under me.

"What the—!" I shot out an arm to balance myself, shopping and phone flying out of my grip. "Shit."

My nose wrinkled as I realized my heel was covered in something disgusting. A small puddle of vomit on the floorboards, the plastic around the potatoes coated with it too. Kicking off my shoe I padded into the kitchen, looking for the source. Another small puddle next to the dog basket where our Wowzer was lying. "Gus . . . ?"

Gus didn't lift his head from his bed as I bent down. His food was untouched. I was about to reach out a hand when the front door slammed.

A figure moved quickly past the doorway, then footsteps on the stairs.

"Miles?" I straightened, crossing the room, my walk uneven with one heel off.

"Dad's coming," he called.

I frowned; normally Miles came straight into the kitchen seeking food, giving me one-word responses to questions about his day.

I moved to the doorway to go and find him, immediately seeing the bag of potatoes which I gingerly picked up with a grimace.

As I carried them to the sink to wash, I noticed the fresh flowers on the kitchen island, orange roses in our best crystal vase. Dan had obviously bought them to mark the day. Another wave of guilt overwhelmed me.

Had he realized this morning I'd forgotten? Again?

No wonder he'd been quiet. The cinnamon swirl, the dejected expression when I'd bustled out.

But it was OK, I could still fix things, I could still stop a repeat of last year.

Work was waiting but I could start the kids' tea instead, that would help defuse things. I went back out to the hallway, wiped the floor, and picked up the rest of the food.

God, had Linda been serious about Arthur? Maybe a quick phone call to her to stress what was at stake? And that bike needed to go. I reached for my phone. Missed calls, notifications, social media apps alight. Christ, sometimes I just needed it all to stop.

Opening Facebook I was instantly distracted by The West London Mums group—a petition to muzzle a local dog, a request for suggestions for an upstairs space, a mum asking about safe sleeping that had attracted 735 comments and lots of angry red-faced emojis. I read and typed and scrolled. Why had I logged on to Facebook again?

The front door went and I glanced up, thrusting the phone behind my back as Dan appeared in the kitchen. "I was just going to put the kids' tea on," I said loudly, walking across the room in my uneven gait and randomly picking up a plastic ladle from the counter.

"I can do it if you like? I got us dinner too." He made no comment on my only wearing one shoe and going up and down which normally would make him mock me, so I knew he was cross. I had to face the situation: apologize.

"Dan," I said, turning to him, "I've been shit. And today, I'm so sorry. I feel bad. I know last year . . ." I didn't finish the sentence, wishing I could erase his hurt expression.

The relief that passed across his face was obvious. He'd assumed I'd forgotten. "It doesn't matter. You've been . . . busy."

"You're busy too," I said, distracted almost immediately by another ping. It could be work, but it could also be strangers getting irate about crib bumpers.

Dan moved across to the sink to start the washing-up left over from breakfast. "Is Poppy back yet? Did she talk to you about giving up Dance?"

"No, and I don't think we should let her just like that, she's so good at it . . ." I said, surreptitiously liking one of my client's photos on Instagram.

"Well she must have a reason, we need to hear it," Dan said, the glass he was holding dripping with suds. "Why is your shoe covered in goo?"

"Hmm . . . ?"" I looked at him and then back at my phone.

"I'll start their tea," Dan sighed.

I didn't fight him for it. "Thanks. I need to deal with this

. . . and I've got a call with our US agent in a bit and then that committee meeting tonight." My voice was soft, I pretended not to see Dan's shoulders fall.

"I was going to make dinner for us."

"Great. I'll be back for it," I added in a hurry, realizing I also needed to write an anniversary letter to him.

"You said you would quit," his voice was low, his grip on the plate in his hand tight.

"I will, really, I'll tell them tonight."

My phone rang. We both looked at it. I blinked.

"Answer it," Dan said, a muscle going in his cheek.

I glanced at it. "It's just Hattie. It's OK."

"You'll only say you have to phone her back later." He took the plastic ladle from me. "Just answer it."

AuthorLou @Emma Did you get my emails? No rush to reply!

Jas @Emma Gah! Have you seen the Guardian piece about Arthur??

Denise @Committee Alan will be joining us this evening so please, a polite reminder to be respectful and arrive on time.

Catrin @Emma. Fucking hell Alan's coming. Denise is gonna wear her Sunday best.

9

3rd December 2009

Dear Emma,

What have I discovered about you this year?

a) You can literally sleep anywhere. The top of a triple bunk in a twelve mixed dormitory even when four already wasted Ozzies are playing the two-up drinking game on Anzac Day.

b) You love the sky. At dawn, at dusk, puffy with clouds, ribboned with pinks and purples. You're always pointing it out to me. As if I don't see it. I suppose I sort of don't. Not in the way you do. Getting me up on my thirtieth to see the dawn was pretty special.

c) You're afraid of fowl. Which is both surprising and hilarious. (That little blue penguin did not "look at you threateningly.")

d) You read voraciously. You just love books. Laughing, crying—totally transported. I envy your passion for them, the light in your eyes when you quote from them. I love your endless attempts to convert me from sporting memoirs.

e) You're kind to me. Even when I'm being a dick. I'm not sure why I'm choosing to bring this up in my romantic letter to you but I still feel ashamed about that night I fell out with you because I thought it was pronounced ex-press-oh and you were adamant it was es-press-oh. I ended up saying all this stuff that wasn't even true—you're absolutely not a know-it-all. And then, when you should have left me on that bench with my pout and my curled fists . . . you didn't. You just came and sat down next to me and leaned your head on my shoulder. You gave me the space to climb down off my embarrassing high horse and apologize. I'm sorry again. And you were right, it is es-press-oh (Yeah I googled it didn't I? See, I am a dick).

f) You make friends anywhere and easily. You're always outside a loo, holding hands with some stranger, subtly waving me away as you hand her a tissue for her eyes. How do you get people to tell you stuff that makes them cry after three seconds of meeting them? You're always doing things for other people. You offer lifts, shared taxis, to drop round a book they might love. You lent that one girl the soft pink cardigan you adored because she was cold and seemed sad. YOU DIDN'T EVEN KNOW HER NAME. *You literally gave her the clothes off your back.*

I know those months traveling with you will forever be a golden time in my life. I'm not sure I could have felt happier if I'd tried. It was a shock to come home. Greeted by my parents and Hattie, their exclamations, their hugs. And God I love my family—I do—but for a second I was overwhelmed with sadness that the magic of being just the two of us was over. It had been completely amazing.

But shit, as you say, has got real for us. And a hostel on the East Coast of Australia is no place for us to bring up a baby.

A baby.

I still can't really believe it.

It's not that I'm not excited—you know I am. I just can't believe that in seven months I'm going to be a dad. A father. Someone's old man. Pot and Pan. Me old geezer.

I'll never forget your face as you emerged from the filthy loo in that hostel in Noosa—the way you drifted toward me like a ghost; I was gripped with fear. What had happened? I knew from the look you were giving me that something fundamental had shifted. We were careering into the "After."

Maybe you were worried how I'd react. I'm not half as impetuous as you, I'm a list-maker. My jobs have literally been about strategy, planning. I know I didn't respond like men do in films: spin you round or cup your stomach. But being that I thought you had food poisoning it was A LOT to take in. And sometimes you need to give the rest of us a moment to catch up with you. When you're flying in, throwing everything at it, you need to give us a second to get our heads round it.

My whole family are over the moon, I'm so glad Mum's surprise spa weekend with Hattie was such a great time to bond (less glad about the fact she brought along those photos—some babies just don't grow hair for ages).

I am excited, Emma. Frightened, obviously. I have no doubt you'll be amazing. I just know I've got to step up to the plate now (sorry, I know you hate sporting analogies) and make sure I don't drop the ball (it's an illness, OK?).

I love you (and the bump) (?!). Shhhhhiiittttttt. I can't wait to see what our fourth year brings us . . .

Dan x x

10

By the time I'd left the room Hattie had rung off. Settling into the office on the first floor, I fired up my laptop, wishing I'd thought to make myself a cup of tea. Skim-reading my emails, I pulled out a drawer, looking for some paper for Dan's letter.

Another agent was asking if I was OK, if I'd seen Twitter. I immediately abandoned the drawer and logged in, searching for the agency handle. A stream of angry responses, many retweeting the incredibly damaging *Guardian* piece. I had to sort this, Arthur was Linda's client but this was our agency and we were, rightly, getting dragged for our lack of response.

A door banged somewhere below as I waited for Linda to answer her phone. No response.

I drafted an email, attaching information on the writers' scheme. This wasn't my job but I needed Linda to understand the seriousness of it all. Partway through I heard voices and lost my thread, huffing as I deleted the sentence. Then I frowned. Because Miles was the one I could hear. And Miles was never the one I could hear.

Opening my office door, I realized they were coming from his room next door, the wood decorated with remnants of some rocket stickers he removed last year as being "too babyish" (I cried). I stepped forward, craning to listen. My eyebrows shot up—Miles was actually yelling.

It was Poppy who normally yelled; she was like me, could fly in, explode quickly. We clashed often, Dan reminding me to give her space, let her come to me. I couldn't help rushing in, never wanting a child to be ignored.

"OKAY . . . (mumble mumble) WILL TALK . . . SAYS HE'LL . . . (something indistinguishable) . . ."

Why did we install fire doors? They made it so much harder to hear things.

"SCHOOL NOW . . . (mumble something) HATE YOU . . ."

"Just don't tell, OK?" said Poppy.

Don't tell?

My whole face was now pressed up against the wood. Miles didn't get angry; he was the most placid child I'd ever known. Even as a baby he just couldn't be arsed to get worked up. His tantrums had always lasted less than thirty seconds before he picked up something else or wandered off distracted by something shiny.

They didn't hear my knock, and by the time I'd stepped inside Miles was standing in the middle of the room, his chest moving fiercely up and down. Poppy stood opposite, feet planted wide.

"Why are you shouting?"

There was a thick silence as they both glared at each other. Miles opened his mouth to speak first.

"Don't," Poppy said.

It snapped shut, his body tense, arms by his side, fists clenched as if he was going to explode upward at any moment.

"Don't what?" I said, feeling the stirrings of a headache. "And why aren't you at Dance, Poppy?" I remembered. "We've paid for the term."

"I quit," she mumbled, not meeting my eye. "And Miles was just angry with me for borrowing his pen. But I've put it back now," Poppy said, her eyes narrowing at him.

"That's SO NOT FAIR I DON'T CARE ABOUT A CRAPPY PEN . . ."

"Miles," I shouted, shocked into being loud myself.

"She's *lying*," he said, twisting to me.

Poppy rounded on him. "OH MY GOD, SHUT UP." Then she twisted to me. "And I'm *not*."

"SHE IS."

"I'M NOT."

I put both hands to my head. This didn't seem like a quick-fix situation and I desperately needed to get back to work, and I still had that letter to Dan to write too. "STOP IT, BOTH OF YOU."

"I haven't done anything WRONG," Miles said, turning and kicking at the frame of his bed.

"Don't kick things, Miles, you're not four!" I yelled.

Poppy was backing away, sliding past me to the door. "And don't think I won't find out what's happening," I called after her as she raced up the second flight of stairs to her room.

I heard her mutter something. Miles was refusing to look at me. My phone started ringing and when I glanced at it, it was Hayley from Charter Publishing.

"Look, Miles, I've got to take this but I want to know what's happened," I said, my voice conciliatory. "Miles?"

He grunted as I pressed Accept, then started gushing apologies on behalf of my agency. Hayley interrupted me.

"What's happening? We need Arthur to issue a statement, Emma, apologize and commit to that scheme."

I put her on speaker as I walked through to my bedroom. I could change for the committee meeting. Save time. And I should check my makeup before my video call with our US agent. I wanted to pitch her Scarlet's novel to sell in the States.

"I know, I know," I murmured, my head stuck in a turtleneck sweater, voice muffled.

"You *really* need to, or this could be the end," she warned as I stepped into the en suite.

My reply bounced off the tiles, "I understand. I'll try my best . . ."

The pause was unbearable as I stared at the phone, then back at my face in the mirror.

"Thanks, Emma. I know this isn't your client, but it's your agency." This final sentence before she hung up triggered another pain in my chest. She was right. I had to try Linda again.

My makeup had faded and I pulled off a piece of loo roll—Dan had obviously bought more—wiping the marks from under my eyes. Then I reapplied my concealer and dashed on an extra line of eyeliner to disguise my tiredness, unable to find my mascara in my makeup bag. What the hell had I done with it?

God, Poppy needed to turn down her music, I thought, as I moved back to the office for my call with our US agent. I texted her with one hand as I adjusted my laptop with the other. I didn't have time to go up there and argue with her.

"Emma, hi . . ."

More than an hour later I was exhausted but tentatively hopeful; the agent had liked the sound of Scarlet's book so would be pitching it in America. I called Linda, repeatedly, and got no reply. Then I answered six of the twenty-nine emails I'd received since lunchtime. At one point, Dan had called me down for the kids' tea.

"Be a sec," I'd called back. I knew I should go; it was about the only time of day we were ever all together. I needed to check on Miles, it wasn't like him to get so upset. And I was on thin ice with Dan too. I made a typo just as Linda returned my call.

"Arthur did not appreciate being blind-sided in that manner. And he will not bend to this wokery."

"But this has really exploded, Linda. It's all over the internet, it's not going away."

"Melissa is being extraordinarily silly over this whole thing. And she needs us more than we need them."

"Well, that's not really true. We're at a vulnerable stage with the recontracting, and if they drop Arthur—"

"Drop him? They wouldn't dare," Linda's laugh turned into a cough. "And we will discuss your disappointing response to all of this in our meeting on Friday."

"But Linda . . ."

She had gone and as I hung up, depressed, I realized I'd missed the kids' tea. Brilliant.

I went looking for my youngest and found Miles lying on his bed looking up at the ceiling.

"Hey," I said softly, sitting down. "What happened earlier?"

"Nothing," he said, swiping angrily at his face.

"It's clearly not nothing."

I waited for him to speak.

"OK. Well . . ." I said, aware of the time I simply hadn't got, the committee meeting any minute, Dan who I needed to talk to too, "we can talk about it at breakfast, OK? We'll sort it."

He didn't reply.

"I've got to go out now, otherwise . . ." I said helplessly.

He rolled onto his side and I felt a lurch in my stomach. Maybe I should stay? See if this was really serious? "I'll come and say good night later, I won't be long," I said, making promises to his back. His digital alarm clock told me I was running late. Shit.

Rushing to my bedroom I tried to shrug off my unease, my instinct whispering in my ear that something was really wrong as I rummaged for a Band-Aid to stick over the rub on my heel. Pulling on jeans, socks, boots, I wished they were pajamas and slippers and I wasn't going back out. Oh God, I still needed to write the letter to Dan.

And I should tell Dan about the kids yelling. Maybe he'd already found out why over their tea?

My phone rang as I was racing down the stairs. "Prompt Emma. Six thirty p.m. sharp," Catrin barked jokingly. "Denise will string you up."

It was only two streets away. "I'll be five minutes, literally. Distract her with talk of the need for speed bumps in Grosvenor Road. She'll lap it up."

Catrin was laughing as I hung up and appeared, puffing, in the doorway of the kitchen. Straightening my shoulders I stepped, attempted to sashay in fact, across the room toward Dan, his back to me at the sink, washing up the kids' plates. Gus lifted his head in greeting as I approached. Give me strength, boy, tell your master I love him.

"Didn't you hear me call you?" he said, not turning around.

The kitchen clock, a large gilt sunflower, ticked loudly above me. The committee meeting had started.

"I'm sorry, I meant to come down but it all kicked off and . . ." I swallowed down the excuses, "I won't be long, OK, and we can have a lovely evening, together . . . alone." I dropped my voice for that last word, trying to inject as much sex appeal as I could into the two syllables. I moved behind him. "I can't wait to celebrate our anniversary properly," I murmured, moving my arms around him.

Gratifyingly the tops of his ears turned pink and his shoulders relaxed. "I thought I'd make us chicken tarragon."

A pang in my chest, one of my favorite meals and Dan knew it. Even cross he was making an effort. For a flash I really did just want to stay there, leaning into him, his familiar smell, his solid body beneath his shirt. We would sit at the table, catch up, the air smelling of warm batter. I'd magically produce my letter to him with a coy smile and a light laugh, "Did you think I'd forgotten . . . ? Not likely . . ." and we'd share a bottle of wine and chat and laugh. Afterward I'd take his hand and lead him to the stairs, moving toward our bedroom, my eyes on him, his dark with desire . . .

Ping, ping, ping. Email, WhatsApp, text. Email, WhatsApp, text. Ping, buzz, ping. It wasn't just the guilt making me tense. I tried to block it out, my grip on Dan firmer, but the mobile was vibrating against his back.

I could feel his muscles tighten, his hand gentle on mine. "I'll see you after your meeting."

Conciliatory—and definitely all I was getting.

Denise @Emma We will be starting promptly in ten minutes.

AuthorLou @Emma So I was thinking that I might call Jane about the font on the cover. My friend said the G looks like a Q from far away and I think he might be right.

CharterHayley @Emma Any update?

11

No wonder Denise had been so insistent on a prompt start. It was an Alan meeting, and she was always fluttery about an Alan meeting. Alan, who owned the playgroup premises and liked to sweep in every month or so with a PowerPoint on something he felt we needed explained. Today he was inexplicably dressed in a brand-new high-vis jacket, stiff creases on the neon-yellow fabric.

"Emma," he pointed me to a chair at the head of the small table, "we wanted to wait for you."

Across the Formica table Catrin rolled her eyes.

Denise's response was clipped. "The minutes, Emma. Let's not keep everyone waiting. Alan says he has timed his casserole and can't stay long and I for one don't want to make him late."

"A slow cooker waits for no man," Catrin called out. Alan shot her a look.

"We have a rota for minute-taking, Alan," Denise was simpering at him, "and tonight the lucky lady is Emma," she explained, as though Alan didn't understand how a rota worked.

"Oh," I feigned regret, "I left my laptop at home."

Denise however had already motioned for Lena, her lapdog in a pale pink Hermès scarf, to push her notepad across the table to me.

"Great," I thanked her weakly.

Catrin snorted and Denise glared at her.

Lena rummaged in her handbag. "Would you like to borrow my pen, Emma?" she offered, passing it across the table. "It's a Montblanc. Limited Edition."

At least if I handwrote the minutes I could also produce a moving love letter? And clearly this pen was expensive so it would look good: classy ink. Dan might be impressed by that at least. He loves stationery.

"Item One," Denise started, "the all-important Christmas party. The children are eager to have us make a decision," she said, her words laced with meaning. "With the party on in just over two weeks, we need to send out the theme for parents to organize things. As you know, last time the theme of gymkhana was rejected."

Alan tutted. "Oh. Shame."

"Apparently *some* of our members believed it to be too 'elitist,' Alan," she said with a sigh.

"I just thought we could probably land on something a bit more mainstream?" I said through my teeth.

"Well, I remember you also put your foot down over anything homemade so I'm not quite sure what you think the children should be wearing? Peasant garb?"

"Oh, I'm sure the mums will enjoy making gorgeous outfits for their children," Alan said, beaming at Denise.

Behind his back, Catrin signaled a gunshot to the head. Lena was too busy nodding agreement to notice.

"*Parents*," I stressed, "have more than enough on their plate without having to create a costume from scratch."

"You're being a kill-joy," Alan sing-songed at me, wagging a finger. "I'm sure many women would want to give up their time for their children."

Lena found her voice, "I could send round a mood board from Pinterest of some ideas to be of help."

"Excellent," Alan said, beaming at her. Lena went pink.

"I would like the theme to be superheroes," Denise said. "Bertie desperately wants to go as Mr. Incredible."

"Well, that sounds excellent. And if that's the theme the children could always go as their mums," Alan said, beaming around the room. "Superheroes all of you. Right," he said, his chair scraping, "I have a lentil casserole to eat and you have plenty to keep discussing so I will take my leave." He straightened his high-vis jacket. "Just wanted to check in on my favorite ladies."

The door shut behind him, and Denise's voice was suddenly as cold as the outside air that blew the paper cups from the table. "We have a great deal to get through this evening," she snapped, "so let's minute a decision. Superheroes," she said quickly. She raised her eyebrow at me, "Any complaint?"

The fight left me as I shook my head and noted it down.

"Oh, and Emma, do note Alan's appreciative comments. If only all men were as understanding."

Catrin gave me a sympathetic grimace. I hope Alan's lentil casserole burned through.

"Now to another vital agenda item." Denise breathed out slowly, "The Teddy Bear Raffle . . ."

I sat back deflated as Lena talked us through it.

Dan was right about this committee. Why was I still on it?

Why couldn't I stop the guilty voice that compelled me to take these things on? I needed to say no.

"What if the teddies have parts missing? We have an adorable bunny but she only has one eye."

"We should be inclusive," Catrin called out. "Bunnies with one eye should not be discriminated against. In fact, we should source as diverse a selection of teddies as we can. Be representative."

I glanced up, a weak smile across at her. "Not helping," I mouthed.

Catrin looked back at me, a more serious expression on her face, asking if I was OK. Normally I sat next to her, shaking at the absurdity of the whole thing, but tonight I kept my head down, robotically finishing the notes, my handwriting as lackluster as my mood.

My numb hand was cramping as the minutes dragged by, the hall colder by the second. I wrapped my coat around me, missing things about the tuff tray or a sunny day or a funny seesaw—I zoned out. And throughout it all my phone was flashing and buzzing and I dreaded seeing what had happened now. I just wanted to be at home, in front of the wood burner, my slipper socks on, a blanket draped over my legs, snuggled into Dan.

Finally I was outside, Catrin at my side.

"All right?" she asked. "You seemed quiet tonight."

"Sorry, yeah," I said. "Just the usual. Too much to do, too little time. Dan's annoyed with me," I admitted, one eye on my phone.

Catrin had met Dan a few times, always made him laugh. "A bit miffed or all-out proper annoyed?" she asked.

"More than miffed," I said, then I sighed. "This is going to sound silly but today is the anniversary of the day we first met and it has always been really important and . . ."

"You forgot."

I grimaced, "I forgot."

Oh God, Hayley had sent me an email, something attached. It was all kicking off at Charter. What had Linda done?

"Want a drink? I brought the car so could drive us?"

"Sorry, Catrin, I've got to run," I said, turning, barely meeting her eye.

"Hey, take care, OK, and remember," she called after me, "you can't do it all!"

Jas @Emma Guardian piece being RTed A LOT—shit this is bad Emma.

CharterHayley @Emma I'm not sure I can stop what's going to happen now Emma.

Claire @Emma Assuming Amelia's book not on the way??

Emma @Dan Meeting done! Just phoning Linda about something. Won't be long!

Emma @Amelia I really need you to send over what you've done so far. Now please.

Amelia @Emma Will do! 😘
But computer being weird! Technology fail 😁

Amelia @Emma I've got someone looking at it tomorrow. So I'll send it over when it's fixed!

Emma @Amelia Can you at least give me your word count?

Emma @Amelia Amelia?

Emma @Dan Coming home now! See you in 2 minutes!

Missed Call: Hattie (2)

Missed Call: School Office (2)

12

3rd December 2010

Dear Emma,

As I write this I've just left you with Poppy. I took you tea to replace the un-drunk tea with the milky film over it. You smiled as I set it down: grateful for any small contribution I make.

You looked so in control: bright eyes, flushed skin, a book in one hand and Poppy nestled in the crook of your other arm, her tiny hand grazing your chest, her eyes rested closed. When you turned the page you didn't even nudge her.

I scooted next to you and you smelled of vanilla.

"Hey," you whispered, tipping your head toward me so it rested on my shoulder.

I felt something in my chest spark to life.

"I can't believe she's ours," you said seconds later. "That we get to be her parents."

I stared down at Poppy. At this tiny person who came screaming into our lives, trying to feel the truth of your words, knowing I should agree. I got up and left.

I've left a lot in the last few months.

I always thought I'd be a pretty good dad. I had clips in my head: me chucking some happy, giggling child in the air, running across sand chasing them. But having Poppy, this tiny, fragile baby—more often crying than smiling—has thrown me. This is the only place I can admit how hard I'm finding it to you. It feels like complaining about a broken furnace to someone who's homeless.

You are the one who should be complaining to me. And you hardly ever do. And when you do it's because the room is literally on fire (I genuinely don't know how that tea towel got there) or Poppy has cried on you for five hours straight or I've managed to heat the milk too hot so she screams at us as we wait those agonizing minutes for it to cool.

You've had to recover from an emergency caesarean, deal with the disappointment of your carefully thought-through birth plan being upended, the early days when your body refused to gear up, crying on the useless health visitor who kept holding up that weird knitted breast and massaging it to show you how to get milk. And all this after nine months of nausea, back pain, swollen limbs, and me on a three-second delay, or barely there at all.

I bring tea, biscuits, toast, tea. Linger in doorways, not knowing how to fix mastitis or stop your trips to the bathroom making you cry out in pain. I can't even seem to help stop Poppy wailing. So I throw myself into more work, get busy, prove I'm helping in that at least.

Sleep deprivation has worn us both down—I was so naïve to think I had any clue what parenting would be like. My Google searches have gone from "best local restaurants" to "can a baby remember things from birth," "if a baby cries for more than an hour is it damaging?," "how many couples break up after their first baby." I did look that up. There are so many times in the last few months where I wouldn't have blamed you, I feel like I've barely brought anything to the party.

I know I need to do better.

When I think of what Mum would say to me it makes me ashamed. I still think of that last visit to the house, her skeletal hand gripping mine. She asked me if it was a boy or a girl. We were going to keep it as a surprise but I told her it was a girl. We both knew she wouldn't live to see for herself.

How does life change like that? One minute she'd been picking us up from the airport waving that garish homemade sign, a little more tired over Christmas perhaps than normal. And then she was sitting me and Hattie down and telling us what the doctors had told her.

Sometimes I see her in Poppy's eyes, the same shade of dark brown, or imagine her in the curl of her smile. It takes my breath away that I can lose someone I love so much, so quickly.

Sometimes I'm floored by a memory—her swearing in Italian in the car when we were kids, her farting so loudly in a tent she woke up Dad and accused him of doing it in his sleep. I pick up my mobile to speak to her, but she isn't there to ring. She isn't there to tell me that I can do this, how to do this. I stay in my dressing gown and pretend not to notice you need something from me. I know I need to do better; I know I do.

I've just returned to the sitting room and you've fallen asleep. The book has slipped from your hands and Poppy is still safe in your arms. I took her from you and rested her down in her Moses basket. Then I draped a blanket over you.

I'm here now. Poppy's stirring. If she wakes I want to handle it, want to help take some of the strain from you. I don't want to freeze; I don't want to panic.

I don't want to be this person.

I'm sorry.

Dan x

unsent

Dear Dan,
I don't have the energy for a long letter. And writing this reminds me of our other letters. I don't recognize the people in those letters.

I've tried SO HARD to be patient. I know how much losing your mum has floored you, but you can't leave the room every time I try and talk to you about her. God, Dan, you're so good at leaving the room or hiding behind "work." It's not work when you come back in drunk from a client meeting in some bar, waking up Poppy, apologizing with wine breath.

I'm sick of feeling like I'm doing this on my own. Your excuses are so shit too. Like I have a fucking clue how to burp a baby. Spoiler: I don't. I really don't. I just try.

Christ, and the questions. As if you're only just learning where we keep bottles or that nappies go in the nappy bin.

And then you seem to find all these jobs to do on a weekend, so if you're not doing your strategy consultancy stuff you're inventing shit to get yourself out of parenting

OUR child. Like the whole day you spent making that photo collage. And it was "for us" so I was the one being unreasonable. But it was another task that took you away from what I really wanted you to do which was to BE HERE.

Oh God, I can't give this to you. I can't tell you this stuff. And I know you don't want to be like this. That grief for your mum, becoming parents, has turned your whole world upside-down. But you're not yourself, Dan, you're lost and I can't get to you. So wherever you are please come back, pleas—

13

I bashed myself on the bloody bike as I flew in, flinging my coat at a hook and missing. My hands freezing from standing in the street on my phone to Linda, finally convincing her to send out the apology.

"Hey," I shouted, "I'm soooo sorry. The meeting went on forever and then the *Guardian* piece about the Arthur thing has totally blown up and I had to persuade Linda to *make* him see sense . . ."

I reached the kitchen. There was no one there: two clean plates, the table laid—but no Dan.

Frowning, I backed out, voices coming from across the hallway. Stepping into the living room I saw Dan sitting on the sofa, Miles in his pajamas beside him.

"Hey, what's this?" I asked. "It's a school night."

Both looked up and Dan gave me a warning look and then plastered a smile on his face as he ruffled Miles's hair, "He's just off upstairs, aren't you?"

Miles nodded slowly as Dan leaned in to give him a one-armed hug. "Night, mate."

"Night." Miles snuck past me in his green striped pajamas. "Night, Mum," he muttered.

"Night." I spun around to give him a hug and kiss but he was already halfway up the staircase, taking two steps at a time. "Love you." Why was he up? Was this to do with the argument earlier? And the school office had phoned, maybe they'd also noticed he wasn't himself.

Dan's tone changed as he stood up. "I made us dinner."

"You know he gets tired."

"I do know," Dan said, gritting his teeth.

"We'll pay for it tomorrow . . ." Was I carrying on like this to distract from the fact I was back so late? "Was he OK?" I asked, my worry about Miles overriding everything else.

Dan moved past me into the kitchen. "He said he just couldn't sleep."

I traipsed after him. "He rowed with Poppy earlier."

"Well, that's not unusual," Dan said.

"I don't know," I mused. "It seemed a bit different maybe?" As I said it a small ball of worry lodged in my stomach. Maybe I could pop up quickly now and talk to him before he fell asleep?

"So did you tell them?" Dan asked, his voice low as he switched on the burner, sugar snap peas waiting in a small pile ready to be boiled.

"Tell them wh—" Dan turned, just as I managed to wipe the blank look from my face, realization dawning, "Oh, um, no . . . but I'll message Denise tomorrow."

Dan's mouth set in a line.

"Wow," I gushed, moving across to the stove and going on a full charm offensive. "That looks amazing," I said, pointing at the frying pan filled with chicken thighs in sauce.

"It might need reheating," Dan said pointedly.

"And sugar snap peas!" I exclaimed loudly, pretending not to hear. "I'll get the wine; do you want a . . ." Too late I noticed his almost-empty white wine on the side. ". . . a top-up," I said brightly.

Dan shrugged, mellowing a little.

"Thanks so much for cooking." I stepped across to the table and then froze when I saw the envelope lying next to my fork. My name in black, a small heart over the "a."

I'd never written the letter. Oh God. I had to write a letter.

"I'm just going to . . . change my . . . boots," I said, backing out of the kitchen and rushing up the stairs.

"Paper, paper, paper," I muttered as I rifled through my bedside table, and then, biting my lip, moved across to Dan's. No paper. Although he did have a little stack of previous letters. Oh God. The guilt worsened. I raised my head up like a meerkat. What was that weird tinny music? It felt so familiar. Where was it coming from?

I could hear Dan calling my name as I raced into the office, snatched up a sheet of paper from the printer tray that I quickly folded up and secreted in my sleeve before heading back downstairs.

Dan looked at my boots.

"I . . . just really like them," I said, feeling like the idiot I was.

He was standing at the table spooning out the sauce.

"Are you all right?" Dan asked.

"I'm great," I said, lingering next to the wall calendar, the number 3 already crossed out with the miniature ballpoint pen Dan kept on the ledge. I quickly reached for it and shoved it up my sleeve with the paper. "Brilliant."

He pointed to my full plate, watching me as I sat down slowly, the heart on the envelope with my name swimming as I tried to think how to avert this crisis.

"Lovely. A letter!" I exclaimed, a wide smile frozen to my face as I pushed the envelope to the side of the table and looked back at him. "We can open them later. Soooo . . ." I steepled my hands and placed my chin on my fingertips, barely waiting for him to settle in his chair. "Tell me about your day? All good? Any new clients? Did you read about the new recycling system? Why couldn't Miles sleep? I'm a bit worried about him. Did the man from SSE fix a date for the furnace?"

"I told you last week that got sorted, he's already been and fixed it."

"Of course you did," I said, brightly. "Great!" I added, the quite-scary smile slipping a bit.

I was distracted for a lot of the meal, my palms dampening as I wondered when he was going to ask where my letter was, the tiny pen slipping down my sleeve every time I moved. I had to get some words on the page. This couldn't be like last year.

Dan was quieter too, his responses to any questions brief, lackluster. I really needed to try and salvage this.

I needed to buy myself some time. "Is there pudding?" I asked.

"Apple crumble."

"Yum," I said, theatrically smacking my lips.

Dan looked a little taken aback.

I'd pitched my enthusiasm too high.

"I didn't make it," he said apologetically.

"I wouldn't expect you to. But . . . I'd love some custard with it. Have we got any?"

"I thought you'd want cream. I bought cream."

"I do," I said slowly. "Normally. But custard would be like the icing on the cake. Ha!"

Dan gave me a strange look as I got up and removed our empty plates and then loitered in the middle of the room. Probably wondering why I wasn't making this amazing custard that I so desperately wanted.

"Just going to the loo!" I sang, racing out of the room.

Perched on the toilet I scribbled some thoughts on the paper, adding an exuberant number of kisses. It was short but it was very loving. One too many exclamation marks but this was no time for perfectionism. I sidled back into the kitchen, Dan's back to me at the oven as I returned the pen to the ledge and slid the folded paper onto the counter.

My insides immediately lighter, I moved to top up our wines.

"What are you doing?" I said, patting his chair. "Come and sit down."

Dan gave me a strange look. "I'm making you custard?"

"OF COURSE! Amazing!"

He turned, walking across the room to place the steaming bowl in front of me, but stopped dead when he saw the folded piece of paper.

He stared at it.

"That was *not* there before."

"Hmm . . . ?""

Reading glasses on, he picked it up, his words slow. "You just wrote this when you went to the loo."

I put a hand to my chest. "I can't believe you'd say that!"

"Admit it!"

"I had it in my bag all day. So I just *put* it there while you were gone."

"I don't believe you, Emma."

"I'm your wife, Daniel."

He waved the paper. "You misspelled affection—"

"It's a tricky word," I stuttered.

"—and it's basically three lines long."

I scoffed, "I don't always have to write really *long* letters. I thought this year I'd—"

"Emma, just admit it, you forgot . . . again."

My chest squeezed tight. "Why are you making such a big deal about this?"

He curled his fists, crumpling the note in his hand. His mood this evening justified, the hurt oozing from him. "Because it *is* a big deal. Or . . ." He paused. "I thought it was. Maybe you don't."

I felt a pang in my stomach to see tears film his eyes. "Dan, don't be like that." My voice was panicked, the memories of last year crashing in as if I was living a hideous déjà vu. How could I have messed up again? This day represented so much to both of us and I'd spent my time on everything else when I should have put this first.

"I'm not being like anything. I'm allowed to be bloody sad."

"Mum? Dad?" A small voice from the top of the stairs.

"God, you've woken the kids," I accused, the anger at myself utterly misdirected at Dan. As I moved to the kitchen door I felt momentarily grateful to escape the pain of his gaze. "Hi darling, go back to bed. I'll pop up and tuck you in, in a minute."

"Were you fighting?"

I couldn't speak for a moment, my throat thick.

"No, darling. It was the telly. Night, night."

I returned to find Dan in his coat, Gus whining for a pee. "Come on, Gus," Dan snapped.

Gus, crouched low, his nose almost touching the floor, resisted Dan's tug on the leash.

"Don't pull on him like that."

"I'm not pulling on him. C'mon, Gus."

Dan scooped up a barking Gus and carried him out of the house. The door slammed.

Christ.

"Mum," Miles's sleepy voice called from the landing.

"Hey darling," I half-whispered. "Sorry, Dad went out with Gus, I'll come up and tuck you in . . ."

He returned to his room.

I looked around the kitchen at the detritus of our meal, at the orange flowers on the central island, at the envelope with my name. I had royally screwed up. Dan deserved so much better than this. And then to be angry at him when I'd been the one at fault.

A loud bang made me jump. The wail of an alarm followed, high-pitched, over and over.

My skin broke into goosebumps as my head turned toward our front door.

What *was* that?

I took a step forward, my thoughts scrambling as I replayed what I'd heard. Where was Dan? I needed to see him. Why did I feel this chill?

Oh my God.

Jas @Emma Our agency's name is mud Emma . . .

Denise @Committee Thank you for your attendance this evening. Am sure Emma will be sending round the minutes shortly.

Catrin @Committee More importantly Denise—how did Alan's casserole turn out?

Denise @Committee Please only use the Committee WhatsApp group for Committee matters.

Catrin @Emma That told me. Hope you managed to get back in time to woo Dan. All else fails you know there is always a 🍆

Hattie @Emma Can you talk now?

14

I left the house without a thought, something propelling me forward. I had to go. That noise. I needed to get to it.

I turned right, the florist and newsagent opposite dark, the streetlamps glowing orange. My breathing was loud in my ears.

A scream. A scream that made my whole body jerk, hairs bristling on my flesh.

Oh my God. I ran.

Flecks of sleet clung to my face and hair as I skidded on icy ground in my boots, speeding toward the sound, eyes straining in the dark. A voice. Someone called something. A bark, nearby. Gus. I knew I was close, felt an icy shiver drip down my neck as I turned right into a side street. Something up ahead that seemed all wrong.

I saw the strange angle of the headlights first, the car bent and steaming, buried in the side of another parked car, Gus barking, circling something large on the ground in the middle of the road. No. No. No. No.

The glass crunched underneath me as I approached, my steps slower now. There were two figures on the pavement bent over someone sat on the ground near the crumpled car: neither of them Dan. "The ambulance is on its way. It's OK, stay there, it's OK."

A terrible keening noise from the person on the ground between them, high, animal. It made my flesh bristle.

I didn't want to keep walking forward but my body seemed unable to stop.

Past the distorted brightness of the headlights, the car's windscreen filled with the whites of an airbag. There was something familiar about it all, as if I'd dreamed it, and yet everything felt totally alien. Across the street a curtain was pulled aside, an orange triangle appearing, a face peering out: an audience as I approached the shape in the middle of the road, Gus still now, staring at it too.

I stopped ten feet away.

Had I known when I first heard that noise? My entire world slowed in the seconds that I saw the shape—the shape of Dan lying twisted on the ground.

"Oh my God, oh my God." My hands covered my mouth.

Dan was lying diagonally across the white line in the middle of the road.

"Dan?"

His head was bent to one side, eyes open and staring unseeingly at Gus who was sat on his back legs, head tilted to the side as if he too expected him to stand up.

"Dan, get up. You're scaring me."

His right leg was bent at an impossible angle, the foot bare. He must have been so desperate to get out of the house he hadn't even put on socks. His shoe was nowhere to be seen. His foot must be freezing, the road glistening with ice. A noise emerged from my throat, and my hands moved around my neck, squeezing. Something sticky and dark pooled around his head. Something glinted nearby. His hated reading glasses, upside-down but perfect on the road.

This wasn't happening. Not to Dan. He'd just been in our kitchen. We'd had dinner. I blinked, his disappointed face swirling in front of me. The dejection in his eyes.

"Dan?"

Gus inched over to his body and nudged him gently with his nose. In that second I knew he'd get up. He'd place a hand on his head. He'd walk home with us. I'd say sorry—I'd say I was so fucking sorry. That it was all my fault, that I should never have rounded on him. I'd shouted at him, oh my God I'd forced him out of that house. He'd have been upset, not looking . . .

Gus nudged him another time. Nothing.

"Please, Dan, for God's sake, get up."

I covered my mouth again, choked sounds escaping from me.

Behind Gus, a disembodied voice. "Are you all right? Do you know him?"

I couldn't do anything but stare at Dan, will him to move, to stop this.

"Dan. Get up. Get up and come home with us. Don't stay out, it's freezing."

Gus bent over him; breathing on his master, a little whimper emerging as if he realized he couldn't bring him back either. I felt ice drip down my spine. Then Gus threw back his head and howled and something broke inside me.

Dan was gone.

15

There was a hand on my shoulder, voices nearby, but my whole world was simply the unreal sight in front of me, Gus's terrible accompanying howl.

"Does she know him? Is that his . . . ?" Did you see it? Call an ambulance."

I don't remember moving toward Dan until my knees scratched on the tarmac, my palms sticky as I knelt by his head.

Someone was asking me questions, kneeling on the other side of him, but I couldn't hear them. I stared at my husband's face. His eyes weren't meeting mine, like a weird game he was playing, something childish he'd do to make me laugh. This wasn't funny.

"Look at me, Dan. Please, please look at me . . ."

The eyes were his, still brown, but I couldn't see the tiny amber streaks that brought them to life. His expression was strange, unfamiliar. His face slack, cheek crushed against the hard ground, two tiny cuts on his chin.

There was nothing there of Dan.

When I looked up, the narrow dark street had filled with people; outside security lights blinked on as figures in raincoats over tracksuit bottoms, pajamas, peered out, some moving a few steps down their path.

Gus had inched toward me, his damp, springy curls in my lap as I reached to touch Dan's face.

"This wasn't what he wanted," I whispered. "He wanted to die in his bed. He told me."

It had been months ago, a conversation after a weepy movie.

"Don't be so morbid," he'd said, drawing me toward him.

I'd wanted to know.

He'd finally relented with a sigh. "With you," he'd told me. I'd called him a psycho and he'd laughed, one of the rumbling loud ones that always made my own mouth turn up at the corners. "No, when we've really lived. In our bed."

He hadn't wanted this.

I was crying, wanting his eyes to look like his eyes again. What had they last seen?

I hoped Gus had been the last thing he'd seen. The adoring face of his loyal, lovable friend. The dog who'd never failed to make my husband smile and soften and spoil. I hoped it had been Gus. Not this scene, not this carnage.

I stumbled to my feet, hands helping me up as I spoke. "I left the kids. I need to go to them. But I'll come back . . ." I reached for a man nearby. "Stay with him, please. Someone needs to stay with him."

The man was nodding quickly, his own eyes filling with tears, his voice gruff in response.

"Yes, love. Of course. Do you need . . . Are you OK?"

Bending down, I ignored him, bundling Gus into my arms. He was so impossibly heavy, fur wet and matted. I staggered under his weight, needing him near me, needing to take him home.

A woman stepped forward. "I'll help, please."

She returned with me to the house, Gus held between us. "He should see a vet. We can tell the police what we saw . . . your dog . . ."

I mumbled thank yous as I closed the door on her worried face. The moment it shut I sank on crouched knees to the floor, my face plunged into Gus's fur. "Good boy, good boy."

"Mum."

Miles was at the bottom of the stairs. It was too late to stop it. I saw his eyes travel down me and I followed his gaze. My top dotted with sleet, hands smeared red, Gus coated too. When I looked up, he was pale in the stark hallway light, the whites of his eyes completely round.

"What's happened? Mum?"

It was his frightened shout that broke something in me.

And I didn't mean to scare him, I didn't mean to make the terrible, awful noise I made but I couldn't stop. I was making my son cry and I couldn't stop.

"Mum. Where's Dad? Mum?"

My name almost shouted forced me to blink, to try to explain. "He was hit. He's . . . he's . . . there was a car and . . . oh, my darling. He died."

My words hit him like they were real things, his face shocked, tiny body crumpling where he stood on the bottom stair. We stared at each other, time still for those seconds, entirely alone in our anguish. Suddenly Poppy appeared, drawn by the noise. She stared past Miles clutching the banister to me with Dan's blood on my hands and started screaming. Which made Miles sob harder, Gus cowering in my lap, shuddering next to my body at the swell of grief. Then they were all in my arms, pressed against me, all of us huddled together, the doormat prickles beneath me.

I tried to reach them all, to crush them both so close I could swallow their pain. How would I do this? How could I do anything without Dan with me? I thought of his body out there in the road, squeezed my eyes closed, but the image didn't leave. I wasn't sure how long we'd been there when the door knocker rattled above our heads, making us scramble backward.

The policeman had sandy hair and eyes filled with pity as he took in our scene.

I couldn't think of the questions I needed to ask. Somehow we'd moved into the kitchen, someone had given me a glass of water. The children were close, reminding me of the toddler years, needing the solidity of their mother, that safety. I couldn't protect them from this night, from anything.

Dan had been pronounced dead at the scene. They'd taken him to the mortuary at the hospital. The driver had been taken to the station.

At that I'd looked up.

Oh my God, the driver, the fucking driver. The policeman's mouth was moving but I couldn't hear him, a hot rage erupting inside me. How fast had they been driving in a narrow residential road? Badly enough they managed to veer into a grown man?

"Can someone be with you all? Is there anyone we can call?"

Numbly I shook my head. I felt the strange, fleeting shame of not knowing where my parents were—Spain? Their Brighton flat? They rarely updated me. And then the blow of telling Dan's dad. The man was already bent double as a widow, and they were suggesting that I wake him in the middle of the night with this?

I couldn't.

"I will, thank you," I said, voice scratchy as though I'd not spoken in years. He needed to leave. I said other things: The children, I need to be with them. Yes, we have people we can ring. Yes, we'll wait for the Community Support officer first thing. Somehow, he left and with his absence a strange silence descended on all of us.

I settled Gus in his basket, his curls still stuck together. The sight making my throat close up. "I can't . . ." I whispered to his solemn face. "Gus, I can't do it." He licked my hand and I let out another sob.

The children didn't want to leave me, and I didn't want them to. We moved through the kitchen. The envelope, with his letter to me inside, still unopened on the table. I stared at it, the small heart swimming.

I never read it.

Where is he? He should be here. He should be walking back into the house. He should be holding his children, holding me, telling us we're OK, not to be scared, it's OK.

He'd never be here again.

Poppy wordlessly got into bed with Miles, both their heads on the pillow, their hair tangled, the same shade of mid-brown. Dan's hair. I stroked their faces, wiped a black smudge from under Poppy's red eyes, feeling a surreal calm as I whispered over and over, "It's OK, I love you. I love you."

Ten and eight.

They finally fell asleep and I wished they'd wake up again as the thoughts crowded in. As I thought of the last things I'd said to Dan. How I'd lied to him, downplayed the day. It was our day, it was important, so important. And I had ruined it. And the last thing he'd known was me dismissing a day that had once meant everything to us.

I couldn't stay in this room, my body shivering as I stood

and slid my hands along the walls to the door, made it into the corridor to cry. I knew I would regret those things until my very last day.

Hours later, still crouched in the hallway, numb and cold, the darkness gave way to a strange gray calm. My head pounded as I groggily got to my feet, stood in the doorway to our bedroom. Dan's work shirt was crumpled half-in and half-out of the laundry basket. Casual. Like he'd shove it in fully later.

I sat down on our bed; the curtains not yet closed. The whole of London was asleep and I was the only one up in the world. It was moments before the birds would shift, flutter awake. The Day After. The Community Support Officer. The day I had to call Dan's dad. Had to call Hattie. Oh my God, poor Hattie.

His pillow was still sunk in the middle; that toothpaste mark I moaned about two (or was it three?) nights ago was still there. I inched across the bed to rest my head on it. It smelled of Dan, of us. I knew I wouldn't be able to sleep. I squeezed my eyes closed, willing this day to be over, willing this day to never end. Wanting my husband back. Wanting Dan.

Missed Call: Unknown number

16

3rd December 2021

Dear Emma,
I'm writing this in our bed. I know I don't even need to hide the fact I am because you won't be up for hours. And if you do come up you might not even notice what I'm doing.

Tomorrow will be fifteen years since we met. That is an achievement, something to celebrate. Well, I think it is. And I used to think you did too.

I'm pissed off but you've yet to realize. I went to kiss you good night but you turned back to your phone so it just skidded onto your chin. And I GET that Arthur Chump, or whatever his name is, is a big deal but actually it's been a really shit weekend watching you glued to your mobile as Twitter explodes because the guy is a complete arsehole.

How is this your job anyway? He's Linda's client. She should be the one staying up into the early hours to prep for a meeting with his publishers. And, from what you showed me, I don't think he should get another book deal anyway—and maybe that will finally make you leave Linda because, oh my God, you keep saying that things will change, but nothing ever does. You have a meeting with her this week but you've had meetings before and they don't seem to make a difference. You shouldn't be in that agency, Emma, and I know you are scared of going—I know you're worried about how people will react—but it will be fine. You need to start seeing what we all see.

I'm sorry, I know these letters are meant to be full of endearments and reflections on our year, but I can't help feeling that tomorrow is just going to pass you by—again, despite everything you said last year. Because, and I know I shouldn't admit this, I've searched for your letter. And I can't find one. And you have shit hiding places—the drawer under the bed under old issues of Grazia *and that shoebox in our wardrobe that is inexplicably filled with single gloves. There is no letter.*

I also stooped to dropping pretty weak cryptic hints this evening and you didn't respond. Why do you think I suggested we watched The Sound of Music *despite the kids moaning about it? It was meant to jog your memory: me, in lederhosen, a busy tube, the 3rd of December . . .*

If you've forgotten again I don't know what I'll do, Emma—because what does it mean? How low on your To Do List am I? Am I just another thing to check off, another thing to manage? I don't want to be that—I want to be the thing, the person, who makes you hop out of bed in the morning, someone you get excited about.

So I won't assume you've forgotten again, I could be wrong. I really HOPE I'm wrong and you're reading this and I'm groveling—but I have this horrible foreboding.

I want you to be blown away that we're still here, still together after all this time. Still having fun, still catching each other's eyes when the kids do something funny (or annoying), still having sex.

A lot of my favorite memories from this year are from last winter. After forgetting last year, you sat down over Christmas and promised me you'd make more of an effort, make time. And you did. You got home promptly so we could eat as a family, you took the odd half-day or late start so we could walk Gus together, get hot chocolate, go for pancakes in South Ken. There was the brilliant day we bunked off to Margate. And I ignored your surreptitious phone checks, and the way your expression would sometimes glaze, because I could see you were really trying.

But things soon slipped. There was always another Book Fair or meeting or phone call. It felt like there always would be. But it's not your job that makes me so angry—I love that you love your work. It's the in-between bits—the Facebook groups, Twitter rabbit holes, the committees, the voluntary schemes—you have to ask yourself, are they really all necessary? Because sometimes, when you're tapping furiously on your phone in the evening, and I'm about to offer a shoulder massage because I feel sorry for you working late, it makes me so cross to find out it's not work at all—you're comforting some stranger in a Facebook group because she got fired. And there goes our relaxing evening because instead of watching a film or talking you're twitching next to me about the poor woman in Raynor's Park who lost her job who neither of us have even met.

Strangers don't need you. We need you. We need to be around more than ever these days for Poppy and Miles. Everyone warns you about the early years but actually I feel like now they're eight and ten they need us more than ever. And you've told me before how much it hurt to realize your parents were never interested in you and the things you did. But sometimes I see you smile, say something vague that doesn't work as a response to what they've said, and I wonder if you realize you're doing the same. I know you're desperate for them to tell you things, to be there for them, but you need to be sure you're really listening.

Sorry, I didn't sit down to get at you. But we've always agreed that these letters are a chance to share our true thoughts every year, a chance to start a conversation. Well I'm starting it, Emma, because if you've forgotten again I really don't know what I'll do.

I love you, Emma, I love you so much. But sometimes I lie here and even when you're next to me I feel alone. And I want to moan to my best friend about it—but that's you. So I'll put it here. Please listen, Emma, please.

Dan xx

P.S. And if you have remembered, and you are just playing this REALLY well, then a) I'm sorry for the rant and b) you'd make a fucking amazing spy.

PART 2

17

I was on my side, facing the window.

The sound of a bicycle bell.

I opened my eyes and winced. A slight crack in the curtains, a shaft of sunlight crossing my face.

I turned over.

"Hey," he said.

I bolted upright, a strange noise escaping from my lips.

Dan lurched back, fear crossing his face as I scrabbled out of the bed and stood panting at the side, dizzy for a moment as I clutched my head. "What the—I don't—how—oh my God." The emotion of the night before spilled out and I half-choked, half-cried the words.

Dan put a hand to his chest. "Oh my God, Emma, what is it? You're scaring me." A tiny, perplexed laugh escaped as he said it, his hair askew, his eyes wide.

I froze, staring at this very real Dan in our bed. The image of the night before, him sprawled across the street, overlaid it all. I'd been lying on his pillow, moments before. His shirt. His shirt had been half-in, half-out of the basket—he wasn't coming back.

Robbed of words, I just stared. His concerned face, so at odds with the slack expression I'd last seen as he lay unblinking in the dark. That had been real. I'd *seen* it, I'd felt his face, stared at his glazed eyes. His reading glasses, upside-down, just out of reach, in the road. What was happening?

Dan scooched back down in our bed, his wary expression fading. "Come back to bed, Emma. The kids aren't even up yet."

I shook my head, a strange tingling through my body. This felt dreamlike. I'd barely shut my eyes, hadn't slept. Sounds faded as I gazed around the room: every line, every color more vivid. The dust mites in the air in the shaft of sunlight, the photo collage above our bed of our babymoon in Paris—the red of the Moulin Rouge, the blue of the cornflower sky behind the soaring Eiffel Tower, and then Dan—his rich brown hair flecked with gray at the temple, head resting back on his pillow, his face only marked by dots of stubble: no tiny cuts on his chin, no bleeding.

I licked my lips, tried to calm my body that was humming with a frantic energy. "Oh my God, Dan," my voice shook, "last night, you were . . . you . . ." If I said it aloud would this mad moment end? Would he disappear? I sat on the bed, edging nearer to peer at him—he blinked, the streak of amber in his eyes catching the light, and this close, I could smell him, that distinctive just-woken smell. Like he'd been there all night. I shuffled backward on the covers.

Dan frowned. "I was . . . I was what, Emma?"

"You died," I said, my voice catching, the ping of my mobile somewhere in the distance.

"Woah, that was some dream to make you react like this," he said, confusion unable to disguise the tinge of amusement.

"No, no, you don't understand," my voice rose, knuckles clutching the bedsheets, "it *wasn't* a dream. You died, Dan.

You were run over. I'm serious!" My eyes filled with tears and my voice wobbled again.

"Emma," Dan said, leaning forward, "it's all right," his voice was slow, soothing.

"I saw you," I insisted, feeling the whole room spin now.

Dan knelt up on our bed and crossed the mattress toward me. I flinched, frightened for a moment about what the hell was happening, what I'd feel if he touched me.

His hand gripped my arm and I stared down at it: solid, warm, real. "I don't . . . I . . ."

"Why don't we just stay here for a bit?"

"I . . ." I whispered.

"You've got time," Dan gave my arm a squeeze.

I moved off the bed, my mind still reeling, my heart racing.

"Ow." My hip knocked into the post of our bed and I felt another lurch of unease as I rubbed at the spot, the same spot . . .

"Are you all right?" Dan reached for me.

"I . . ." I backed away, watching him as he left our bed, moved slowly past me to the bathroom, a curious expression on his face.

What was happening to me? Had the shock given me hallucinations? Was I so desperate to see him that I was tricking myself that I could? God, all I wanted was for this to be real, for last night not to have happened. But it was impossible, I shook my head and leaned backward, unable to resist another look. Caught the sliver of him in the bathroom door, his back to me as he brushed his teeth. His arm, smooth, unharmed.

He caught my eye in the mirror and gave me a foamy grin, white bubbles. I couldn't help the small smile back. If this was all in my head it was better than the alternative. Maybe I could gift myself this moment back with him. I drifted to the door, still staring at him.

He spat his toothpaste out, the water running. "We're out of loo roll by the way. I'll pick some up today."

I barely heard him, still just gazing as if seeing him for the first time.

This was incredible. Oh my God, if this was true . . . I swallowed down the insistent voice that told me it hadn't been a dream. I needed it to be a dream. I couldn't live without Dan.

He twisted the shower on, looking at me over his shoulder. "Emma," he laughed. "You're white." He stepped toward me, his lighthearted look slipping when he took in my expression. He wrapped his arms around me; he smelled of toothpaste and sleep. I allowed him to draw me to him, his arms firm around me, the side of my face resting on his chest. "It was obviously a bad dream. A really bad dream. I'm fine. Feel me. See?"

I allowed myself to believe it. Clutching him, the incredible familiarity of my husband's body, his solid frame, his heart alive next to my ear.

He disentangled himself and went to remove his T-shirt, but I couldn't help it. I stepped forward, needing to touch him again, to remember what it was like to have his arms around me. This would end and I would want more. Always more of him.

The cotton of his T-shirt was soft as I hugged him fiercely from behind, my throat closing, the tears so close to the surface. The mirror was steaming up, the shower pounding as he let me stay like that for a few moments.

"Emma . . ." he said, his hands moving to mine, his fingers gently releasing me.

"I love you," I mumbled into his back. Because, if this was going to end, if *this* was the dream, I wanted those to be the words I said to him. I shook my head, images of our row last night, my fervent desire for that not to be the last thing I did and said. "I love you," I repeated, my voice breaking.

He twisted around. "Emma, I love you too. But it's OK. Really." He paused, looking at me seriously, "So I'm going to get in this shower now."

"Be careful!" I said suddenly.

His laugh was loud and strange in the small space, then his eyes grew darker as he looked at me. "I will be extra careful."

He stripped off and stepped in the shower and I was frozen to the spot, not wanting to leave him but not sure what else to do. My hands gripped the top of the sink, a couple of orange powdery dots left which the water hadn't washed away.

From our bedroom my mobile pinged again, and like Pavlov's dog even in this bizarre moment I found myself moving to pick it up. I couldn't resist a look back at him, naked, not a fresh mark on his body, just the tiny scar on his left temple from his fall a decade ago. How had my mind done this? When would it end? Would it end? Please don't let it end.

I reached unthinkingly for my phone, tapped at it automatically, and then stared at the screen for a second before I really saw what was written in front of me.

Monday.

It was Monday, 3rd December.

Again.

Denise @CommitteeChat 6:30pm tonight. Please don't be late.

Catrin @Emma Denise is totally referencing you.

Denise @CommitteeChat The rota states that Emma will be taking the minutes this evening.

Catrin @Emma God forbid you fuck up the rota. Lol.

AuthorLou @Emma Sorry it's early. And you so don't need to reply quickly. I don't want to be *that* author. I've just been on Amazon and I've got 2 new reviews today! But one of them was a 1 star that said the binding is loose and I was wondering if I need to ask Amazon to take it down?

18

What. The. Hell.

I stepped backward, collapsing on the foot of our bed, still gaping at the date. Then I stared around, reaching for Dan's mobile, tapping on the screen.

Monday, 3rd December.

I put it down slowly.

Impossible.

"What the . . ."

It couldn't be. I hadn't just imagined an entire day. Was there something wrong with my brain? What the hell was happening? Oh my God, if this was true then he was really here, really alive. Could I be that lucky?

A noise above my bedroom: muffled laughter. This was it. I was going crazy. I'd had one of those things, what are they called? A psychotic break? I'd splintered away from reality.

I opened my phone again, checking messages on every platform.

The woman couldn't pick up the bike.

The committee members were talking about meeting that evening.

Amelia was on Instagram, red cocktail in hand, star-jumping on the same sand. The photo had been posted two hours before.

This was not happening. Could you have a déjà vu this strong?

I could hear Dan turning off the shower, my brain still trying to figure out what was going on. I felt like a contestant on one of those Derren Brown shows where everyone would reveal they'd played their part in some screwed-up social experiment.

I pulled on clothes, the white shirt, burgundy corduroy skirt. They were rumpled but clean. I frowned staring down at the heels and boots. I lifted my heel, felt the smooth skin with my finger: no rub from any heels. I reached for the boots, as Dan reappeared.

"I'm going to check on the kids," I said slowly, eyeballing him as I pulled them on and left the room, then sticking my head back inside, making him jump. "Sorry, it's just . . ." I didn't add anything, just watched him standing in his towel, chest bare. He was really there, in our bedroom. I ached with the desire for it all to be true. A dream, a really vivid dream.

"Perv." He grinned, removing his towel, but I couldn't find a smile back. Dan gave me another perplexed look.

Leaving him I moved down the corridor and peered round Miles's door. No Miles, just an unmade bed, rumpled space duvet, mismatched pillow, and a thousand sharp and tiny pieces of Minecraft Lego on his rug. Hand on the newel post I moved up to Poppy's room, pausing only briefly at her door where she'd stuck a penciled KEEP OUT sign, softened slightly with some quite artistic pink flowers. It still made me sad. I mustn't let her keep me out. I thought of her need last night, her pressed into my side when we thought the worst had happened. I shook my head: a dream, just a dream.

I knocked and went in.

"Mum," she whipped round, just dressed in her training bra, pants, and school tights, "What the—!"

"Sorry," I averted my eyes, wondering for a quick second when she had become self-conscious in front of me. "I just wanted . . . to see you."

Poppy gave me a not completely friendly face in response and reached for her school shirt. Her face was smooth, no blotches, no tears. No sign she had had anything other than a good night's sleep.

She hadn't slept in Miles's room, curled around him. She hadn't been trembling in my arms last night. Nothing had happened.

"Let's have breakfast all together," I said quickly. "Come down soon, OK?"

"Sure."

"I'm serious, Poppy—one minute, OK?"

"OK," Poppy said, one arm in her shirt.

I left, heading down the stairs quickly, wanting to see Miles, to see he was all right, to hold him. He was sitting in the kitchen when I got in and didn't look up as I rushed across to the table he was sitting at, planted a kiss on his head. I imagined him bundled into my arms in the hallway shaking with pain and fear, my sticky hands, desperate thoughts.

He looked up, his eyes wide.

I pulled out the chair next to him and sat down on it. I couldn't resist reaching for his face, tentatively testing the water. I'd been stroking his head only hours before. He'd been broken. He was so close to Dan, adored his dad. "I'm sorry about last night," I said.

He frowned and looked at me. "S'OK."

He looked down at the table, as I studied him. "I ended up liking it anyway," he mumbled. "Maybe we can watch the end tonight?"

It was my turn to frown distractedly. "The end?"

"That girly film about all the kids wearing curtains. It wasn't actually too bad."

I straightened. "Oh." The film, *The Sound of Music*, we'd watched on Sunday night, bunched all together on our big L-shaped sofa. Well, bunched together before I'd crept away to finish sorting the Arthur stuff, the film I'd turned off so Poppy and Miles wouldn't be late for bed. "Yeah. The girly film . . ."

Was it really possible?

"So, you don't remember, um . . . anything special about last night?" I checked.

Miles looked up, a startled expression on his face. "No."

"Nothing about . . . Dad?"

"No," he said, giving me a strange look.

A dream. It had to be. There was no way the kids wouldn't remember. They'd been so broken; I hadn't been able to shield them from any of it.

Dan appeared in the kitchen and moved across to the fridge. "Hey Miles."

"Hey," Miles said, dragging his eyes away from me.

I stood, moving away, staring at the wall calendar that announced it was Monday 3rd, a miniature ballpoint pen on the ledge, a three that Dan had yet to cross off. Because the day was just beginning.

"Cereal?"

"Yeah."

How? I jumped as Dan touched my shoulder, a practically empty milk carton in his other hand.

"I'm just going to go and get some milk," he said, grabbing his keys from the counter next to me.

"No," my voice was shrill and Miles and Dan jerked to look at me.

I put both my hands on Dan's chest, shaking my head. "No, please don't."

His eyebrows shot up, he gave a worried glance over at Miles. "Emma," he said, removing my hands.

"No, please don't go anywhere, please. I'll sort breakfast, just stay here, OK . . ."

"But I want to get you a—"

"I know, I know," I said, my voice rushed and high. I needed more time. If this was really real, I needed more. "Please don't. Just stay. I want us all to have breakfast here. Together. Now."

Poppy appeared in the doorway dressed in her school clothes, "Where's my blaz . . ."

"Look!" I said cutting her off, my arm thrust out. "Poppy's here too," I said. I couldn't stop this strange manic energy as it seized me. "I'll sort breakfast. Cereal for all!" I said, as my whole family stared at me.

I got down more bowls and poured the cereal in them. "Everyone at the table," I trilled, trying not to notice the look Poppy and Dan were exchanging.

They all obeyed in silence.

"There's not enough milk," Miles said.

"Hold on," and before anyone could say anything I took the milk and rushed to the sink. "It'll just be like skimmed," I said as I poured tap water into the dregs that were left.

Poppy wrinkled her nose. "Gross. I'll have an apple," she said, reaching for the fruit bowl. I put the bowls down on the table and ushered everyone to sit. As I stared round at my family I realized I couldn't remember the last time when we had all sat together like this. "Well, this is nice," I said.

Miles dolefully picked up a spoon and Poppy bit into her apple. Dan smiled at me and I beamed back. Silence, apart from the tick of the large gilt sunflower clock as the seconds passed, as I looked round at them all in happy disbelief.

"I don't think I should go to work," I said.

Dan's brows knitted together. "Didn't you need to get to that meeting? You were up past midnight preparing for it," he said, brow furrowing.

Was that it? Tiredness? Was I so tired I'd imagined the whole day, that terrible night? None of them remembered anything. They really thought it was Monday. It *was* Monday. How could it be possible if none of them remembered it? For the first time my chest felt a fraction lighter.

"Emma?"

"Maybe we should all stay here? In the house? Together?"

Miles looked up, curiosity replacing his current morose expression.

"I've got a meeting with a new client at eleven," Dan said slowly, not meeting my eye as he spooned cereal into his mouth.

"What's going on? Why are you eating cereal with basically water?" Poppy asked, her eyes narrowing. "And why do you want to stay home?"

I didn't reply.

She looked at Dan.

"Nothing's going on," Dan said, a warning look at me. He was right, of course; I couldn't tell the kids . . . "Well, Mum didn't have a great sleep," he added.

Poppy kept munching her apple, eyeing me closely.

"I didn't," I said, my phone pinging.

And maybe it really was that. I couldn't deny it as I stared at the notifications popping up on my phone—it *was* definitely Monday. Unease prickled as I read the notifications, guessing the next one to appear, but I swallowed it down. Didn't they say we only used 5 percent of our brain or something? Unexplained things did happen.

"I don't mind staying home," Miles said.

Dan looked sharply at him.

Poppy rolled her eyes, "Well, I need to go to school. I need to talk to Gee."

Miles was watching her, saying nothing. She gave him a wild, round-eyed look and he looked down again.

As Dan asked them questions about their day I zoned out, staring round at them all. It was just a strange morning. After a strange night. A terrible night, a hideous, vivid, frightening . . . dream. It was OK. He was here. He was asking Miles about his math. His low voice steady, familiar. It filled my whole heart to hear it. Oh my God, this was real. My chair scraped as I stood, making my mind up. This was incredible, a miracle. My muscles unclenched. He was here, he was with us all. Nothing had happened.

"How about you get to work, get through things quickly, and get back to us so we can all sit down together later?" Dan said, reaching for my hand and squeezing it.

I could hear the apprehension lacing his words, I'd obviously panicked him. And I didn't want to worry or scare the kids. Whatever was going on had obviously all happened in my head. Just a very, very real déjà vu. An extended one.

I needed to believe it, will it to be true.

"I'll see you later then," I said carefully, "I'll go to work."

"Good idea," Dan said, his shoulders dropping. I felt a flush at seeing his features relax. I shouldn't be burdening him with my panicked delusions: that wasn't fair.

"All right," I said, lingering as I collected up my things.

"Have a good day."

"OK," I said, needing a few more seconds to really convince myself.

I bent to kiss both children, relishing Miles's warmth, not embarrassed by Poppy's squirm, and then I moved round to Dan. Leaning down I kissed him long and hard. Poppy made "ew" noises behind me. "I do love you," I said again, feeling my chest expand at his surprised expression. "So much," I added. Scared my voice was going to break again, I backed away.

I moved through to the hall, another glance over my shoulder at them all watching me from the table. My family.

"Ow."

The handlebars of the bike got me as I reached for my coat. I could hear them all talking in the kitchen as I squeezed past it.

"Mum's being weird."

"Yeah. Really weird."

"She just loves us," I heard Dan reply as my hand stilled on the doorknob.

I do love you, I thought, closing my eyes for a moment. I love you so much.

AuthorLou @Emma Sorry! Should have added it to my last message. So I've just been on Goodreads and someone has 1 starred it saying that they think Carl is a bit rapey. Do you think I should mark their review as offensive?

AuthorLou @Emma He's not rapey is he?

AuthorLou @Emma Sorry! Last one I promise! Should I worry that I've got no reviews yet on the Waterstones site? I've checked other authors who had books out in the same week as me and some have got over three so far. Does it matter?

Jas @Emma Gah have you seen Amelia's Instagram? I want to be her.

Hattie @Emma Time for a catch-up at lunch?

19

3rd December 2011

Dear Emma,
I'm sorry.

Writing this today, when we're not actually together, makes my chest hurt. But there was no way I wasn't going to write it. I'll always write a letter to you today, wherever I am, wherever you are.

You've deserved better from me, so much better. I replay some of the worst moments of the last year over and over in my head: see myself in the living room staring at Poppy on her playmat, eyes screwed up, little fists flailing; I see you sweeping past me to scoop her up, whisper in her ear. I see the look you give me as you leave. I hate that I'm the man that made you look like that. I told myself you knew what to do, that you were better at it. I didn't want to admit you'd learned through practice, failing and trying.

We were all struggling. That awful Christmas back home

in Suffolk that didn't feel like home anymore: the ghost of Mum in every room, Dad valiantly trying to pretend he wasn't falling to pieces, you sad because your parents had forgotten to phone from Jamaica, had yet to even meet their first grandchild, Hattie quiet and low.

I visited Mum's grave, promising her I'd do better in the new year. I admitted the things I couldn't say to you. I left brought lower, knowing I wasn't being the dad she'd want me to be. I stopped sleeping, fear making my flesh clammy. Mum had been taken just like that, after the shortest illness. I'd stare at your profile in the darkness. What was stopping anyone taking you? Taking Poppy? A gray dawn would leak in, another day of tension, worry.

It's been more than six months now in this new life without you. When that last fight finally wore you down enough to tell me to leave. You didn't mean it but I ran with it, wanting the excuse of your words, knowing I deserved them.

You didn't do this to us. I know you saw us as a team. I let you down.

But I want to do better, be better.

I want to ask if I can see you both more? I've been to the GP who has helped and I've booked to see a new therapist. Hattie's been brilliant too—I'm so lucky to have her, I know she wants me to piece myself together. I pump her endlessly for news of you and Poppy. I love hearing her stories of what you all get up to. I want to be in those stories again.

I'm so sorry I've hurt you. I want to make it up to you so badly.

You were just here, dropping Poppy round, her hair in bunches, yellow leggings with zebras I've never seen before.

Your hair is longer, your eyes red rimmed. I wanted to snatch up your hand and beg you to come in too but, like a coward, I've let you leave.

I want to be brave this year. I want to be the man you deserve.

I'm going to seal this letter now and drop it straight to you before I change my mind.

Because this day is the day I met you and you were the best thing that ever happened to me.

I'm sorry I haven't always been the best thing for you, but this year I'm going to turn that around.

Dan x

20

I sent Dan a text almost as soon as I left the house. "*Love you. Take care.*" He would see right through it; would know I was anxious. I just couldn't shake the feeling that something was seriously wrong. I wanted to turn and run back, step inside and triple-check. I needed this to be real.

A bell.

I stepped back hurriedly.

"For fuck . . ." The cyclist glared over his shoulder at me and I felt my whole body lurch. It just couldn't be. How?

Standing on the pavement I put my hands on my hips and breathed out slowly. A woman with a terrier in a tartan coat passed me, an inquiring look on her face. I didn't remember that dog. It was a coincidence, the cyclist, surely?

Crossing the road I entered the tube, standing on the escalator staring hard at the people moving up and down. It smelled the same—but the tube always did. There was a man in a padded coat, a rucksack slung over one shoulder. A child's face peeking over the top of the escalator. A woman in a lurid blue faux-fur coat, headphones over her ears. A man in an overcoat hurrying down one side, a couple of older ladies talking, one staring as the man pushed past.

I checked my phone, amazed to see the messages appear. Have I conjured them because I've seen them before? How does this work?

I stared at the Committee thread. There was no way I'd be going tonight, not when I needed to be home. Exiting the tube, I stared for a second at the wash of blue sky. Had that cloud been in the shape of a turtle yesterday? The café was pretty empty and I moved inside.

"I'm not sure I should have caffeine," I said, almost to myself.

"Headache?" the barista asked sympathetically.

"Something like that," I said, chewing my lip as I stared at the chalkboard behind him. "I'll have a freshly squeezed orange juice, please."

"My mum has the bad migraines," the barista said, pouring some oranges into a plastic machine. "Have you got the pain pills? I think I've got some, I should not really give, but if you haven't?"

"Oh no, I'm all right, thanks though," I added.

He got the tongs and picked up a blueberry muffin, popping it into a bag. "On house." He smiled at me. "Hope it helps." I noticed again the gap in his front teeth.

"Your smile reminds me of my daughter," I said suddenly.

"That is nice," he poured the orange juice into a cup.

"Sorry," I said, feeling heat in my cheeks. "Weird day."

He laughed, "Not every day I look like young girl."

Thanking him I looked at my phone. Ignoring the twenty-seven emails, I opened the message from Hattie. "*Time for a catch-up at lunch?*"

"*Please yes*," I typed back, leaping at the opportunity to talk to her.

Hattie, yes, Hattie was the person to turn to today. She's always been there for me, taking my side even if I didn't deserve it. She once sent me a new Clinique Black Honey lipstick because I'd told her I was gutted I'd lost mine. Another time, she cut short a weekend break in Wales she'd been looking forward to forever to see me after I'd called her crying the night before. I needed her, I needed my friend.

The office was empty and rather than head to my desk I found myself wandering along the hallway and up the stairs, treading carefully between the stacks of books balanced on either side of every stair, past wonky frames of book covers, faded photographs of authors, and Award Ceremonies from the Nineties on the wall.

Linda's office was on the first floor, along with a dark-paneled room packed with old filing cabinets and lever arch folders filled with yellowing royalty statements. There was Linda's desk, red light on the printer blinking, landline telephone that must be the last left in London, brown ashtray overflowing and giving the room its stale stench. I picked up the mug with the hares on, which she knew I'd been looking for, that clearly said "World's Best Mum" and was not given to Linda by her three white rats. (Yes, she has rats. They have red eyes and a custom-made cage that cost her over £800.) A centimeter of long-ago coffee sat in the bottom, a cigarette butt stuck to the thick white film on its surface, which made me place it straight back.

Her empire. And a room I wanted to visit in a few days so that things would change around here. I'd been fobbed off at similar meetings in the past but maybe this time I could be brave enough; the prospect of it suddenly seemed smaller and less scary in the grand scheme of things.

A buzz from the door, the waiting taxi visible in the street below through the smeared glass. I stared at the car, the same vehicle, another car turning down the road toward it. Had that one been red yesterday?

Then there were voices in the hallway below and I moved back down the stairs. There they both were: Linda in her hideous fur coat, Arthur still dressed as two thirds of a traffic light.

"Gemma."

I was pleased to be far enough away to avoid the accompanying kiss.

"It's Emma," I corrected, which would have been frostier had I not bent to pick up a pile of Hungarian editions of a WWII saga that I'd knocked off the bottom stair.

"We had to go—"

"Coffee. I know. Poor Arthur can't abide granules, can you, Arthur?"

"I . . . cannot."

"Well, the taxi's waiting again so shall we get on?" I said briskly.

"Do we have to go?" Arthur pouted. "I'd much rather take you beautiful ladies out to lunch."

"Oh Arthur! So naughty! It *is* an absolute bore. But Emma here has *assured* me she's got it all under control."

"The meeting is going to be fine," I announced with a dismissive wave of my hand. I didn't add "but the bit afterward will take all bloody day to fix" because today there was no way I'd let it. Anger flared within me as I remembered the wasted minutes on the phone last night that had made me even later for my dinner with Dan.

"After you," I indicated the door.

Linda gave me a strange look.

The honking had begun and I saw the taxi driver lift both his hands, prompting a vertiginous feeling for the hundredth time that morning. Would today be exactly the same? And was it like the tree falling in the wood? If I wasn't there would it still happen? Arthur had just said "To our chariot," so I was fairly sure I had my answer.

I froze before stepping into the taxi.

But that would mean.

If it was all the same, that meant . . . I closed my eyes, and my head swam again with a cracked headlight, his leg, his head . . .

Denise @Emma Please can you respond to the messages on other thread.

Denise @Committee I have yet to hear from Emma. We will need a volunteer to take tonight's minutes if Emma is indisposed.

Lena @Committee I will Denise!

Catrin @Emma Hey, you AWOL? One way of getting out of taking minutes. Thank God for Lena. (Hope all OK?) x x

AuthorLou @Emma I called the office just to check something. Jasmina tells me you have a meeting—if you're in town I can totally meet?

Emma @Dan Just checking in with you! Message me back OK!

Emma @Dan X X X

21

Seeing Hayley in the lobby of the publisher did something to me. The urge to tell someone, a friend, overwhelmed me. Launching myself off the sofa, I squeezed her tightly. Her body remained rigid.

"Can we talk after?" I whispered, desperate to share.

"Do come up," she said, avoiding my eye, her voice stiff.

I hadn't stopped thinking in the taxi, trying to work out what it all meant. If everything was the same at least I had time. Doubt still snuck in so I messaged Dan anyway, relief overwhelming me as I saw he was typing a response. Linda had been glancing in my direction, barely reacting to Arthur's rant about young female crime writers.

"Are you ready?" Linda's tight grip was on my arm, a rictus smile in place as we followed Hayley across the polished foyer to the lift. "You have prepared. You said you would."

"I did. I'm more than ready." I recalled the vital papers I'd worked on, freshly printed and left . . . at home. "Over-ready! It'll be like I've done it all before." The laugh that followed was high.

Oh God, the fart in the lift. It seemed worse today. I wrinkled my nose. "Fart," I said suddenly. Three people twisted round to look at me.

Ding.

Hayley led the way and Linda held me back, "Emma," she hissed. "What is going on?"

"Nothing," I said. OK, I wasn't sure I was OK. My insides felt like they were unraveling, my head too full of questions.

Hayley was waiting for me outside the conference room, an eyebrow raised when I lingered. I stepped forward, mouthing I NEED TO TALK TO YOU, but she just looked puzzled. When I walked past her into the room I managed to whisper an ominous "Help me" and that made her look up sharply.

"Talk after?" she whispered back.

I nodded so heartily I thought my head would fall off my neck.

". . . he is tired of life; Samuel Johnson."

"Bet old Johnson never had to catch the tube in rush hour though, am I right?" I said as I sat, and the two women at the table lifted their heads in unison.

I snapped my mouth shut. I just needed to survive the meeting so I could move through this weird day, get back to Dan. I glanced down at my phone, heart warming at his text in response to mine.

"Mr. Chumley. Thank you for coming in to see us this morning. Obviously, we would like to address the quite serious situation that arose this weekend."

This was surreal. Everyone looked super solemn and I felt as if I was leaving my body and watching us all around that glossy table.

"'I would much rather be stuck in bed with her, not her book. There'd be more action.'"

Was this real? What would happen if I jabbed my pen into my ar—

"Ow," I shrieked, grabbing my arm.

Everyone swiveled toward me, Melissa's speech tailing away.

"Sorry," I whispered, holding up my arm. "Just . . . checking."

"I was speaking privately to another writer."

"Twitter is never private."

"I realize that now," Arthur said pompously.

I didn't mean for the laugh to escape. Everyone craned to look at me again.

"Sorry," I said, Linda's look shriveling my insides, "I um, was thinking, of something funny I heard . . . the other day . . . about . . ." I looked around wildly and stared at the river, "A boat."

"Right," Melissa said, frowning and shuffling papers. "Well, there is nothing amusing about all this. And I'm sure the author on the receiving end is not laughing."

Her hand curled into the familiar fist. Only this time I felt it was directed at Arthur *and* me.

"My tweets will stick to the prospects of Leeds United and vintage cars."

It was his smug expression as he leaned back in his chair that did it.

"Or you could come off Twitter altogether, Arthur?" I suggested, my voice bright.

Arthur snapped to attention, Linda's eyes narrowed, and Melissa shot a look at Hayley.

"What I mean to say is," I cleared my throat, realizing things were going wrong, that I could affect things and needed to be careful here. I tried to remember what I'd pulled off yesterday. What had I said? "I know you take these things very seriously. So Arthur is going to pay a large amount to a scheme. A scheme for women. Writing women." That was it!

Arthur spluttered; flecks of spit spattered on the glass tabletop.

"Yes, that was it, Arthur will apologize, come off Twitter, make a sizable donation and—"

"I'm going to do no such thing," Arthur said, the pasty face going puce.

"Yes Emma, I am not quite sure what has come over you," added Linda, "but the good folks here know that this isn't a crime. We can get things sorted out. A few people seeing a tiny chirp is hardly cause for alarm."

"The tweet was seen by a far-reaching audience; it is still being shared." Melissa's voice was brittle. "It's utterly unacceptable and if Mr. Chumley, or you, cannot recognize that, we really will need to reconsider whether we wish to continue in this partnership. We haven't yet finalized the new contract, and we can pause that process while we consider our next steps."

She sat back again, her own team staring at her. This was not how it was meant to go. Shit. Linda looked really angry now. Oh bollocks. Could I salvage this? Did I even want to? I thought of our mortgage, of the stress caused if I lost my job. Dan and I were just getting sorted financially; last year we'd started saving, actual savings for a rainy day like sensible adults. But it didn't have to be the end. I just needed to be brave.

Arthur clearly felt more confident. The self-satisfied looks had been replaced with steely eyes and squared shoulders. "I won't be bullied into an apology for something I said in jest and which has now been deleted."

Linda patted her cloud of hair. "Any other publisher will be biting my hand off to publish, Arthur. Have no worries on that score."

"If you really want to take a stand in this way . . ." Melissa said, her eyes flashing behind purple frames.

Arthur's peacock chest jutted out. "I cannot live in this new fascist world, where we're too frightened of saying anything lest it cause offense in some way."

"Asking our authors to respect each other on public platforms," growled Melissa, "is hardly fascist."

I found myself nodding feverishly at Melissa's words.

"The woman couldn't take a joke!"

"Mr. Chumley, if you cannot see your words were not a joke I am afraid we, at Charter, have a serious problem."

Arthur tipped his chin up. "Then I can write my words with another publisher. And my fans will follow," he added with a flare of his nostrils.

Linda darted a look at him. I realized she looked concerned for the first time. Would it be easy to find him a new publisher, and one who paid as much? His last few books hadn't sold in the same numbers as his previous works, and the stink of this would follow.

"Wait, wait, wait . . . This isn't what is meant to happen," I said, rubbing my temples.

But no one was listening. Melissa was muttering and moving paper around, her partner was struck dumb, Hayley was completely bug-eyed, and Linda was gaping like a fish.

Arthur bounced to his feet and stormed out of the room, Linda sharply following. I scuttled after them, shooting an agonized look at Hayley.

As Linda got into the lift with Arthur she held her hand up. "I need to talk to my client alone," she told me, and then added in a hiss, "I will talk to you later today."

I bit my lip.

"Hayley, see Emma out of the building." Melissa had followed us, glaring as if I'd been the one to tweet offensively.

"I'm sorry, I . . ." I stopped. I couldn't fix this. And I shouldn't be disloyal or say anything that might be mentioned again. I worked for Linda; Arthur was her client.

Hayley stood grimly next to me in the elevator.

"I really need to talk to you," I said, turning to her urgently as she pressed the lift down.

"I can't, Emma, I'm sorry."

"No, no, not about Arthur, well sort of . . . the thing is . . ."

Hayley spun round. "Emma, I've got to go back upstairs and help fix all this. I don't have time to be a friend."

I nodded mutely. "Of course," I mumbled, feeling horribly tearful suddenly. "Of course."

Hayley bit her lip. "You're not dying or anything like that, are you?"

I looked at her with watery eyes and then forced a smile on my face, "No," I said carefully. "No, not dying. It can wait . . ."

Dan @Emma Just out of my meeting Emma, all good. See you later. X

AuthorLou @Emma I'm just around the corner from Charter, just relaxing in a café—writing of course! If you're free . . .

Jas @Emma Hope the meeting was OK and we're still in a job. X x Your author Lou called btw—she's . . . quite a lot isn't she?

AuthorLou @Emma Oh my goodness, Waterstones in Piccadilly haven't stocked my book. I thought they stocked everyone. Should I ask the publisher or just speak to the manager now?

Denise @Emma Lena has agreed to be the backup but I have left your name on the rota for the minutes. Fair is fair. We are all busy.

Emma @Dan Still good? All fine? Love you! X X

22

"Hattie, thank God." I launched myself at her the moment she appeared in the café, the hug tight and a little too long.

"All right," she said, extracting herself and taking one step back. "Good to see you too, Ems." Hattie wasn't one for big shows of emotion. "You're a hugger," she'd once told me, "I am very much not." It was funny really; she and Dan had such a warm family, yet it was me with my cold upbringing who was desperate to pull everyone I loved into my arms.

I half-dragged her to our table. "I ordered you a wine, I figured we needed a glass. OK, I needed a glass," I gabbled, sitting down and watching impatiently as she draped her green woolen coat over the back of her chair, tucking her handbag under it.

"Why are you being crazy intense?" she asked, noticing me tapping my foot, making the table jiggle.

"I'm not," I protested, a fraction too loudly. The waiter in the reindeer ears looked over. "OK," I admitted, gulping wine, I was almost down to the final mouthful. "I need to talk to you."

"I need to talk to you too," Hattie said, her face drawn as she sat down, a black-and-white-striped sweater in contrast to her blonde hair.

"Hattie," I said, a flash of guilt. Hattie never really pushed herself into the center of things—sometimes I'd have to remind myself to ask her questions or we'd spend the whole catch-up on me. She was like that, always topping up my wine with a follow-up question. But I was so desperate to explain, today really felt like it *had* to be about me. "Honestly, I'm freaking out. So today, right? Isn't today," I said, leaning across the table to her. "It's not Monday, it's Tuesday. Well, it *should* be Tuesday but it's not, it's Monday. Again."

Hattie lifted one eyebrow. "Um . . ." she lifted her glass of wine, then returned it to the table shaking her head. "No, I'm sorry, I'm already lost."

"It's Monday again. Today. Everything is happening all over again."

"Yeah. That's how the weeks work," she said, giving me a funny smile. "It's Monday every Monday."

"No, you don't understand," I said taking a breath; the waiter swiveled his eyes as he passed carrying a tray with two mugs. "What I mean is I have lived today before. I lived it yesterday."

Hattie's forehead creased. "What? Like déjà vu?"

"More than that. Like I literally lived it all. But no one else seems to have."

"What do you mean? So we did this yesterday? OK," she said, a tiny smile playing on her lips, "what did I order?" She lifted up the menu and waved it at me.

"No," I said, realizing she wasn't taking this seriously. I needed her to understand. I suppose I couldn't really blame her—what I was saying was mad. Would I believe me? "I didn't see you yesterday."

"But you're seeing me now?" Hattie said slowly, as if talking to a child. "Isn't everything the same?"

"No, I didn't . . . we didn't meet yesterday."

"Did you ignore me yesterday?" Hattie said and sat back. "Cow!"

"I was really busy."

"But you're really busy today. Because today is yesterday," she pointed out.

"Well, yes, I am, but now, well, does any of it matter because I did it, or didn't do it, or can catch up if I haven't and . . . Oh GOD." I finished the wine. "I can't explain."

The waiter appeared, summoned perhaps by my empty glass. "Ready to order? Our special today is a Prawn and Gorgonzola Pasta and our Soup of the Day is Leek and Potato."

"We're still deciding," Hattie said to him, giving me a curious look.

"I'll give you some time."

Hattie nodded distractedly.

We sat in silence for a second, my face glum and Hattie's perplexed. She was the first to speak. "So why do you think it's happening?"

I looked up at her. "Why what?"

"Why today?" she asked. "Why has your brain fixed on today?"

"I don't think my brain has fixed on it." I knew she was humoring me; I knew Hattie too well. She was earnest and logical and didn't believe in anything otherworldly. When her mum had died she had never taken comfort from the friends saying she was in heaven looking down. She would always point to her head and say, "She lives in here now, Emma." She would recall memories with a fond smile. Her mother lived on every time she spoke about her.

Hattie bit her lip, looking to be swallowing back her next

few words. "So has anything happened that's so terrible?" She gave me an encouraging smile. Too nice to shut the conversation down when she could see I was clearly fretting about it.

"Yes, actually . . ." I said, a couple nearby looking up from their meal. I quieted, realizing with a sinking feeling that, of course, Hattie was the one person I couldn't tell. How could I admit what happened when it would be telling her I saw her brother die? That we rowed, that he got run down and it was . . . sort of my fault.

I thought back to a shaking Hattie bent over Dan in a hospital bed a decade ago, her hand clutching his, pale face jabbering as she tried to explain what had happened to him. I slumped in my chair. I couldn't frighten her all over again. She'd been devastated then, quiet for weeks when she'd been faced with the thought of losing her big brother. And Dan was here, he was alive . . .

"Well, what happened?" Hattie asked.

I licked my lips, buying myself time. "I had a fight with Dan," I said slowly.

"Well, that's OK," Hattie said, "Everyone rows now and again." She glanced away then, fiddling with the sleeve of her sweater. "No one knows what goes on behind closed doors, do they?"

"I guess not," I said, distracted for a moment by her strange expression.

"So that doesn't sound too bad, then. Just . . . don't row," she said, her face clearing as she gave me a small smile.

I squirmed in my chair, desperate to go on but aware how upsetting it might be for her. She adored Dan. I had a flash again of the road spattered with glass, his cheek flat against the hard ground, that strange familiar feeling creeping over me. Something about the scene that struck me now as being important . . .

"No one knows what really goes on in a relationship," Hattie continued.

"Yeah," I was distracted, still lost in that hideous moment from the night before. Outside the café a dog barked and I thought of Gus's howl. I shivered.

"What was it about?" she asked.

"Hmm?"

"The row?"

"Oh." I swallowed, shaking my head to dislodge the images. "I forgot our anniversary."

"But it's not your anniversary. You got married on the twenty-sixth of August. I know because it's the day after Mum's birthday." She said the last bit quietly and I couldn't stop myself reaching across the table to squeeze her hand. I knew how much they both missed their mum. She had been the sun they'd all orbited. I might not have known what that felt like, my mum was barely a planet in my solar system these days, but I wanted to be the kind of mother she'd been.

"So?" Hattie said, typically removing her hand and straightening. Never one to put her own feelings first.

"It's the anniversary of the day we met," I said, leaning back again, "We write letters to each other."

Hattie swallowed quickly. "I remember that. Wow, you really still do that?"

"Well, we're meant to, but I didn't," I admitted. There was no way I would be making that mistake again today; I would carve out proper time to produce one. "He was rightly upset. It's always been really important to us," I explained.

And it had always been important. It had happened so naturally over the years. Dan's letters always funnier than mine, but more honest in many ways. Some of those early letters had really altered the course of our relationship—an opportunity to truly reflect on where we were and what we needed to do. He'd even written me one in those bleak months when he'd moved out. Hand-delivered, it had been the sweetest, saddest letter. And when I'd heard he was in hospital the next day I just knew I had to race there. That letter brought him back into my life at a point where I really thought I'd lost him.

"It's a lovely thing to do. You two have always been sickening." She gave me a small smile, but why did I feel the words were delivered with an edge?

"You can talk, Ed buys you a present anytime he leaves your side for a second!"

Hattie's smile slipped for a second and I remembered again that she wanted to talk about something. Was something wrong with her and Ed? I knew he found the medical stuff they'd been going through hard—it was a lot of pressure to heap on a relationship.

"So you've forgotten again," Hattie pointed out before I could ask her.

"What?"

"Well, if today is yesterday then . . . you've forgotten it's your anniversary again."

"No, well yes, sort of. Because I haven't forgotten, obviously."

"So you can fix that today at least? Avoid the row."

I could avoid the row. My chest ached as I wondered if I could avoid the rest. God, I was desperate to tell her the truth. But I'd seen the impact of her mum's short but devastating illness. Could I really land her with the thought that she could lose the brother she adored?

And it hadn't actually happened, I reminded myself. He was there this morning, not a scratch on him; he'd replied to my WhatsApp less than an hour ago: it really *was* Monday. If I didn't say it, I wouldn't hurt another person.

"Maybe that's what your dream was about?" Hattie mused. "Giving you a second chance?"

"It wasn't a dream," I said desperately.

Hattie pressed her lips together, tucked a strand of loose hair behind her ear.

I bit my lip. "But maybe you're right, maybe it sort of was . . ." Could that be it? A really intense experience to remind me about today? Not mess up like I did last year? Write the letter, pay attention, fix the promise? It was possible, as possible as living it all before.

Hattie tipped her head to the side. "Emma," she said carefully, reaching a hand out and smoothing her napkin. "You've been so busy lately. Well, I know you're always busy. Dan told me he's barely seen you." She didn't meet my eye. "Have you wondered whether maybe it's just stress? This thing . . ." She waved a hand. "Maybe it's a bit of a sign you need to ease up a little, take some time for yourself?"

"It's not a thing," I insisted. It was true I had been stressed. The endless juggle of work and home life, my upcoming meeting with Linda that loomed, the Arthur mess over the weekend amplifying the fact she still saw me as her dogsbody. I had to bring about change, and yet I was terrified to upset things.

The waiter appeared at that moment disrupting my thoughts, my blood pressure already rising again as I thought about what I had to do. "Have you had enough time, ladies?"

I looked at him, the café fading away as I glanced across at Hattie, worrying at a strand of her hair, something distant in her eyes. "Have we ever?" I replied.

Jas @Emma What happened? Linda is M-A-D. Has she killed you and buried your body?

AuthorLou @Emma Hi, hi, so I was talking to another author and she said that her marketing department are printing her book cover on tote bags—can we ask Jane if they can do something like that for me?

AuthorLou @Emma Do you know anything about Facebook ads? She says they really worked for her last book. I think I should ask Jane for some.

AuthorLou @Emma Also! Last thing! (Sorry!) Bookbub—apparently these seriously help boost sales but you need to be nominated for them, and the category is really important too. Maybe we could jump on a call with Jane and discuss? Are you about? You're so quiet today!

Denise @Emma If Lena does take the minutes tonight it would be good if you could volunteer to take her slot in two meetings' time.

23

3rd December 2012

Dear Emma,
Writing this sends me spinning back to this time last year and the night that changed everything. I'd written you that letter then gone out, trying to break through my cloud of depression, as well as finding an excuse to drink. It was some friend of Hattie's house party where I knew almost no one, and after losing Hattie, I'd been wandering aimlessly—bottle in hand, still smarting from the fact I was spending our anniversary without you, nervous about the letter. Had you read it yet? Would it make a difference?

I'd been out on the balcony, back against the handrail, telling some story to some stranger I didn't care about. Arms wide, I'd been gesturing extravagantly when the bottle fell from my grip and in a jerky movement to try to catch it, I'd overbalanced and lost control completely. Hattie had appeared in the double doors to the balcony and I saw her wide-eyed look as I slowly tipped back, arms windmilling as I tumbled over the edge. I heard her terrified shout as I fell.

You visited me in hospital the next day, cried by my bed when Hattie told you what had happened. She'd phoned the ambulance immediately. In the minute it took to race down the stairs and outside to me she believed I'd be dead. How could I have survived a fall from that height? The paramedics couldn't believe it either—a broken arm, rib, a small gash on my temple to show for it—I was told how lucky I was—if I'd landed a different way . . .

I told Hattie I couldn't recall any of it, but that isn't true. I remember falling backward, I remember the thoughts I had as I fell through the air.

That fall transformed everything for me. Life looked different after that night. I'd wanted to change but that night gave me the strength to do it.

I felt able to be there for you and Poppy. I made a conscious effort to remember the things I needed, stop asking you stupid questions, no more playing dumb. When Poppy cried I held her, felt her tiny body shaking in my arms over a broken biscuit/a lost polar bear toy/when she wanted the orange plate, but then didn't want the orange plate. I joined her tea parties, played endless rounds of that plastic monkey game, delighted in hearing her laugh, seeing her turn to me to share the joke. She dragged me back into the light.

The therapy helped; I stayed the course—no more running from the room with flimsy excuses about oversized dream catchers. And she's good, Hattie was right. Talking to her about Mum, the pain and shock of losing her, facing up to how I'd behaved in those months with you and Poppy released something twisted and messy inside me.

The medication, the sessions, allowing me to finally see that I had hope, that I had a future.

And with you? No big gestures, no rushing in. I knew I needed to prove I was worthy of you, reliable, turning up when I said I would, listening, following through on promises.

Did it change for you? Do you believe it now?

I lived for those days with the two of you in between my other life, the sad single-dad bachelor I knew I never wanted to be. I asked you out, doing things backward: date nights in gastropubs, a quiet brunch, holding hands as I walked you home. The second first kiss in Wimbledon Park, Poppy up ahead pointing out ducks, clumsy, you'd caught me by surprise, the warm glow that filled me up all the way home. And then the day we were planning Poppy's birthday party, and you simply asked if I'd like to be there when she woke up. I still can't think about that without choking up.

You let me stay. I love being home, still amazed that the fog has cleared. Your shapes are defined, the colors more vivid. When I ask you a question I can hear your answer. Old jokes resurface. And every time I do another thing for us I can feel myself being pulled back toward a world I used to inhabit full-time. Finding joy in Poppy's giggle, a shared look, a story from your day, you nestled into me on our sofa, the warmth as I stare down at your profile.

I still worry about us—that you'll never quite be able to forget what I did—but I'm determined to make a life for us now, have seen a glimpse into another, duller world. I was pleased when the landlord gave us notice—OK, OK, after the initial shock (I'm a planner, Emma!)—it meant a fresh start somewhere new. And it's lovely to have Hattie round the corner—I'm glad she's broken up with Ed, I never quite got him. You love it too—two of you with TV voting rights is deadly—I've watched more X Factor *than a man should.*

I hope you know now that I'm not going anywhere, that you can trust me again. I really want to share the load. I want to do more. You don't always have to be captain of our ship—I can steer it too (sorry this has suddenly gone very nautical) but you are my best mate (OK, that one was deliberate).

As for work, maybe you should take some time to think about what you really want to do. I should know more than anyone about needing to do something you love. I feel like a new man, landing on my feet with Matt. He was always full of big plans during our business degree. I didn't even know sports marketing was a thing, but I feel so at home in this world. I want that for you too. And you were doing everything on your own for too long—this is your time to lean on me.

I love you, Emma. I think of the nights we spend together. Every part of our bodies touching, you press yourself tightly into me, smelling of coconut shampoo, murmuring into my neck. You are still the most beautiful woman I know—you've grown out your hair, your bangs separating in the center, long enough to be tucked behind your ears. Sometimes I see you swaying in our living room to the music you love to play or adjusting an earring over the mantelpiece mirror and I get that sucker-punch feeling I got on that tube all those years ago.

For the first time in a while I'm looking forward again, not in the past with Mum, or crippled with indecision in the present. It is no exaggeration to say that I think you've saved my life this year. I genuinely don't know what I would have done without you.

You are my very favourite human.

I love you Emma,

Dan x

24

Hattie and I ate lunch in a disjointed way after that, periods of silence punctuated by half-started conversations. Me battling whether to tell her, unable to focus too long on anything else. My head woolly from the wine meant my thoughts were even more disconnected, another headache starting.

Hattie seemed to pick up on my strange mood too, and when I pressed her for news she just waved a hand away, "Nothing much."

Was she holding something back about the tests she'd been having? Or was her quiet mood nothing to do with that? Hattie was rarely stressed about work; she worked in HR for a US tech company that gave her loads of autonomy and flew her out to LA for the odd conference. Maybe she wanted to discuss Dan and Ed; that awkward Sunday lunch had really brought it home how much he and Dan didn't like each other.

I looked at her half-eaten food but didn't push her. I knew I should have but kept losing myself in the memories of the previous night, picking up my mobile to check for more messages from Dan, then simultaneously feeling stressed as work and WhatsApp pinged away reminding me that life was moving on regardless. We spoke in a shallow way about work, the kids, Christmas plans, as if we were acquaintances and not best friends.

I told myself if I could get through today I could probe Hattie more tomorrow; I'd be sure to see her, to check on her. I loved Hattie. Loved her so much. I knew how lucky I'd been to find not only the man I loved but a best friend too. And she would tell me if something important was going on. Wouldn't she?

We said an awkward goodbye at the tube near the top of the escalator Hattie was about to descend.

"And you really are OK?" I said, grabbing both her hands, someone skirting us with a loud sigh. "You'd say if you weren't, wouldn't you?" Did I just want her to agree because I knew I couldn't quite face it if she wasn't? Is that why I let her go, knowing something wasn't right?

There was a moment just before she turned away when I thought she was going to say something.

She opened her mouth to speak and I lifted my eyebrows.

But she just snapped her mouth shut and removed her hands from mine, mumbled, "Bye Ems, love you. And take care, OK?"

"You too," I said, seeing her eyes slide from my face. I moved right to the District Line, feeling hollow. And I never left Hattie feeling like that.

"Jas," I called, stepping through the office door.

Silence.

I glanced at the hooks, no creepy fur coat there.

And then I remembered. "Jas, it's OK, they're not here." I marched down the hallway and wrenched open the loo door.

"EMMA! What the—!"

She was there, wide-eyed in the dark, hand on her chest, mobile light glowing.

"I was just—"

"Here hiding from Linda and Arthur, yes?"

Her shoulders dropped. "That is, um, exactly right." She peeped out of the loo fearfully. "How did you know?" She dropped her voice, "They were pretty loud before. It didn't sound good. Then I thought they'd gone but I wasn't absolutely sure."

"I suppose they could be here," I mused, watching her dart back into the loo, eyes wide with terror. How was I to know? If the meeting had gone differently, maybe their reactions were different? Although instead of a celebratory boozy lunch Linda was probably planning their next move over the red wine.

"Oh my God, say they left!" Jas hissed at me.

"No," I said, voice dripping with sarcasm, "Arthur is right here behind me with his hand on my bottom." I gave a bark of laughter.

Jas frowned and tilted her head. "Are you all right? I take it the meeting didn't go well?"

"It did not," I confirmed, and then, I couldn't help it, I started laughing wildly. "Wow, it really did not."

"Hold on," Jas said, bending to scoop up the letters and books on the loo before squeezing past me. "Tell me everything. I'll make you a coffee. I got new pods because—"

"Arthur can't abide granules?" I said in a loud and high-pitched voice.

Jas slowed down on her way to the kitchen. "Yes. And you're being . . . odd."

"Odd is about right," I said, following her the few paces to the kitchen. Books were piled so high in the corridor it always felt claustrophobic moving around the building.

"So Arthur didn't charm them?" she asked, reaching for a mug. "He is the actual worst."

"He is the actual worst," I agreed, reaching for the paper bag on the side.

Jas pressed a button and the coffee machine started to rumble.

"So," Jas said, her palms up, "what happened? How bad was it?"

I waved my hand dismissively. "He threatened to change publishers, but look, that doesn't matter . . ."

Jas's jaw dropped open. "Change. Publisher. Leave Charter? Are you for real?"

"Yes, but it really doesn't matter," I repeated, voice rising again.

It was Jas's turn to get loud. "Shit. This is serious. We should be panicking. What if no one else wants him? Emma, why aren't you panicking? You normally panic before me. Do you remember when we thought we'd deleted that pitch document we'd worked on all day and I had to make you breathe into the wastepaper basket? And the time we thought we'd been on mute in that Zoom to that American editor and you'd said cunt and I had to style it out for you and blame it on our connection because you just totally froze and I could see all the whites of your eyes and the American editor thought you were having a stroke . . ."

"Jas, JAS," I called loudly, moving my hands to either side of her face and squashing her cheeks together.

She stilled, coffee forgotten.

"OK, Jas, I need you to listen to me. Other stuff is more important, OK? I need to talk to you."

Jas nodded, her lips pushed into a pout.

"So," I said, releasing her and turning to lift the paper bag in front of me like a sacrifice. "I know what's in this bag."

Jas stared at me, "It's a—"

"SSSSSHHH!!" I said loud enough that she jumped a little. "Sorry. OK," I said, feeling my breathing quicken, "I know this is an apple turnover."

"Okaaaaay," Jas said.

I opened the bag and spoke to it dramatically like I was some amateur magician, "Ha!"

"I bought it for you," she said slowly.

"I know you did," I said in my Wisest Woman voice. "You bought it for me and you were hiding in the loo from Linda and Arthur and . . . and . . ."

Jas was frowning again. Then I spotted her mobile. "AND," I shouted, "you were reading a submission on your mobile that you love, or . . . or you don't love but . . ." I tried to force my brain to recall her wording, "But you think it's good. Or the worst. WITCHES, something about witches."

At this Jas's eyebrows lifted, the small silver hoop in her left one flashing in the light of the small kitchen.

"Oh," I added, "and you want to talk to me about audiobook contracts. Something very modern and hip and I can't recall the exact details."

"Wait," Jas had put up a hand. "Wait, Emma, EMMA," she called over me scrabbling around for more examples. "What's going on? Why are you having a nervous breakdown? You're freaking me out."

Jas handed me the coffee that had been sat in the machine, the familiar scent strong. "Drink this. Catch a breath and tell me how you seem to know everything today. You're like the frickin' Oracle. What's that about? Have you done yoga again? You're always odd when you've done yoga."

"No, no yoga."

Jas waved impatiently. "Drink."

I couldn't drink, I needed her to understand, "I'm not guessing, Jas. I'm not guessing. I know this because I lived it before. Literally before. We talked yesterday, which was today, and you were in the loo and I found you and you gave me an apple turnover and . . ." I took a breath. Hattie hadn't really believed me; and I hadn't been able to tell Hattie what I was really fretting about anyway. ". . . the whole thing. It's a repeat. I'm repeating the day."

I put my coffee down on the side and waited as patiently as I could.

Jas was quiet for a really long time.

Finally she said, "This so happened in a book I read. Where this man kept waking up every day and reliving it."

My body relaxed a fraction. She hadn't dismissed it completely. "*Groundhog Day*," I confirmed.

"No," Jas shook her head, "it was called something else."

"OK, maybe, but it was based on the film *Groundhog Day*."

"I've never seen that. Is it good? It's an old one, right? Is it black and white or color?"

"Are you serious?"

She looked entirely serious. "Did they restore the color?"

"It was never not in color," I said, my own problems forgotten for a second. Moments like this really brought it home that we were not the same age. Laughter bubbled out of me, "Color, for fuck's sake: it was the nineties."

Jas gripped and sipped her own coffee. "OK, so it's Groundhog Day."

"No, I don't think so. I mean, it's only the first time it's happened so I think it's just a one-off, maybe?" Christ. Could it be Groundhog Day? No, I dismissed that idea. No, it was just a freakish event, an anomaly. Something to give me pause, like Hattie had suggested.

"Maybe it's all a coincidence?" she suggested.

"It's not a coincidence, well, if it is it's like ten thousand coincidences."

"Maybe, like, the meeting went so badly it has put you into shock?" Jas suggested.

I gave her a disdainful look, "I'm not *that* sad."

Jas was really quiet for a long time. I could hear the tick of the wall clock, the faint hiss of a bus outside the office. Then she looked up at me. "OK," she said and shrugged in a sort of relaxed way.

"Do you . . . believe me?" I said, feeling this enormous wave of relief.

"Yep. That's pretty freaky shit."

I nodded. Distracted for a moment because her believing me somehow made it scarier. That this was a thing.

"I'm not sure why though," I said, recalling the previous night, the images making my skin prickle, my stomach swirl with nausea.

"Well, what happened?" Jas asked. "There has to be some reason, surely?"

I looked at her and exhaled slowly.

"What is it?" she asked.

"Dan . . . Dan died. I saw him, he was . . . dead. Last night, at the end of the day."

Jas couldn't stop both her hands reaching up to her face. "What?"

I couldn't reply, not quite trusting myself, just nodded.

"I love Dan," she said.

"I know you do." The laugh was choked. "I mean I LITERALLY know because we had this exact conversation yesterday about how much you like him."

"How does he die?"

I couldn't stop my eyes filming over, my breath catching. "He gets run over. In the street near our house."

"Fuck." Jas's coffee tips and splashes on the linoleum of the kitchen. Righting her cup, she stares back at me.

"I know," I said, swallowing, feeling the weight of it all once again. "I know." The panic swelled within me.

"Well, it's obvious . . ." Jas said, placing the cup on the side. "You have to save him. You've been given a second chance. That's . . . that's pretty amazing."

And I felt a heat spread through my body as she said it. She was right. Other things might go differently but I couldn't let that happen. This was the point. It had to be why.

I'd been given a chance to stop it.

Hattie @Emma If you've got any time later can we speak? Sorry, I know we've just had lunch. It's not urgent. Love you. X

Denise @Emma I take it from your lack of response that that is a no. We must all pull our weight Emma.

AuthorLou @Emma Another author told me about this piracy site but my book isn't on it. But is that sort of bad? Like, it's not good or popular enough to be pirated?

25

Jas shooed me out without many more words. "Go home and check in on him, yeah? Like why hasn't he answered your last few messages?" She chewed her lip.

"No, I messaged earlier and he replied. He just thinks I had a bad dream."

Thinking about Dan reminded me about the letter again.

Jas's face was not convinced. I knew what she was thinking and then I was gripped with a terrible fear too. I pulled out my phone, my shoulders relaxing a fraction as I looked at my last message. "See, look, the blue tick means he's read it."

"What if his phone is with like the police or something? Oh my God, call him, Emma, this is stressing me out."

Her panic made my own flare. I hastily rang his mobile, Jas staring wide-eyed at me. Her shoulders slumped when she heard him answer.

"See," I said, relief coursing through me too as I held out my phone to her in triumph. "Not dead!"

"Emma? Emma? I'm working," came the voice. "What is it?"

"Just checking . . . checking you are . . ." Don't say not dead, Emma. "Checking you are . . . on track to be home at the usual time."

His voice lifted a fraction. "I am." Was that hope?

"Great. I'll pick up food."

"Cool."

Jas was miming something in front of me. Both hands in front of her like she was holding the imaginary handles of a bike, her body wobbling urgently from side to side, and then she sank to the floor, her tongue out of her mouth to the side.

"Er . . ." I stared down at her as she craned her neck upward, an urgency in her brown eyes. "But don't hurry," I added quickly down the phone.

Jas nodded.

"Don't rush. There is no rush. Be careful. Like appropriately careful. Not speedy. Or, you know, reckless."

"Er . . . OK. I mean I don't aim to be reckless. I'll be chill."

"Great," I said as Jas did a thumbs-up from the floor. "See you soon then . . . And Dan?" I added.

"Yeah?"

"I love you."

"I love you too, Emma," his voice was infused with warmth for a moment and it filled me up.

Emma @Dan Just heading home! See you later! Can't wait!

Dan @Emma OK! Love you! You are messaging me a lot today!

Emma @Dan I just wanted to keep you abreast of my movements.

Dan @Emma Breast lol.

AuthorLou @Emma Also, I heard that Jane might be pregnant again. Well, I wasn't sure but on Chloe (her assistant)'s Instagram I saw a photo at Clive's book launch last night and Chloe was holding a wine but Jane was holding a water and I wondered.

AuthorLou @Emma Not that that's a problem! I mean, is it a problem do you think? Who would I move to?

Scarlet @Emma Lou keeps sending me DMs on Twitter asking about you. She can't get hold of you. I've reassured her you'll just be busy. Hope all OK. X

Denise @CommitteeChat I have edited the new minute-taking rota to reflect these latest changes.

Catrin @Emma Denise loves the rota so much she wants to marry the rota. Hope you're all right mate X

Jas @Emma Lots of luck. Let me know all good, OK? X X X

26

3rd December 2013

Dear Emma,
I'm currently writing this with a full French press of coffee and a Chelsea bun as I watch Miles, trapped in baby prison (aka the Sweateroo) which has been the best £30 we've ever spent. You're with Poppy at soft play. So we all know who the loser is in this scenario.

After my coffee I might settle down with the Sports section of the newspaper—JOKE—I will obviously clean the flat like the excellent human I am, otherwise we'll be found in a few weeks' time buried alive by Lego, broken crayons, and that fucking plastic elephant that seems unbreakable despite my numerous attempts on its life.

I know the last few months haven't exactly been glamour and, yes, our conversations mostly revolve around poo, but I'm pretty happy right now. Who even are we? Me bent over a nappy studying the contents like a witch checking entrails, you fascinated by my findings—sometimes asking follow-up questions!

And things are changing again. I know you're going to miss Hattie when she moves away and it will be strange without her round the corner but she's not going far. And I think she needs to do it, her and Ed have been so on/off/on/off it's good she's finally made a decision. And I know you won't believe me but he's growing on me. That comment about his eyes was petty, you can't really not trust someone because of a look. Mum used to say it about her neighbor Pauline but it was Malcolm who ended up leaving her so what did Mum know really?

Ed and how much we'll both miss Hattie aside, I want to make plans too, get a house, start geeking out over Farrow and Ball colors. Dad's insisted we take a share of the money from the sale of the house. I felt resistant at first, but he's right, she would have loved to know she was helping us build a home with our own kids. I want a large kitchen with a table we can all sit round rather than a breakfast bar. I want somewhere with loads of light and room to breathe and our own bathroom so we don't have to navigate foam letters and toy ducks to have a bath. I'm desperate for a place with adequate storage.

Before you panic I'm not going to make you leave London, move to the sticks where we know no one, and pop out another few children. I know you love London, that you love your friends, feeling at the heart of things. Trips to comedy nights at the Soho Theatre, mouths agape in the Dress Circle in the West End, weekday trips to the Tate Modern with Miles strapped to your chest, a coffee with a friend on a sunny South Bank afterward. You adore London and you really live in it, unlike some people who never leave their part of town—you don't mind taking tubes or trains to people's houses in the arse end of wherever, saying "I can read my book."

*I love you, Emma. I love you for your wonderful energy and your outlandish hand gestures, and the light in your eyes when you want to share something funny. I love your obsession with bad American TV (*Charmed *IS bad, Emma, no matter what you say, and yes you have got me into it but that doesn't make it a good program). I love you even when you get caught up in another plan or scheme and just expect me to fall into line with two seconds' notice (*coughs* the petition about gendered clothing).*

I love the way you are with Poppy and Miles. Your endless patience as Poppy learns to read, mouthing the words at her encouragingly until she gets it right. I know it is taking up all your energy not racing ahead or doing it for her. I love the way you wear Miles around the house when you're hoovering, or when you're settled on the sofa, your hand stroking the soft down of his hair as you read and he sleeps.

I love the way you fit neatly into me when we hug or kiss. I can't get to sleep now without you in bed with me. When I feel the mattress sink down I automatically reach for the soft warmth of you, for the weight of your arm across my chest, your breath steady on my shoulder. The smell of you.

I love everything about you, Emma Jacobs.

Seven years and no itch here,

Dan x

27

Our empty house yawned around me, the silence foreign and peculiar. The bike was still resting against the wall, handlebars a hazard. As I squeezed past it I noticed the small puddle of vomit on the floor.

Oh, poor Gus.

I peered into the kitchen, everything wiped down, winter sunlight slicing the air, highlighting the freshly wiped surfaces, the bright of the orange roses in the center of the island. Gus was still lying in his bed as I approached. He would have been for his walk, which was why he looked so lethargic.

Dan worked a few minutes away in Matt's fancy outdoor home office and always found time to return to walk Gus—before I became an agent and the kids were young it had been my job, Dan joining me when he could. Gus, faster, bouncier, with fewer gray hairs then, would skip between us both, under the arch of our hands as we ambled in all weathers. Dan had carved out time for them and last year I'd done the same, trying to join him when I could. I felt a flicker of sadness that we'd let that slide, or rather I had. I was the one with the all-important Arthur meeting, the urgent edit, or reading I hadn't finished over the weekend.

For a second I felt a sad rush for one of those gorgeous spring walks—a cornflower-blue sky overhead, the green stems of daffodils about to burst through, the first early snowdrops. Us in coats and scarves, hands reaching for the other without a thought, unfathomable to walk along without holding hands, and conversation about the kids, work, the day, our future. I loved those walks. The lump was in my throat as I bent down to stroke Gus, my hand lost in his springy curls. He lifted his head and looked at me. His food bowl was still full.

"You all right, boy?"

Taking a cloth I cleared up the vomit, not much. Perhaps he had a stomach upset. I should ask Dan if he'd noticed anything. Gus stood up and padded behind me curiously as I took a mug of tea into the conservatory.

I used to love sitting in here, a submission on my Kindle, the light streaming in as I looked out on our garden. These days it seemed perpetually filled with drying clothes and junk—abandoned scooters, piles of books, a punctured soccer ball. Outside the garden was more jungle than manicured lawn, weeds pockmarked the patch of grass, crept through the cracks between the paving stones, climbed the bricks of the house as if trying to get inside.

I cleared a space at the table, placed my mug down as Gus nestled close to me. Picking up my pen I began, "Dear Dan . . ."

I wouldn't forget the letter today. I filled it with my thoughts from those walks with Gus. I wanted to capture the feeling I always got when Dan and I were alone, his arm slung casually over mine, his profile in laughter. That we were the only two people that existed on the earth, joined together with so many invisible ties. That tug when I had first looked up on the tube, the shock of his expression, something in his eyes that seemed so simple, so straightforward. *I found you*, I'd thought.

As I signed off I blinked back the tears that had formed there, thinking of Jas's words, that my strange experience was a kind of premonition, that I could stop what might have been. Certainly things had been different—the outcome of the meeting for starters. So things could happen differently, things could be stopped. Yesterday hadn't happened, not really. It was just a terrifying insight into a different version of today. I clung to that hope as I picked up the envelope and placed the letter inside. Nothing had happened. It was a warning, a what-might-have-been.

The front door went and I twisted in my chair, Gus lifting his head too. He might be feeling a little under the weather but he loved the kids, adored Dan. And he was nosy to a fault.

I saw Miles arrive in a whirlwind and called out to him. He started, the look on his face reminding me about yesterday's row.

"Hey, come and say hi."

His steps were slow, his eyes wary as he appeared in the doorway. "I got back a bit early," I explained, thrown for a moment as I took him in, the slightly too short school trousers—when had he grown again? Hadn't we just bought those ones? His hair, a little long around his ears. His face seemed thinner, his expression more mature.

"Dad's coming," he mumbled, already twisting away as if he was about to leave again.

"How was your day?" I smiled, removing a pile of books from the seat next door to me and patting the houndstooth cushion.

"S'OK," he said, not meeting my eye.

A thread of worry streaked through me; this was Miles who always had something to say about school. They'd watched a volcano explosion, Albie had put an eraser up his nose and it'd got stuck, did I know that tarantulas could live for two and a half years without food?

He hadn't sat on the chair but was scuffing his toe on the floor next to it. His eyes seemed red-rimmed in the brightness of the conservatory. "Miles, have you been crying?" I asked, realizing the moment I had that my voice had been too dramatic, the question making him wince.

"No," he scowled, and his fists curled at his side.

"Sorry, you just look . . . upset," I said, reaching a hand out to him.

He shrugged it off, and then I really knew something was wrong. Miles was always the first to scoot to my side when he was tired or fed up, still held my hand when we walked down the street to the little supermarket. My loving boy.

"Did something happen at school?" I asked.

A momentary pause gave him away, "No."

I couldn't seem to stop myself. "You seem angry," I said. "What's happened? You can tell me."

He paused. I could see the strained muscles in his neck as he tried not to look at me; he seemed to be physically having to keep his feelings inside. "I can't," he said, kicking at the leg of the chair.

"Miles? Look, I know you're angry with Poppy," I said, in a rush.

His head snapped up.

"And that's not like you. So," I made my voice gentler, coaxing him into a confession, "do you want to talk about it?"

The pause seemed to last an interminable length, Miles's eyes darting from left to right on the floor, his brain clearly working overtime.

"I want a best friend," he said suddenly, his voice startling me with its passion.

I frowned, not expecting that admission.

"You've got loads of friends," I said soothingly. "You're always being invited on play dates and—"

"But I don't have a best friend," Miles said, his expression drooping. "Everyone has a best friend and I don't."

"You don't need a best friend," I insisted. "I don't have a best friend. Well, I had one, Jules, but she moved to Australia, so sometimes," I added, "best friends can emigrate."

"Aunt Hattie's your best friend," he pointed out.

I didn't protest. He was right, of course. When had I realized that too? When instead of phoning Jules for advice, I'd phoned Hattie? Although some friend I'd been today. I would call her after this, check in again. I hadn't replied to that last message . . .

"And Dad."

"Dad?"

"Dad's your best friend," Miles said gruffly.

"Well, yes," I admitted, a lump building in my throat. Miles was right. So right. I swallowed down the ball of panic. "But my point is," I said, trying to get back on track, "you don't need one now. It's good in life to have lots of friends. My best friends came later."

Miles still looked desperately sad. And I thought back to the argument he'd had with Poppy.

"And how does not having a best friend have anything to do with Poppy?" I asked aloud, causing another panicked glance from him in my direction.

"It doesn't."

"Look, Miles," I said, trying to keep my tone even. Don't leap on him, Emma, don't be accusatory. Dan was right; sometimes my desire to demonstrate how brilliant a mother I was meant I flew in too fast, too fierce. "Have you told me everything? Maybe I could help?"

His expression was morphing again, his edges harder, his eyes determined. "You can't help, no one can help."

"I'm sure I ca—"

"It's too late," he half-shouted, tears springing into his eyes as he turned and raced out of the room.

"Miles," I twisted, hands on my chair. "Miles . . ."

I was halfway to the stairs when Dan walked in, his hair askew. "Hey," he said, coming forward for a kiss.

I was distracted, my mind on my upset boy, and the kiss missed its mark, just left of my lips. "Miles is not OK," I said.

Dan's expression changed. "He was a bit quiet on the walk back."

"I'm going to find out what's going on," I said.

"Why don't we start tea? He'll tell us in his own time."

I wasn't listening, already stepping past him to the stairs. How could Dan do that? Sit on his hands and wait? I felt a physical tug toward them when they were upset. I wanted to wrap them up, cuddle them, make it better. That wasn't bad, was it?

Miles was in his room, dolefully connecting a tiny piece of plastic to another, heart clearly not in it.

When I stepped inside he tensed, didn't raise his gaze. The room was stuffy, the curtains not fully open from that morning.

I moved to crack open a top window. "Miles," I said, trying to sound relaxed, "you know you can talk to me about anything. I won't get cross."

"I haven't done anything," he said, his voice filled with hurt; it made my chest ache.

"Well, clearly something is bothering you."

The small plastic construction he'd been working on collapsed and he stared at it as if he might cry.

"Come on, Miles," I could hear my voice, probing, insistent.

I sat on the bottom bunk, plucked at his navy-blue duvet cover, couldn't resist straightening it.

"I can't," he said, so quiet I almost missed it.

His head darted up as we both heard noises below. The front door, a mumble of indistinct words, footsteps two at a time on the stairs.

Miles looked at me, a strange mix of emotions on his face, eyes rounded. I wondered what on earth had happened.

"Oh my God, what have you told Dad? You better not have told them anything . . ." Poppy swung into the room.

She hadn't seen me sitting on the bottom bunk of Miles's bed.

"Mum is going to go mental if she—"

Poppy sensed me there, spinning round, one hand flying to her chest, "Oh my God, Mum!"

"Poppy," I said, my voice sounding a note of warning.

"I didn't see you there." Poppy straightened, grabbing a piece of hair to chew.

"Why am I going to go mental?" I asked, my voice low.

I could see Poppy scrabbling around for an excuse. Desperate eyes swiveling to her brother. It hit me that something was really going on. I felt a mixture of anger that I was being excluded from this mystery, sadness that neither of them had told me what it was, and resentment that it was me out of the two of us who would go berserk on hearing it. Sometimes I wanted to be the fun parent but I was so often the one chivvying everyone along, nagging them about forgotten lunches or permission forms or remembering to drink water/wear sunscreen/a hat/take your gloves and don't lose another pair please they're expensive.

It wasn't even that I did lots more of the parenting; Dan just didn't seem to notice certain things, or care. An unironed school skirt, a forgotten pencil case, too-long hair—these were things he didn't appear to see. And sometimes I wondered why I did. Would it all unravel if I could sometimes just let the small stuff slide?

There was a peculiar pause as no one really knew what to say. Poppy was practically leaping from foot to foot, clearly wanting me out of the room and as far away as possible.

"What is going on?" I asked, not meaning my voice to sound quite so teachery.

I looked at Miles, his face still angry, hurt—he pursed his lips together as he stared at his older sister. He'd always doted on her, following her around like a shadow when they were small. "Me too" after everything she did and said. "Me too." He used to giggle if she showed him the slightest whiff of attention; even if she pushed him down, it delighted him. He was constantly checking over his shoulder to see if she was watching.

"'Oppy, 'Oppy."

"Nothing," Poppy said quickly, unable to stop the glare at Miles.

"Nothing," Miles agreed in that whisper-quiet voice.

"It's clearly not nothing."

Neither was budging and I didn't want anything ruined, not today. This thing between them could wait, just a day. I needed to get through the next few hours. It couldn't be too big, surely? Not a matter of life or death. I blinked, that hideous possibility rising up within me. No.

"I really need you two to come downstairs and be nice to each other. OK? Just for this evening. It's . . . important to me. Please."

I canceled the video call with our US agent, wanting to be there at kids' tea. Everyone seemed miserable as Dan and I watched the kids eat, Poppy pushing fish fingers around her plate and Miles staring off into the distance. I was tense, clutching my mug of tea, practically scalding myself as I stared at Dan moving around the room. Alive. Trying to cajole our children. He was weary too as they left the room and he started to wash up.

"Something's up with them," I mused.

"Maybe I'll get more out of them when you're at that committee meeting," he said. "Don't you need to leave?" he asked, glancing at the sunflower clock.

"No, it's fine. I'll stay."

I pulled out my phone to send a message.

"Is it canceled?"

"No."

He turned, his head tilting as he looked at me. "Did you finally leave it?" he smiled.

"No."

His forehead wrinkled. "So why are you not going? If you have to go, you should go."

I couldn't help the irritated sigh. Dan was always like this. Normally it was great, it meant that the kids knew if they signed up for something they had a responsibility to do it, they owed it not to let people down. Now, though, I felt like letting people down. And I had been to the meeting already so it really wasn't letting people down in the strictest sense.

I shouldn't get cross with him now, not today. Guilt bubbled up and caught me off guard, tears thickening my throat. I'd been cross with him last night. God, how could I even think to row with him after last night?

"I'd like to be here with you," I said, my muscles tensing with images from the night before.

"That's sweet, Emma, but why don't you head out, tell them you're quitting, and then come home. I can do the kids' bedtime and we can have our dinner."

I chewed my lip, not keen to leave him. "I'm not sure."

"Honestly, it will be fine."

"Will it?" I said, my voice rising. "Will it really?"

"It will," he said earnestly, "go."

"Something's definitely going on with the kids."

"Well," Dan said in the patient voice again, "if it is I'm sure it will come out in its own time. We just need to trust them."

"Hmmph."

"Go, Emma, and I'll see you later."

I did still have time. And it was round the corner. Dan was right, I could finally leave it and be back long before I needed to be. Maybe this was a chance to do what I should have done months, years ago.

"OK," I said, making the decision. "I'm going to be really quick," I said. "I'm going to quit, Dan. Tonight."

"I'm sure," he said, in a voice that I realized meant he really didn't believe me.

"No," I said, moving over to him and forcing him to look me in the eye, "I'm serious. I'm going to quit. I should never have carried on this long. You were right."

His mouth twitched.

"What?"

"You never tell me I'm right."

"Shut up," I said, leaning in to kiss him. Our lips fitted together so easily. I closed my eyes and absorbed the warmth of him. He was safe here, I reminded myself, he wouldn't leave the kids alone in the house. He wouldn't head out into the road. And I could do this small thing for him, for us.

He patted my bottom with the ladle as I pulled away.

"Check the conservatory," I said, scooping up my bag and heading for the door, narrowly avoiding the stupid bike. "There's something for you on the table," I shouted, enjoying feeling the smile on my face as I thought of him finding that letter while I was gone.

This was better. Today was better. It would be fine.

Catrin @Emma YOU'RE CUTTING IT FINE MS. JACOBS. ALAN'S HERE DON'T YOU KNOW!

Denise @Emma Alan has arrived in the hall Emma.

Lena @Emma Denise has told me to find out how long you might be. Alan is here.

Catrin @Emma ALAN IS HERE. I REPEAT ALAN IS HERE. DENISE IS WEARING HER WHISTLES DRESS WITH THE FLOWERS. THIS SHIT IS SERIOUS EMMA WHERE ARE YOU?

28

The hall was only two streets away but by the time I arrived I'd felt my whole body seize up again. Nothing is going to happen, I assured myself. I can do the same as yesterday. As long as I'm back in good time. It's fine.

I regretted going the moment I arrived. Alan had yet to take his seat, the high-vis neon jacket almost blinding me as he stepped forward to clasp both my hands in his.

"Emma, we waited," he said, drawing me over to a chair at the table.

"Alan was gracious enough to wait for you," Denise called.

"And I can't be too long at this little gathering, ladies," Alan announced, lips pressed together. "I've got something in the slow cooker."

"You know, Alan, this little gathering," I said suddenly, "runs the playgroup for you, without which you wouldn't pay your mortgage."

He blinked twice as I moved chairs to sit down next to Catrin.

"All right, Emma," she whispered, quietly shaking with laughter. "Vive la révolution."

Alan was looking rather morose in his neon-yellow get-up as Denise stared across at me.

"Well," she finally found her voice, "Emma, when you are quite settled we will begin. Lena, the new rota reflects that you will be taking the minutes this evening. Emma will be taking them in two weeks' time."

"Emma won't be, I'm afraid," I said, taking a breath and straightening in my seat.

"And why is that? I have edited the rota," Denise said with an irritated jerk of her head.

"I can't take them because I won't be here," I announced.

Denise stopped. "The new rota clearly says . . ."

I felt the usual flicker of panic. I'd never liked letting people down, wanting to be reliable, steady, to be there if I'd said I was going to be there. But as I looked round at their surprised faces I remembered where I could be. At home, with my family, or seeing a friend. Why was I so worried about offending people I barely knew?

I thought of the missed calls from Hattie, who'd been by my side for years through so much of my marriage, the pregnancies, when I'd been upset about Mum not seeing the kids. Hattie who'd never pestered me to see her, never asked for anything. And I'd taken that for granted, like I had taken lots of things for granted. And I was making excuses not to talk to her, but allowing myself to be cowed by the Denises of the world.

I thought of Miles, lonely and sad at home. What had I missed while being caught up with stuff like this?

And then I thought of Dan.

"I'm stepping down from the committee," I said in a rush, knowing I needed to do this quickly, otherwise I would end up apologizing, going back on myself.

Denise and Alan both started talking at once. "The minutes! The correct protocol! My casserole! You can't just . . ."

"Women on this committee have often proved to be notoriously flaky, not you of course, Denise, not you."

Denise was too cross to respond to him, still just staring me down.

"I thought mums were all superheroes," I said, turning to him. He frowned and I was just about to leave but the heat was rising in my cheeks, and actually, what the hell? "And we're not flaky, we're overworked and expected to juggle an insane number of things with fuck-all thanks. Alan, you don't even come to most meetings! I've been trying to leave this committee for two years but no one will listen. So, I'm doing it now, while you are."

"But . . ."

Denise and Alan were both speechless, Lena was biting her lip.

"I'm sorry, I really am," I said. "But I am sure you can agree things without me anyway, and put a call-out for other volunteers. And I've done my time, more than my time," I added. And with that I stood again, grabbed my things, and left the hall. By the time I got to the door Denise was already instructing Lena not to minute the contents of my outburst ("Of course, Denise") and Alan was telling Catrin that some women just couldn't handle responsibility.

The street was darkening as I stepped back outside, lamps glowing orange as I turned for home past Catrin's car, her cherry-red Ford Focus.

"Hey Emma," came a shout from the steps, and Catrin was there, arms wrapped around her. "Wait."

I turned, watching her take the steps two at a time toward me, "Er, drama llama, check you finally releasing yourself."

"I did," I said, a small laugh. "I just realized I've been wasting my time on the wrong things," I admitted.

"Well, I'm glad. Some of our kids actually attend the group still—aren't yours basically voting now?"

"Not quite," I said, a pang as I thought of Poppy and Miles. They were growing up so fast and I'd been missing it, missing those everyday moments. I'd always promised myself I wouldn't be so caught up in my own life that I would miss theirs—how had I let that happen?

"Well, I'll miss you, but go! Go now before Alan explains why he's wearing a high-vis jacket," she said, with a wide smile and a quick hug.

"I will," I said, feeling a weight drop away as I realized people understood, people that I liked would get it. That someone else could step into the breach.

"Be free!" she called after me as I turned toward home, toward Dan. "Be free!"

Missed Call: School Office

29

"You're back." Dan turned, wooden spoon in hand, something bubbling on the burner behind him. The kitchen smelled of tarragon. He was here. Of *course* he was here.

I moved toward him, pleased to see the wide smile on his face, the natural way he reached for me.

"I quit," I mumbled into his chest, the cashmere soft on my cheek.

He pushed me back with both hands. "You did what?"

"I quit," I said, trying to be casual but giggling when he deliberately dropped the spoon on the floor with a clatter and put both hands on either side of his face.

"Very funny."

"Emma, this is huge," he said, scooping up the spoon. "I thought you'd be running a Teddy Bear Raffle into our retirement."

Something about the line made me wince, the casual assumption that we'd both be around, breathing, together, when we were retired. We'd said similar things a hundred times but this time it caused a frisson of panic.

"Thank you," he said, in a more serious voice. "I know that wouldn't have been easy."

"Where are the kids?" I asked, looking around the room.

"Poppy went upstairs to her room already and Miles is in his pajamas watching *How to Train Your Dragon* for the eighteen-thousandth time," he said, turning to stir something on the burner. "You're right, he's been a bit quiet. I was about to take him up."

"I'll do it," I offered.

"There's wine and a romantic dinner in it for you. And . . ." he said, looking at me over his shoulder, "probably some after-dinner action—if you know what I mean." He waggled his eyebrows at me.

For the first time all day something loosened in me. This felt normal, this felt real. Nothing bad was going to happen.

"Sounds good."

"Don't be too long. And thanks for your letter," Dan said, his voice lower. "It really meant something."

I was still smiling as I entered the living room, Miles curled up in a ball in his green striped pajamas, pressed in tightly to the corner, something he'd done forever.

"Hey," I said, sitting down next to him.

Miles turned off the TV without me asking. He waited there, in his ball, the pose making him look younger than his eight years.

"I don't want to go to school tomorrow," he said, his voice quiet.

Frowning, I looked at him. "You love school!"

He didn't look at me, just shrugged.

Miles did love school. They both loved that school—Poppy was in her last year and was one of the prefects. Miles was always full of facts, science experiments, games in the playground, how Mr. Fry had been bitten by his son's hamster, what he had for lunch. And he adored the fact his big sister was two years ahead of him, got her friends to wave at him and say hello. Or she used to.

"Well, you have to go, I'm afraid, it's sort of the law," I joked, nudging him. I opened my mouth to say more, and caught another whiff of the rich, herby smell from the kitchen. My stomach churned in nervous delight, dinner with Dan, something that less than a day ago had seemed forever impossible.

Miles was still looking very serious.

"You just need a good night's sleep," I said, ruffling his hair. I glanced toward the kitchen again. It was fine, don't think about it, it's all going to be fine.

Miles swatted my hand away.

My eyebrows lifted; Miles was normally so placid. "There's no need to be like that."

"Whatever," Miles said, getting up. "I'm going to bed."

"I'll tuck you in," I said, standing too.

Miles shrugged again and skirted round me to the door.

Dan emerged from the kitchen as we passed, half a smile on his face as he saw Miles in the corridor. "You all right, Miles?"

I made a cutting motion on my neck but Dan missed it.

Miles paused for a second, opened his mouth.

"Just one of those days, isn't it, Miles?" I said, chivvying him up the stairs. "Come on, let's get your teeth clean."

He resisted my nudge for a moment and then let me guide him up.

Dan watched him go. "Night, Miles."

He didn't reply.

Miles didn't meet my eyes in the mirror as he cleaned his

teeth, or when I offered to read and he said he was tired. I knew I was giving up too quickly, wanting to be downstairs tonight. Guilt nudged at me, but the desire to return to Dan was too important to ignore. And I'd be a better mum tomorrow. I leaned right over his duvet and kissed him on the forehead.

"I love you, OK?"

"OK," he said, looking at me with those solemn brown eyes.

Closing his door softly I took the stairs to Poppy's room, sure for a moment I could hear voices inside. Was she watching something on her laptop? She was *not* allowed to do that on a school night. I had a tiny moment of relief that I felt more myself, my usual irritations and worries eclipsing the strange daydream I'd been in a lot of the day. The voices stopped when I knocked, footsteps on the floor as I pushed open the door. There was something in front of it, something heavy—her school rucksack, which meant it took me a few more seconds to get inside.

"Hey," I said.

There was something slightly off about the scene. Poppy was lying in her bed; her eyes swiveled to me as I entered. Was she still annoyed with me from earlier? I couldn't put my finger on it.

I moved toward her, past her desk, her laptop shut, good, a large round light on her desk illuminating half the room. Dan must have bought it for her.

Her duvet was pulled up tight and her face was angled away from me toward the window.

I sat on her bed, noticing her knuckles tighten on the duvet.

"Are you OK, Pops?"

"Yeah, all good."

I suddenly recalled a detail from all the other terrible details of last night, something that made me frown: wiping a black smudge from her left cheek.

"Are you sure? Has something happened?"

"No," Poppy said quickly.

"Between you and Miles? You normally get on and he seems quiet . . ."

"Oh for—!" She exhaled loudly rather than finish the sentence.

"What is it?"

"I don't know, some boy in his year is being a di—being not nice," she corrected quickly. "Or something, I don't know."

"Oh," this revelation surprised me. Miles was well liked, always so easygoing he just fell in and out of different groups with no problems. But why would that make him angry with Poppy? Was he blaming her for not protecting him from it? He'd often relied on Poppy to step in for him. "He's my little brother," she'd announce. She'd always been proud of it.

"Also, I've had some missed calls from the school," I said, remembering my phone. "Maybe it's worse than you think."

Poppy seemed to freeze as I said it.

"Pops?"

"Mum, I'm just really tired, OK?"

Frowning, I tried to recall what I'd heard earlier and yesterday. What was going on with them? Could it wait? Should I be more worried?

Thinking of yesterday, today—whatever—made my stomach tighten and I glanced at Poppy's alarm clock. "I need to get down to Dad," I said.

"Cool."

"But Poppy," I said, putting a hand on the duvet, feeling her body stiffen as I did so, "you would tell me, wouldn't you? If it was important? I hate you two not getting on."

"Course," she said. Was her voice higher than normal? Why

wasn't she looking at me? She rolled over on to her side so my kiss ended up on her shoulder. "Night."

"Night," I said slowly.

I loitered for a second at the door, feeling remote from my daughter. What was she not sharing with me?

I couldn't shake it as I emerged downstairs, accepted the wine Dan offered.

"They're both being strange," I admitted.

"They barely spoke at dinner," he said.

"And the school rang. You don't think something bad has happened?"

"Well, I can check at drop-off. There's always some drama, you know what it's like to be that age. Poppy's phone's been lighting up every few seconds this evening."

"You didn't give her the pho—"

"I didn't give her her phone, Emma. I know the house rules," he said. "No phones after eight p.m. or . . ." He grinned as he drew a finger across his throat.

"Good."

"She sees you breaking that rule often enough though," he said, in a quieter voice, and then held up a hand. "Sorry, sorry, it's our anniversary and I shouldn't say it."

"I don't." I snapped my mouth closed. The truth was he was right. I did often answer my phone at night: send an email, it could be our US agent, news of a deal; a quick check on my socials, a click on the authors I represent—like, reply, retweet, message—or the editors I want to submit to; or read the article I'd starred in the day but hadn't actually got round to reading. "OK, fine, I do," I admitted. "But with my job I need to be—"

"On social media a lot, I know," he cut me off. "You don't need to explain. I get it, and our job doesn't work like that.

And we're blokes so we don't, you know, share stuff," he said, the irrepressible smile back.

It was a lovely dinner, easy, great food, the white Rioja Dan knows I love. At one point Miles appeared in his pajamas, lingering for water. Dan handed him the glass and watched as Miles sipped at it. "All right?" he asked and Miles glanced back at our table, at me. "Go on then," Dan said softly, "back to bed. I'm wooing your mother."

We'd finished the wine and he'd watched me read his letter, short and loving, no heart above the "a" today, a different letter from the day before? The words seeming all the more poignant. Dan was so delighted by mine, rereading some of it in front of me, "I was so worried you'd forget again!"—and I felt ashamed as I recalled the day before, that I had. I got up and started loading the dishwasher.

"I can do that tomorrow!"

"You cooked," I said, glad to be busy, trying to assert normality. Nothing was going to happen, I reminded myself, scraping our plates into the bin, noticing a torn envelope, the half of a heart above an "a." This is just a normal Monday night, I told myself, stacking plates, putting a fork back in the cutlery drawer.

This was the evening we were meant to have: Dan relaxed, his features soft in the lamplight. Us reminiscing about other evenings like this, anniversaries where we'd actually left the building and gone for a meal, or a night in a hotel. The one where we'd ended up in a nightclub, Hattie emerging from the spare room after babysitting to find us both passed out on the sofa the next morning, shooing us upstairs before the kids found us.

I smiled at that and sipped my wine, kicked off my boots, and finally felt my muscles unclench. The hands on the large gold sunflower clock moved round, the big hand on the 5, 10, 15. Then I noticed the tiny flecks on the window suggesting the weather was worse outside, my body tensing once more as I thought of the feel of the sleet of my skin the night before. Dan was leaning back in his chair, and apart from a few extra lines around the eyes, across his forehead, he looked the same as when I'd first met him. In the light his hair was darker, no gray. He was still so young.

"You're staring at me, Emma."

I bit my lip, a laugh a little too late.

"I'm being silly," I said aloud. I reached for him, a swell of love for him. His familiar face, the tiny scar on his left temple, the creases at the side of his mouth when he smiled.

"You want to get on this, yes? You want a piece of this?" he joked, standing up, his chair scraping the floor. Gus let out a whine from his basket.

"And you can," Dan teased, leaning forward and kissing me. He tasted of apples and wine. I closed my eyes. "But first . . ." he added, "I need to take the dog out for a pee."

My eyes snapped open as he laughed.

"No, don't."

"He needs his walk, Ems," Dan said.

"I know but . . ."

"I won't be long, OK?"

"You'll be back soon," I said, almost to myself.

"Super soon if you want the sex with me, yes?"

I wanted to laugh, normally I'd laugh, but the sound was stuck in my throat.

"I do," I squeaked, swallowing down the sudden nerves.

I was being silly. Of course I was being silly.

I wasn't being silly.

"I'll come with you," I said, standing quickly.

"Someone should stay here, the kids are in bed," Dan said, putting a leash on Gus.

"We won't be long," I said. "Let me put on my boots. Wait there."

I dived quickly under the table as Gus barked.

"He really needs to go, Emma, it's fine, I'll be quick."

"No," I said, pulling on a boot.

But Dan had already scooped Gus up, marched to the door with him. "We'll be two seconds, stay here."

I stood up, second boot in my hand. "No!" I shouted, the word desperate, terror rising in me. I bashed into my chair, urgency making me clumsy. Dropped the boot, scooped it up again. I moved quickly across the room holding it. "DAN. Fuck," I said to myself, pausing to tug on the other boot, panic making my fingers slippery. "Fuck."

"Mum?" A voice from the landing.

I skidded into the corridor, saw Miles at the top of the stairs clutching Tigger, dizzy with the feeling of déjà vu. "Miles, go back to bed."

"Why are you shouting?"

"I'm not darling, please," I said. "Please just go back to bed." My voice was high, breathing fast.

"I want to—"

"Miles," I said, so loud he stopped mid-sentence. "I can't . . . I—"

I didn't have time for this. Needed to go.

Panic roared in my ears as I turned back around, bumping into the bike, "Dan, DAN . . ." My hand reached for the front door.

"Mum?" Miles's voice, more urgent now. "Where are you going?"

There was no missing the bang. My body jumped involuntarily.

The wail of the alarm following immediately, screeching in my head over and over again as I made a terrible noise. Stepped forward, backward, forward again.

"No," I whispered. "No, oh my God. No."

I stood, staring fixedly at the front door, barely listening to my son behind me.

"Mum?"

Dan'll come back. He'll come inside. He'll tell me about the crash. Wow, he'll say. Did you hear that?

I stumbled backward, clutched the kitchen doorframe.

He's going to come back. He's going to come home. He's not out there. This isn't happening.

This isn't real.

"Mum? Where's Dad?"

Missed Call: Unknown number

30

3rd December 2014

Dear Emma,
I knew you were bored of being PA to Brian, building contractor, and wannabe professional darts player (who knew!). There were just too many days when I'd walk in and you'd be playing with your hair—I liked the side plait, no, I didn't think you should get a bob, it's not going gray—or holding a hairbrush and pretending to be interviewed by Kirsty Young on Desert Island Discs *(I know that's what you're doing, it's not a big flat, Emma) not to realize. But you were SUCH a Secretive Susan about the new job—how had I not noticed the eight different interviews? (Worryingly you could be conducting a long-term affair and I would definitely not cotton on.)*

Linda from the Morton Literary Agency knows what's good for her. And to be made an Associate Agent after about two seconds flat just shows it. It does seem to be your dream job—despite the fact your boss is a bit unhinged

(I mean, the warning signs were there—who gives someone a job because they can do six down on a cryptic crossword?) and it's not exactly sitting around reading all day, in fact you never seem to get round to any of the free books you're sent.

But the best thing? You love it. You've shelved the hairbands and hairbrush and now you are emailing or reading or editing or managing a crisis. You love being in the book world.

And you need to stop worrying about Poppy and Miles. They are the least neglected children in London. Now that Matt's brought in Amard, I can work from home more—I feel too young to have an assistant, but man, I love the power. The kids adore Hattie who plays endless games with them and ignores ALL my healthy food instructions. We're doing well, and you need to trust us more. Poppy is still going to come to you with her worries ("what and when is my next snack") and Miles is not going to forget who you are! You're being dramatic when you say things like that. Can I be honest? Sometimes you panic if you're not needed. Because you worry that your children won't know you are always there for them. But they will grow up knowing ABSOLUTELY that they are loved, that you are interested in them. History will not repeat itself.

Things should also get easier in the new house. So, as long as the chain holds and no one gazumps us (I'm so up on housing jargon these days), we'll get more space so we're not tripping over each other all the time. I think you crave that more than any of us—I forget sometimes that you were brought up in that quiet, adult home with your own room, the ability to find a space just for you.

And fine, yes, I'll admit the main reason I want it is for its storage space alone—you know how a big attic gives me a hard-on. And this one has wooden loft boards and fucking integrated cupboards in the eaves. Imagine how much of your crap we can put up there (*beloved belongings). I'm going to buy sticky labels for the cupboard doors. Do you know what? I'm going to go all out and finally buy a laminator for home, because HELL YEAH that small box room is going to be our home office.*

I mean obviously I'm going to have to work to kick my Rightmove habit (I'm down to twenty clicks a day, I think that's healthy, yes?) but I'm so excited to get in there and make it a home. I know it's a bit of a fixer-upper but you're right about the light. And I know you have designs on that window seat, a perfect reading nook you called it. And an EN SUITE, Emma, no more sharing with those disgusting small people who splash everything. Two sinks. A sink each. We've basically made it.

The kids are so on board. Miles has taken his role of building inspector pretty seriously. I mean, yes, he is slightly All the Gear and No Idea but to be fair to him, his little hammer did alert us to that dry rot in the gross pink haunted house and he looks good in his little yellow hat. Formal. The estate agent looked pretty alarmed to see an official with us.

Although we might need to manage Poppy's expectations. Yesterday she asked about the swimming pool. She has expensive tastes which we might need to rein in. (How does she know what a jacuzzi is? Who are her friends? We need to do more due diligence on these people. Or, at the very least, get in with their parents who sound wealthy.)

But it's happening, Emma, we're moving to our own place and we can decorate it and not have to ask a landlord if we can paint a wall a slightly wacky shade or put up some pictures. It will be OURS.

I love you and I hope this makes you as happy as it makes me. God, I am so glad I met you all those years ago.

Dan x

31

I was on my side, facing the window.

The sound of a bicycle bell.

I opened my eyes and winced. A slight crack in the curtains, a shaft of sunlight crossing my face.

I turned over.

"Hey," he said.

A split-second of confusion as I struggled into a sitting position before the thoughts came crashing in. The sobs came thick and fast, my hand stuffed into my mouth—habit from the times I used to cry when the kids were small and I didn't want them to hear.

I heard Dan's intake of breath before his weight shifted and he folded me into his arms, drawing my head to him. Tears dripped onto his T-shirt as he waited, his whole body coiled to prepare for what was coming.

"Hey," he soothed. "What is it? You're OK. You're OK," he repeated into my hair. "What is it?"

I couldn't speak, the exhaustion of the night before, and the night before that, and the fear, like a hard stone inside me, that this was real, this was happening.

"Wait," I said, stopping abruptly. Needing to know but already knowing. "What day is it?"

Dan leaned back and frowned and then his face broke into a warm smile. "You know what day it is! It's Monday the third of December. Happy Anniversary," he added, his voice tentatively testing the waters.

I couldn't do anything but nod mutely. It was Monday. Again.

The sobs subsided and I stayed put, Dan still holding me, sneaking glances but remaining silent. My head was crammed with questions. Thank God he was still here. I hadn't known if he would be. I thought I'd lost him, failed to keep him safe. But how was he here? How was it still Monday? My eyes felt bruised with tiredness, the stress of two sleepless nights. I couldn't make sense of anything. "We can stay here awhile, we've got time," he said finally as my mobile pinged from its spot on the chest of drawers.

I rubbed at my eyes, sniffed.

"Do you want to talk to me about it?" Dan offered in a low voice. "Maybe I could help."

It was the way he said it, his troubled expression filled with concern, his reassuring encouragement, which forced tears to leak from my eyes once more. I thought back to last night.

How had I still let him go? I'd known, I'd *known* it was real. I should have told him everything then, explained how it had happened that first night, what leaving the house might mean.

"Emma," Dan said gently, "what is it? Talk to me."

"It's . . ." I looked up at him, bit my lip. How could I do that to him? How could I tell him he'd died, that his death wasn't a one-off, a strange premonition, a dream?

How could I tell him that when I'd heard that bang I'd known I'd lost him all over again? That I'd had to usher Miles and Poppy back to bed, eerily calm, desperate to shield them from it all. Do that at least.

How could I tell him what I'd seen when I'd finally snuck out. A few more vehicles this time. More people around. I'd stood shivering, staring at Dan still there in the middle of the road, a couple weeping on the pavement nearby. I needed Gus, needed him away from there, tried not to look again at Dan's frozen expression, as I picked up Gus and clutched him to my chest. A woman was crying in a police car as I staggered home and I felt a searing hatred for her.

How could I tell him that hopelessness had swallowed me whole as I held Gus on our sofa, fiercely rocking him, willing time to turn back, to do it again? Not feeling Gus's comforting licks as I realized this time he had died because I hadn't stopped him leaving. That this time it was my fault, the pain a hundred times worse. I'd driven myself half-crazy waiting for morning, terrified of what it would bring. Gus stared at me with doleful eyes until the gray morning light appeared, and I closed my eyes for a second on our sofa.

I blinked, forcing the images out of my mind. "I think I just had a terrible dream," I said slowly and carefully.

Dan frowned, studied me. "A dream?"

Swallowing, I twisted to look at him. "I'm sorry. I didn't mean to scare you."

Dan pulled me closer, his familiar scent making me well up again. Something inside told me to stay quiet, to give myself space to think. Hope a grain of sand inside me. I gripped him firmly, my nose buried into his body, his scent. Thank God he was here at least, he was here, I had more time to think, to sort out whatever was happening.

Dan pulled back, a last check. "I'm going to have a shower, I won't be long."

I nodded dumbly.

He kissed me on the top of my head and got out of bed. I listened to the shower, trying to order my thoughts. He returned, throwing on clothes, the same navy-blue cashmere sweater. I remember how it had looked only a few hours before, almost black against the tarmac of a residential road. I squeezed my eyes shut, willing the image away.

He lingered, seeing perhaps that I was wobbling once more.

"Go," I said, ushering him out with a hand and a half-smile.

The moment he left I pressed the balls of my hands into my eyes and breathed out slowly. Head groggy from tiredness, I inched out of our bed, bumping our wooden bedpost as I passed it on the way to our bathroom. "Ow."

Rubbing my hip I gave a strangled laugh. "Of course," I said aloud, as I moved into our bathroom.

I looked dreadful, pasty and drained, my brow puckering as I leaned forward and stared at my face in the mirror.

"What's happening?" I asked it, breath fogging the surface.

The tiny orange dots still peppered the sink as I turned on the tap, splashed my face with cold water, rubbed at my teeth.

The shower was too hot but I stood under it until my skin was pink and I was lost in steam. I felt detached from reality, a thin veil separating me from everything around me, reacting seconds later to things staring me in the face.

There was Miles at the table, oblivious of course to the drama of yesterday. His eyes sallow still, as lackluster as poor Gus lying despondently in his basket.

"Dad left for milk."

I moved across to him and leaned down, enclosing him in my arms.

"Mum," he squirmed.

"Sorry," I breathed, my voice choked as I stood, remembering his face last night, his worry when I'd been shouting. Dan arrived back, meeting my eye with a sympathetic smile. He slid the milk bottle over to Miles and handed me a paper bag.

I stared at it for an age, the bag warm from the cinnamon swirl inside.

Dan knelt down next to Gus's basket. "You all right, boy? Off your food?"

Then he looked up at me, standing inertly, paper bag in hand, dumb expression on my face. "I'll sort the kids, you can get going, I'm starting later this morning. My meeting with that new client isn't till eleven."

"Yeah, yeah, I'll . . . go," I said, "I'll go to work too." I needed to get out of the house, away so I could think, plan.

Dan stood, head tipped to the side, "I'll see you tonight," he said, a smile warming his face.

I nodded at him, seeing him as if from afar. A flash of sound in my head, a siren, unbidden, forced me to take a step backward. "I love you," I whispered. "I love you both."

Frightened I would cry again, I backed away, barely remembering to pick up my bag and put my mobile inside.

Stepping into the corridor I looked down at the bike, reached over it to get my coat. Wordlessly I left the house, leaning back against the front door and squeezing my eyes closed, the paper bag still gripped firmly in my hand.

Denise @CommitteeChat 6:30pm tonight. Please don't be late.

Emma left @CommitteeChat group

AuthorLou @Emma Sorry it's early. And you so don't need to reply quickly. I don't want to be *that* author. I've just been on Amazon and I've got 2 new reviews today! But one of them was a 1 star that said the binding is loose and I was wondering if I need to ask Amazon to take it down?

AuthorLou @Emma Sorry! Should have added it to my last message. So I've just been on Goodreads and someone has 1 starred it saying that they think Carl is a bit rapey. Do you think I should mark their review as offensive?

AuthorLou @Emma He's not rapey is he?

AuthorLou @Emma Sorry! Last one I promise! Should I worry that I've got no reviews yet on the Waterstones site? I've checked other authors with books out in the same week as me and some have got over three so far. Does it matter?

Emma blocked this contact.

Jas @Emma Gah have you seen Amelia's Instagram? I want to be her.

Hattie @Emma Time for a catch-up at lunch?

32

Shoving my phone in my bag, I walked to the tube slowly, looking around me as if seeing for the first time. A normal day. A Monday. No one else was reacting like the universe was playing some horrific trick on them. So why me?

Approaching the road, I noticed the cyclist a few moments before and slowed right down; the woman with the dog in tartan stopped and tutted as she almost walked into me. The cyclist swept by, the whir of his wheels, the flash of his neon top, a slight hiss in the air. I twisted my body to watch him continue down the road, signal, and turn left. What could I change? What could I affect?

My chest ached as I chided myself again for messing up so badly, how different today might have been if I'd stopped him leaving the house.

The tube was the same. The man in the padded coat had a slightly sad expression on his face and I stared back at him for a second in mutual torment. I wondered what his story was. What would he think if I told him about the last forty-eight hours? What would any of these people think? The woman in the blue faux-fur coat, headphones over her ears, wouldn't believe me, surely. The child peeking over the escalator at me might, but then he probably believes that Father Christmas really does deliver presents to a billion kids in one night. The man in the overcoat hurrying down one side might scoff. Would the two women watching him take pity on me?

I exited the tube into the street, blue sky above, the turtle-shaped cloud, the stripped, small tree ahead stark in its winter beauty. The sight brought a lump to my throat.

I moved on automatic to the café, realizing as I approached the counter that I was still clutching the paper bag with my cinnamon swirl inside.

The barista was waiting, an eyebrow raised as I looked at him, the tattoo winding around his neck. "Hazelnut latte?" he ventured when I hadn't said anything. "And a blueberry muffin." That smile, the gap in the teeth. I thought of Poppy, the rigid way she'd been lying in her bed, the dark smudge on her cheek, the orange dots in our bathroom sink—of course—the details slotted into place. But that didn't make any sense. Why?

A discreet cough as the café bell went. How long had I been standing here?

"I'm sorry." I jerked to attention, aware suddenly that my latte was on the countertop, a muffin in a bag. I rummaged for my purse.

"On the house."

"I . . . Thank you," I said gratefully, alarmed to feel the sting of tears. Perhaps he noticed too as his expression turned to concern. I turned to leave and then looked back, "Can I ask? Sorry, I know I should know. What is your name?"

The smile again. "Jurek."

"I'm Emma," I said, not wanting to leave the warmth of the café, the kindness of this virtual stranger. For a second I wanted to tell him everything, to sit in the steamed-up window, the smell of coffee beans strong, and unburden myself. But another customer was waiting and Jurek was too polite to move me on.

"You take care, Emma," he said. "The muffin will help, yes?" and the connection warmed my stomach.

I didn't want to go to the office. To see Linda and odious Arthur. But where to go? I slumped onto a bench farther down the street, the graffiti announcing D hearts F. I felt my hand tingle with the urge to change the F to an E. Dan hearts Emma. Emma hearts Dan. What I felt for Dan was so much more than that—what was I meant to do without him? He was my husband, my best friend, he was my ally in parenting. He'd seen me at my very best (tanned and happy winning a pool competition in a Sydney bar) and very worst (vomiting down myself and into a coal scuttle at Hattie's thirtieth birthday party).

Miserably I sipped my latte, heart not in anything, the familiar flavor taking a second or two to even register. Resting the cup on the bench, I pulled out the cinnamon swirl, examining it. Flakes escaped into the bag as I bit into it. The explosion of flavor prompted the memory of a particular day, barely being able to swallow the pastry for feeling.

A Saturday morning, in those early foggy days of Poppy when it could have been a Saturday or a Tuesday, midnight or midday. Time didn't make sense, the days long and dark and disjointed. Poppy slept, I slept, Poppy cried, I cried and laughed and soothed and cleaned and tried to support Dan. He'd been struggling with fatherhood, with life. He was deep in the middle of grieving for a mum he'd grown even closer to in the last few years. He barely registered his newborn daughter, emerging from a daze as I handed her to him to cuddle, to change, to hold for two seconds.

Bewildered, he would look down at her, his face softening as she clutched a thumb with her tiny fingers. Then wordlessly hand her back after a few moments. "She wants you."

"Dan."

He was frightened, I could see it. Frightened of the dangers everywhere for the precious new member of our family. Frightened to hold her, to love her. I was frightened too but someone had to do it, to put one foot in front of the other. And God it was hard, and sometimes I just wanted to scream at him to notice us, come back to us.

Anyway, that Saturday he'd appeared, showered, clothes clean, eyes bright. He'd paused in the bedroom doorway. Poppy starfished beside me in the bed, me on my side half-asleep, one hand on her chest as it rose and fell, steady, calm, serene. Tiptoeing in he handed me a plate.

"You said you loved them."

Returning a few moments later with a mug of tea, steam curling into the air as I slowly sat up. We sat on either side of her and Dan cheersed me with his own mug.

I'd told him I loved them. Cinnamon swirls reminded me of my gran, when I'd stayed in her Dorset cottage when I was tiny, the smell of them filling the galley kitchen. Every day began that way, cross-legged watching the small circles of dough rise in her oven. She'd remove them and we'd eat them warm at her small circular table. A day on the beach stretching ahead. I hadn't seen Gran after that visit; Mum and her had stopped speaking to each other—an argument I was never privy to—my parents were like that. Private. Had their own arguments with each other, family members, neighbors. Even if it concerned me. It was like I wasn't even there, didn't have my own thoughts or feelings about it. And by the time I'd been old enough to see Gran under my own steam she had died.

"I'm sorry," he'd said quietly over our sleeping daughter. I looked at him, at his haggard face that had aged ten years in two months, the solemn expression, the tears that filmed his eyes. "I'm sorry, Emma."

I'd bitten into the pastry then, the explosion of taste reminding me of family. Something hard, a kernel of resentment, dissolved inside me and I reached across Poppy to lay a hand on him. "It's OK," I said, "it's OK."

I thought back to those days, to a Dan so utterly different from the one I lived with now. The Dan who shuffled around me, face gaunt. He'd been ill, so swallowed up by grief and anxiety he never slept, lying tortured in the dark. I'd find him sometimes when Poppy stirred, eyes open and bloodshot, fixed to a spot on our ceiling. Looking slowly at me as if it was 2 p.m. or 2 a.m., oblivious to the world around him.

He'd left us. We'd had a terrible row, God, I'd let rip, it still makes my heart ache to think of the things I snarled at him—and then he left.

Hattie had practically moved in with us, doting on Poppy, giving her bottles, burping her, playing with her as I cried for Dan, asked her if I'd forced this life on him. She'd chastised me for worrying about him. She was of course grieving herself, but she seemed better able to talk about it.

The Dan who had left us had long since disappeared; in fact, it was hard to reconcile the two men. The accident he'd had, his drunken fall from a second-floor balcony that had put him in the hospital, seemed to jolt him back into being.

Today he couldn't be more different. I mean, yes, his obsession with stationery is an illness, but this Dan is calmer, more comfortable in his skin. In recent years he negotiated hours with Matt that meant he was always back to see the kids, often working from home. He put us first. I stopped chewing; the pastry dust in my mouth as I thought of that Dan, who loved us, splayed in the street.

Dropping the remnants in the bag, I felt nausea swirl in my stomach. God, what was happening? I was going mad; maybe I was the one who had died and this was some test? Some purgatory?

I'd never felt more alone.

"Emma?"

It was a second before I realized the voice wasn't in my head. Jas was standing in front of me in her woolen teal coat. "I thought it was you! I was sent out to buy—"

"Coffee," I finished in a flat voice, the last two days suddenly swooping back into my vision.

A line appeared on Jas's forehead. "Exactly. Arthur can't ABIDE granules, Emma."

"He's such a waste of space," I said.

"Well, yes, but he, you know, helps pay our wages . . ."

"It's gross that someone like him gets all the success. I've got authors with a million times more talent, who are actual decent human beings, and that sleaze rakes it in and we all have to fawn over him while he's online being a misogynistic twat."

Jas was quiet for a moment. "I agree. But not the angle you're going to go for in the meeting, OK? He's lovely, right. He respects all women. He loves all coffee." Her laugh was nervous.

I shrugged, wondering quite what I was doing on that bench, outside that office. I didn't have to go to that meeting. I didn't *want* to go to that meeting.

"Oh, and talking about nice authors," Jas said, "I really want to give you the opening pages of Ernestina's latest draft—honestly, Emma, I'm obsessed, I really think it's special. I think it might be ready to submit. I'd love to know what you think. I mean, I know you barely have time to read but—"

"Ha," the laugh interrupted her, half strangled, half sobbed.

Jas leaned down toward me. "Emma? Are you all right?"

"Send the pages," I said, my voice low, my body slumped on the bench.

"Oh, I will. Thanks. Um . . . Do you need to get going for that meeting now?" Jas asked, lingering next to me, a worried expression still on her face. "I think they're both waiting for y—"

"I don't feel well," I explained. "Can you tell Linda . . ." I stood up, decisive suddenly, "Tell her I'm not well. I can't . . ."

I trailed off as I walked away. My coffee cup abandoned on the bench, Jas staring after me.

"Emma!"

I held a hand up in a wave but kept walking, back past the café, past the tree, and out of the sunshine into the bowels of the tube.

Opening my phone I ignored the notifications, the pings from Instagram. Lou stressing about her cover, Amelia in her hammock, Claire the editor asking where her book was, the emails from clients and editors and publicists. Denise. All of them.

I headed to the internet and typed into Google.

I couldn't lose Dan. I needed to know what was happening. I knew where I needed to go.

Missed Calls: Linda Office (8)

Missed Calls: Hattie (2)

Missed Calls: CharterHayley (3)

CharterHayley @Emma Emma, where are you?

Denise @Emma Did you see the Committee messages? Please respond.

Denise @Emma I do not wish to alter the rota for minute taking. Emma, please confirm your attendance.

Unknown number @Emma Hey it's Lou! Am on my Mum's phone because my messages weren't getting through!

Catrin @Emma Denise losing her nut in the main group—all OK? I've told the woman I'll take the minutes. (This is a clever way of wheedling out of them though.)

Unknown number @Emma Hi! It's Lou again! I haven't seen a response from you but my Wi-Fi signal is not great. So I am around if you have tried to email, phone, or message.

Jas @Emma Really hope you are OK. Call if I can help with anything. Take care. X

Dan @Emma X X X

33

"I have a head injury," I said, aware of the queue of people behind me, the bleeding shin of a boy about Miles's age, a man lying on the floor whimpering, his back clearly in spasm, the arm of a toddler clutched tightly by his mother. Two paramedics passed me, heading out through the sliding double doors. I licked my lips, trying to feel emboldened as the receptionist looked at me skeptically. "I urgently need a doctor," I said, my voice pitched too high.

The man glanced up at my head, clearly not cut, oozing, or even mildly bruised.

"I fell. Blacked out. I need a doctor urgently," I said, the lie coming easily. I did need a doctor. And what was I meant to tell him? The truth. If I could just see a specialist, end all this while Dan was here, while everything could be fixed.

"You fell," he shifted in his chair. I felt a tiny flush of triumph.

"I did."

"Where did you fall?"

"In the road," I said, waving a hand.

The receptionist looked up, alarm crossing his features. "Have you been involved in a road collision?"

"No."

"But you fell in the road."

"Near a road," I corrected. "I fell near a road; I must see someone."

He narrowed his eyes at me. "Did you really fall?"

I swerved the reply, "I need a head specialist. A brain specialist. A brain injury specialist. Is there anyone in the hospital that is a specialist in the brain?"

"You want an appointment with someone in neurology? Your GP will refer you to the appropriate doctor. We only see emergencies."

"No," I said, leaning forward and almost falling through the glass barrier that separated us. "Please, you don't understand. It really *is* urgent; I really do need to see someone. I can wait. Please."

Perhaps it was the earnest look or the desperation tingeing my voice, but I could see the man relenting. He let out the smallest of sighs before staring at the computer in front of him.

"You'll need to fill in this form. The wait is four hours. Priority cases will be seen first which . . ." I swear he sneered, ". . . might mean your wait time is further delayed."

"Thanks, thank you," I placed a palm on the glass, tears pricking my eyes, as if I was in an airport lounge about to watch my one true love fly away.

The receptionist just nodded and bent to look past me.

Wandering to the row of pea-green bucket seats bolted to the floor, skirting past the groaning man with his back in spasm and trying not to see the droplets of blood on the speckled plastic linoleum beneath a man with a gashed lower leg, I sat, feeling all eyes were swiveled to me and my supposed injury. But something was going on, something had broken, a circuit in my brain or something surely that would explain the last forty-eight hours, or the fact I thought I had lived them.

Avoiding the curious glances, I settled in the seat. When the kids were young I enjoyed going anywhere sans children: GP waiting rooms, the optician, the pharmacist because they always had the longest queue like they made the drugs from scratch in the back. I'd revel in the moment to read, to think, to just be alone, without any interruptions.

I wasn't sure any story could distract me from my thoughts today. I *was* the story. As I stared at the wall opposite with its endless peeling posters, reminders to Wash Your Hands, I wondered what the doctors might discover. Because they had to find something, surely? Maybe they'd give me an MRI, get the other doctors in to have a look at the results, fly in a specialist, Skype an American doctor, see if the US had any cases like mine. I'd become one of those case studies in medical magazines. My hope ignited as I stared at the clock, willing time, for once, to move faster.

People came and went, the man dripping blood, the man in spasm, all disappeared, the swish of the double doors making me look up every time. My stomach was empty, the latte and cinnamon swirl hours ago now, but I didn't want to leave this spot, this chance to be cured. I wouldn't just be saving myself.

Slumping in the seat, eyes sagging even under the fluorescent bar lights, I bolted to attention as I heard "Emma Jacobs?"

"Yes, yes," I said, scurrying after her, boots slippery on the gray linoleum of the corridor.

We moved into a small square side room and she sat in a swivel chair looking at some notes.

"It says here you've had a head injury," she said, a tiny frown. I wondered what else was written there.

I licked my lips. "I have, well, I think I have, you see . . .

this is going to sound crazy but honestly it's true . . . I have lived today before, twice in fact."

The nurse's frown deepened.

I didn't give her time to interrupt. It was vital I got her to understand I was telling the truth, that this was *serious*. "I basically go to sleep and I wake up and everything is the same. Time hasn't moved on. None of the past twenty-four hours has happened."

I paused, my chest going up and down, up and down.

The nurse looked momentarily dumb. I was worried she was skeptical. I mean, I'd be skeptical.

"So I think someone needs to look inside my head. Maybe I'm really ill, like a tumor or something, and it's making me believe that everything is real—it feels absolutely real—I mean it *is* real, you see, my husband dies. At the end of today. So he has died twice now but he is totally fine."

The nurse took a slow breath and my eyes widened. Oh God, please let her realize I was telling the truth.

"I can absolutely see you think what you're saying has happened but—"

"It has happened," I didn't mean to shout it. She flinched. "I'm sorry," I can't help gesturing with both hands now, "you don't understand. Please, I promise, I can't go out of here without seeing a doctor. Please."

The wait felt interminable. I'd already been at the hospital for over four hours but I couldn't leave now and give up.

"I'm not sure how to help really," the nurse said, her gaze slightly to the right.

My shoulders slumped. Of course she didn't believe me. I knew I hadn't explained it well enough.

"I can refer you for psych evaluation," she scribbled something on a form.

I would have liked a neurosurgeon or someone who spent their days opening up people's brains, but maybe someone who had studied the brain was the answer. "Yes please. Please." The triage nurse gave me a peculiar look; I suppose most people in for psychiatric evaluation weren't always so keen.

I left clutching my sheet of paper like a lottery ticket, led to a different, smaller waiting area with no blood on the floor or people moaning. The whole day seemed to pass, the winter sky outside now a mass of cloud, the light fading fast. I pulled my coat around myself and rehearsed what I was going to say.

When my name was called I stood up, put my shoulders back, and followed the doctor into her consulting room. I needed to sound sensible, legitimate, level-headed, NOT crazy. She was curly-haired with a line of magenta lipstick and she seemed to take an age to settle herself in her chair.

"I'm here because I think something really serious has happened to my brain, my mind . . ." I exploded dramatically.

She tipped her head, birdlike, to one side and sucked on her pen. "Start from the beginning . . ."

She didn't want to refer me for a scan, or any test. "Let's see where we get to with talking."

I tried to keep my voice even, my gaze steady. I sat on my hands to stop any wild gesticulations that would have me pegged as unstable.

She made notes and she asked whether I'd been particularly stressed at work. How were my relationships? Was there anything causing me emotional distress?

"Just seeing my husband die," I said, almost petulantly. This was not going how I'd rehearsed. Why couldn't she take me to an MRI scan? I asked again and she swerved the question.

"Is there a reason you're intent on focusing on your

husband's mortality? Are you worried about your own mortality?"

I knew this was all getting me nowhere. Through the course of the consultation I sagged into my seat, the energy leaking from me. No one could help me. I suppose I'd known it really. That whatever was happening *was* happening. So all I could do was take control back, change the only thing that mattered. Not screw it up again.

I got up when she was mid-sentence. "I think I'll go home," I said.

She glanced at the notes. "I could refer you to your GP for some talking therapy?" she suggested.

I nodded mutely.

"They'll be in touch," she said and I thought—when?

Dan @Emma Hope the super-important meeting went well. See you later x x

Hattie @Emma Lunch?

Catrin @Emma All OK my fave committee member? You left the group and, as fun as it is watching Denise lose her shit over it, I hope all's fine? C X

Missed Calls: Linda (8)

Missed Calls: Jas (2)

Jas @Emma Hey, bit worried as can't get hold of you. You didn't seem yourself this morning. Do let me know you're OK X X

34

My phone was red-hot as I headed home in a weary daze. Barely taking in my surroundings, everything muted around me. I felt totally lost, inconsequential. I couldn't face the emails and messages that had built up throughout my day. Editors, authors, mothers in the committee, even Hattie's missed calls. I didn't have the energy to face them. And what would be the point anyway? It's not like anyone would remember any of it.

The house was quiet as I stepped inside and called out. When Miles returned I practically pounced on him, pulling him toward me for a hug. The feeling of having my boy, real in my arms, was so comforting I almost started weeping in the hall corridor. His hair tickled my face; I was shocked that both my children were growing up so quickly.

"Mum," he squirmed out of my clutches.

"Sorry," I said, releasing him and trying to smile. "Come into the kitchen, tell me about your day." I knew I sounded desperate, pleading, and Miles gave me a sideways look. "I've got chocolate," I practically shouted, knowing I'd offer him anything to step inside. I've got the goods, my boy, whatever you want I'll get it—just talk to me.

Miles shrugged and moved inside and my insides expanded.

I opened the cupboard to pull down a secret stash of Twixes that I hid from everyone. Miles's eyes rounded as I blushed and offered him one. I remembered days, months ago now, Miles and I at the kitchen table together after school with a plate of cookies, him doing homework, me replying to emails. I couldn't remember the last time we'd done that.

As he opened the wrapper and sat at the kitchen island I stared at him, my brain awash with the exhaustion and confusion of the last few days. He bit into it and I recalled his sad anguish, his worried face, the anger that had erupted toward Poppy.

Dan returned but quietly backed out of the room, his eyebrows raised, his face conveying: "I'll be close by if you need me." When did Dan and I say so much with an expression? The thought gave me a momentary thrill—I didn't have that kind of connection with anyone else—the ability to say so much with a look. To meet his eye in a room of people, or across a dining room table and know just what he was thinking. Two lines deepening either side of his mouth signaled quiet amusement, his fingers twitching meaning he was bored, a look in his eyes that meant he loved me.

I inhaled deeply, Miles looking up. I didn't want to think about Dan, didn't want to break down now.

"Difficult day?" I ventured, pulling myself back to the present.

Miles swallowed the piece he was eating, a slight wave of panic passing across his face. "Not really."

"A mother," I began, tracing a finger on the table, "mentioned something happened today. At school." I looked up, eyes innocent.

Miles's face paled as it always did whenever he was caught out. He'd never been a deceitful child, immediately fessing up to the smallest crimes. I recalled the time on a train to somewhere when he was five years old. The ticket officer had asked for our tickets and I had produced mine. "He's four," I explained, nodding to the inspector, waiting for him to move on. Tickets were free for under-fives.

Miles had looked at the ticket inspector. "I'm five," he said in a loud voice. A man opposite glanced up as I straightened in my seat. "Sorry," I said, laughing airily, "he's four."

Miles had frowned. "I'm five. My birthday is May, May the tenth," he insisted.

I could feel heat creep up my neck, into my cheeks. A woman opposite was staring.

He tugged on my arm. "I'm five, Mummy."

There was a momentary pause as the ticket officer looked at him, looked at me, and then, with a small wink said, "Kids, eh?"

I could have melted into a puddle of shame. But I hadn't been cross with him then and I certainly didn't have the heart to be now.

"So? I asked. "Is it true?"

He gave me the smallest of shrugs.

"Is someone being unpleasant?" I asked, trying not to display my rage at the thought another child was hurting one of mine. I remembered a moment with Poppy in the park. She must have been five or six. A girl she went to school with had been playing with two others. She told them in a loud voice not to play with Poppy. I'd never known anger like it—the red heat of it mixed with heartache for my baby.

"Liam was being mean," he said, his eyes sliding over the surface of the table, unable to meet mine.

"Being mean how?" I imagined a playground scuffle, a tug on a sweater, a nudge in the ribs. I was already plotting a hex on the bully.

"He was . . . saying stuff. About . . ." Miles stopped, licked his lips. "About what Poppy did . . ."

I frowned then, not expecting that.

Just then the door went and Poppy herself, after some grunting about the bike in the corridor, appeared in the kitchen.

"Hey?" she said, eyes narrowing as if she sensed our collusion.

Miles looked stricken; his hands clenched on the kitchen counter.

"Miles tells me someone was being mean about you at school today."

Poppy's mouth fell open and then she turned to Miles.

"Oh my God, did you tell Mum?" she accused.

"I didn't," Miles panicked.

"Tell Mum what?" I asked.

"Nothing," they both chorused.

"It's obviously not nothing," I said, my voice rising over them. "Poppy," I said, "what did you do? What's it got to do with Miles?"

"It hasn't. It's Holly's stupid brother stirring shit up."

"Poppy!" The swear word, unfamiliar in her mouth.

"Whatever, it's not fair Holly has totally started all this and now I'm the one getting in trouble."

"He showed me them," Miles burst out.

"They deserved it."

"It's really bad."

"Showed you what?" I called out.

"They started it," Poppy said, fear crossing her face. "They weren't meant to find out it was me, OK?"

"Well now I can't go back to school," Miles said.

"You? What about me?" Poppy looked really upset.

My head was throbbing, their voices clashing as I tried to make sense of what they were saying.

Miles looked bereft. What had Poppy done? It couldn't be too bad, surely? A drama. I mean, this was primary school. And yet I felt a creeping dread in my stomach.

"But why did y—"

"Shut up, Miles," Poppy said, her body quivering as she spoke.

"Poppy, what is going on?"

"Well, he's obviously been telling you." There were tears in Poppy's eyes.

"I didn't," Miles insisted.

"A mum said something."

Poppy looked pale. "It's just stupid school stuff."

"And school rang me." Fine, this was not *strictly* true. They hadn't rung me yet but they had been calling—maybe it wasn't Miles they were phoning about?

Just then Dan appeared, a smile slipping from his face as he saw us all in the kitchen looking mutinous.

"What's happened?"

Miles had half-stepped behind me, a shield to Poppy's wrath.

"It's nothing," she yelled, and Dan took a step back in surprise as she stormed past him upstairs.

"Don't let her leave," I said, moving to follow her.

"Woah, woah, wait, let her go, you can both be hotheads," Dan said.

"What's that supposed to mean?" I said, like a hothead.

Dan looked weary. "I just mean sometimes we need to give her some space to come to us . . ."

I did, I thought back to yesterday. It didn't work. She doesn't say anything. But there was no way I was arguing with Dan. Seeing him in front of me, alive, here. The horrific pain of his death floored me once more, rowing with him that first night, allowing him to leave last night. A shiver ran through me. If I could stop the car, him going out to the car, then it wouldn't happen. It couldn't happen. I needed to get out of there before I frightened them all.

"I'm going to go and get changed," I muttered.

"Emma," Dan's voice was a warning.

"I'm just getting changed, Dan," I said, squeezing my eyes closed as I left the room.

I couldn't face this today; there was something in Poppy's face that scared me a little, something adult. If I pushed it what would I unravel? I felt like I was losing my handle on things, like everything I'd known was shifting beneath me. I couldn't be sure of what was real or what was not. And I loved Poppy and Miles so much, I wanted to keep that thought close to me while I got through this day, while I concentrated on saving Dan.

I was dragging my feet up to our bedroom, time moving so slowly as I changed into harem trousers and a loose sweater. I didn't go back downstairs when he gave them their tea, lied and said I was working as I closed the office door and sank into the chair. Why did it feel that everything was spinning out of my control? What was going to happen in a few short hours? If it had happened twice, surely . . . but if I could stop him going? That idea solidified. That was what I had done wrong: I had literally sent him out to his death.

And what if he had died and I hadn't woken up here again? I would have had to live with the fact I'd known and basically killed him. I shut my eyes, willing that thought down.

Tonight I would force him to stay inside. There was no way he could be run down if he wasn't in the street.

This new idea gave me energy to emerge for our dinner, Dan frosty at my disappearance. But how could I explain without breaking down? Or worse, triggering an argument? The meal was stilted, Dan quiet. Miles had appeared, loitering at the bottom of the stairs, Tigger dangling from his hand, sent packing by Dan who was clearly not in the mood to be messed with.

I felt overwhelmed, a terrible foreboding as I pushed the food around my plate. I had, of course, forgotten to acknowledge our anniversary and Dan had barely said a word to me.

"I know why you're quiet," I said in a low voice. "I didn't forget, it's just . . ."

Dan pushed his chair back. "I'm going to sit next door," he said, no offer of pudding, no offer of another glass of wine.

"I'll wash up," I said, moving to clear the plates and then changing my mind and following him out of the room. Just in case he changed his mind. I wanted him in my sights this evening.

I sat down on the sofa next to him. "I'm sorry I forgot," I said slowly. "Well, I didn't forget, but it's hard to explain. Well, not hard but you won't believe me. I even went to the hospital about it actually . . ."

Dan's whole demeanor shifted at those words. He turned toward me and immediately put a hand on my leg. "The hospital? Why? Are you ill? Is there something you're not telling me?"

"I'm not ill, well, I don't think I am. I'm just, the thing is . . ." Oh God, I needed him to understand, to take me seriously. "I wake up and it's the same day all over again . . ."

His forehead wrinkled.

"I know it sounds impossible. But it's true."

"Like . . . a memory thing?" He clearly wasn't getting it. "What did they say at the hospital?"

"Nothing much," I said, my head dipping onto my chest.

"Hey," he said, drawing me to him. "Don't be upset. We can work this thing out. It sounds neurological maybe?"

I knew I needed to say more, but Dan was warm and I felt overwhelmed and he was stroking my arm as I rested against him and I just wanted to stay there awhile. My eyes were drooping, my head full. I felt as if I hadn't slept for days.

Dan slipped his arm out from under me a while later. "I'm just going to take Gus for a pee," he whispered.

"No! No, I'll do it," I said, sitting straighter, adrenaline surging. "I'm not sure he's quite right." Shame flashed through me that I hadn't taken Gus to the vet's yet. "You stay here," I said, "I want the fresh air."

"OK, well," Dan said slowly, looking a bit bemused, "I'll just sort the stuff for breakf—"

"No, leave it," I said, voice high. "Stay and relax. Please. I won't be long."

"If you're sure," he said, picking up his almost-finished wine glass.

"I'm really sure," then I knelt down. "You have to promise me," I said; Gus whined softly in the background. "Promise me you won't move from this sofa?"

Dan sipped his wine and gave me a strange look. "Er, I promise."

I turned and went to get Gus's leash. "And promise me you'll stay in the house?" I said on my return.

"Where else do you think I'd go?"

"Nowhere," I said. I forced a smile. "I just, well, I just want you to relax. And I'll see you soon, OK?"

He waggled his eyebrows again. "Oh I see," he said, "softening me up for some sex later. OK then," he said, and I tried to smile back, ignore the nausea swirling inside me.

I moved across to Gus quickly, putting the leash on him. He gave me a doleful look and I gave him an encouraging tug. "Come on, boy," I said.

A quick pee, I thought, we'd be back in two seconds. Gus wasn't exactly looking like he was in the mood for a walk. I coaxed Gus forward and then stopped in the corridor as I stared at the leash in my hand. What if the premonition had been a warning for me? What if it was going to be me splayed in the road?

I dropped the leash, stepping back into the living room. Dan was in profile on the sofa where I'd left him, his nose with the tiny bump where he'd broken it ruining an otherwise perfectly proportioned face. I took a breath, a few steps forward, and reached down to kiss him.

Gus barked from the corridor.

"I love you, OK? Whatever happens."

"OK," he said slowly.

"I'll be as quick as I can." What time had it happened? Had the moment passed anyway?

"See you soon then," he said, watching me carefully.

I nodded, unable to find the words for much else. Dan lifted both eyebrows. I knew I was being mad. I couldn't help it. I gave him one more kiss. His eyes crinkled at the edges.

Leaving, I bundled Gus into my arms, squeezing past the bike with him to the front door.

The air was cold as I put Gus down and wrapped my coat tightly around myself and walked down our path to the gate, sleet on my face like an icy mist.

There was no way I was walking in the direction of the crash. What if someone *had* to be run down? I didn't want that to be true but I wasn't risking it. I turned the other way, pressed against the wall, alert, past parked cars, houses with orange windows underneath a starless sky. My breath clouded in front of me as I looked around, tense for any sound.

We moved slowly and then all of a sudden Gus flopped down on the pavement, his weight slumped on to the cold, wet stone. The leash jerked in my hand. I bent down to ruffle his fur; he really didn't seem himself. My shoulder hurt from the wrench of the pull.

I heard the bang as I was crouched over him and squeezed my eyes closed as if waiting for an impact. A second passed and my whole body shuddered as I opened my eyes, feeling Gus's fur tickling my face. What did this mean? The car had still crashed. Should I run to check? No, I knew it was the same noise, that unmistakable sound of metal and glass.

That meant it had happened. And Dan was in our house.

I quickly lifted Gus, carrying him awkwardly back the few paces to our house. We had barely got half a street away. I felt a huge swell of relief.

"Oh my God, thank God, thank God." I sped up.

Dan had stayed, he wasn't in that street, his leg at a strange angle, the terrible dark pool spreading beneath him. He was back in our house, I'd told him to stay there. He would have stayed. And I was fine. I hadn't been hurt. And he was safe. For the first time since it all started, light burst through. I wanted to shout, to throw my head back and howl. I couldn't feel the cold sleet on my face, didn't care, just needed to get back, back to my husband.

I put Gus down and let him gently into the house. Thank

God, thank God, thank God. I wanted to cry and laugh and mostly cling to Dan, tell him over and over again how much I love him, how much I need him.

"Dan?" I stage-whispered. "Are you there?" Had he gone upstairs? I didn't want to alert the children. Wanted this moment for us. No reply.

Everything was quiet as I lifted a damp Gus up and placed him in the now-empty kitchen, laying him down in his bed for the night.

I stroked him as he nudged me with his head, and yet . . . . Something about the quiet sent little ripples of apprehension over my skin. But I'd heard the bang, and I *knew* he'd been here. He wasn't in the road; he wasn't in the road. He wasn't dead.

Somewhere outside a distant siren was wailing. I didn't want to think about that scene. Who was affected. We weren't. And it was over. And tomorrow I could focus on other things, not exist in this hideous cycle. I could listen to Miles and Poppy and be a better mother. I could phone Hattie, be a better friend. And I'd cherish Dan. Stop taking our life together for granted. My shoulders dropped as I walked out of the room and along the narrow corridor to the sitting room. Back to him.

Hearing quiet chatter of some sport commentators as I approached, a smile formed on my lips. It was over. Oh my God, I'd done it, I'd saved him. That was what it had all been for, to give me this chance. And I'd done it.

"Did you hear that?" I said, voice light.

Then the smile faded. Dan's head wasn't resting back against the sofa.

My mouth snapped shut as I realized he wasn't in the room at all. The television was playing to nobody, a man putting a golf ball on a smooth green somewhere sunny.

But he wouldn't have, he promised . . .
And then I saw him.
A foot.
Dan *was* in the room.
He was lying on the floor next to the sofa.
And he was dead.

Missed Call: Unknown number

35

3rd December 2015

Dear Emma,
I should spatter the pages of this letter with Farrow and Ball because it seems to be all we've done this year. But it's coming along, isn't it? I mean, the first month where we basically just cleaned wasn't fun. And the sagas over rotten joists/crumbling bedding around the chimney stack/the fact the house was probably last wired in the early seventies didn't end in any (major) rows. Is it because I look so attractive in overalls? Or is it that you are simply too exhausted to leave me?

Making you Head of Interior Design was a decision I did not take lightly (Poppy's mood board had real promise) but you nailed it with the myrtle-green cupboards and the massive shiny gold sunflower clock I thought was "a bit much." It really does draw the eye—the kitchen looks amazing. Sunday brunch around the table with the kids and you sat on the window seat, eyes closed as the sun streams in, is absolutely my favorite time of the week.

I'll gloss over the low points (fine, I was not "trying something new" in the bathroom, I should have called a plumber earlier; and to be fair to Miles, paint rollers DO look like toys), but we have survived the stresses of it largely intact. Our own house. I still get a thrill when I step inside the hallway (I know, I know, I need to sort a coat rack, I will) and realize it really does belong to us (*mainly the bank). OK, so it has cost us a teeny bit more than we budgeted for (hi dry rot!) but we have just about kept our heads above water.*

Due to cutbacks it did mean you finally relented to a family camping trip. And I know you love a bed and clean sheets and INDULGENCES like hot water, Emma, but you have to admit that week in South Wales was pretty awesome? All I can see when I close my eyes is that stretch of sand, us clutching hot pasties in paper bags as Poppy careered around, hood up, sand stuck to her feet as she laughed and dug and raced back to tell us something, "a massive seagull just ate that man's ice-cream, someone said they saw A SHARK yesterday . . ." And Miles just toddling after her on his chubby little legs. "Poppy, Poppy, me too, me too"

Our silent looks as we sent one or the other into the fray.

When did we learn to communicate so much by a look? Sometimes it gives me such a buzz, to catch your eye, your expression, and know precisely what you are thinking. Share the amusement with the slightest twitch of your mouth or the smallest raise of one eyebrow. He's an idiot. You're an idiot. I love our kids. I told you so. I love you. Your turn: I'm reading.

That holiday does feel like forever ago now though. The frantic PACE of our lives continues to shock me—that wall calendar makes my eyes cross some days (although I do wish you'd respect the color code system). New nursery, new school, new set of parents, new authors, new clients, new house . . . sometimes it's actually hard to catch a breath. Sometimes that scares me because I see Poppy—five now, taller, as if she just shot up in the two seconds it took me to turn around, or hear Miles use a new word ("Fantastic, Daddy!") and get a sudden pang for when he couldn't talk or walk or take his nappy off and pee over the newly laid kiln-dried timber floorboards.

Thank God for Hattie when you're reading a manuscript over a weekend or poring over those old contracts looking for new ways to make Linda money, rights that have yet to be sold—she really does need to appreciate you more—I am not sure an aunt could love her nephew and niece more. I can't wait for her to have her own kids; I know how desperately she wants that for her future. I know I should stop needling Ed about it but what is he waiting for? He knows as well as I that Hattie wants to start a family. Sometimes I just don't get why you like him so much. You and Hattie are so quick to point to his shitty dad, but lots of people have sad stories and don't act like the world owes them.

I'm not getting at you about work by the way—I hate it when we row about that but sometimes it feels like we just never see you. And I'm sorry for the times I pretend not to understand that the launch parties or author dinners are work—but it's hard to share you. You hate turning people down or disappointing people—I get that, but I suppose I'm just reminding you that I'm still here, wanting to see you, spend time with you. Sometimes I worry you don't feel the same.

Do you want me to tell you the thing I love most about your job? The way you talk about books to our children. I love how they can see you really adore something that isn't another person, but something that is just for you—that lights you inside. You still get lost in stories, their bedtimes stretching on forever. I creep up and listen at the doorway, sit on the top stair sometimes, not wanting to go in and get you all to make room for me. I hear your animated voice, making Poppy do her little piggy laugh, Miles press his hand to his mouth.

As I sit and listen, I think, God I love this new house and our kids and the fact that we're transforming it into a home for them.

Most of all Emma, I love you, so very, very much,

Dan x x

36

I was on my side, facing the window.

The sound of a bicycle bell.

I opened my eyes and winced. A slight crack in the curtains, a shaft of sunlight crossing my face.

I turned over.

"Hey," he said.

I couldn't reply, just met his eyes with mine.

"Wait," I said, getting out of bed, swerving the bedpost, and crossing the room to my phone.

Monday, 3rd December.

My shoulders slumped, the phone limp in my hand. So I'm not in control of this thing. I can't stop it happening. Everything I do is pointless. I'll end up back here.

Dan looked disgruntled. "Come back to bed, Emma, the kids aren't even up yet. You don't have to look at your phone now."

I returned to bed without a word, Dan's eyes widening as he folded me into his arms.

I swallowed, not wanting to acknowledge the deep-rooted fear inside me. That whatever I did didn't make a difference: that Dan would die. Again.

"What do you want to do today?" I asked, curling up against his chest, the cotton of his T-shirt soft and smelling of him. He was here, he was in bed with me. That I could control.

Dan craned his neck to look down at me, "Oh my God, are you kidding me? You wouldn't come to bed last night—again—to prepare for the meeting. The Super-Important-For-My-Career-Meeting, the Must-Impress-Linda meeting. So I assume we've got about ten minutes before we have to deal with the kids, and you have to get to work to hold vital meetings in the book publishing world. Fifteen at a push," he said, drawing me back toward him. "But, fine, yes, I do have one suggestion we could do in fifteen minutes if you want to hear it?"

"It goes badly," I said numbly.

"Er, are you talking about sex?"

"No, there's no point, the meeting doesn't go well."

"OK, Mystic Meg. You can't know that."

"It doesn't matter," I said, my voice dull.

Dan twisted round fully this time, meeting my eye. "Hey? Of course it matters. I was only teasing about the meeting. I know how much you care about this. Go on, seriously, I can sort the kids if you need to get on. I hope it goes brilliantly. Go and save the day. That woman is lucky to have you."

It started as a giggle and then turned into a sort of shaky laugh. "OK, great, I'll go . . . again."

Dan was frowning at me, "I'll take a shower and then run out and get us some breakfast."

I turned to him with a serious expression. "Thanks in advance for my cinnamon swirl."

Dan smiled, his forehead puckering. "You're being bizarre," he said, heading into the bathroom.

I laughed again, kind of manically, and then lay back against the pillows.

Ping ping ping, my mobile was buzzing from its spot in the corner of the room.

"Ping, ping, beep," I said aloud and laughed again.

The laughter died on my lips when Dan returned, patting his body from the shower. How often had I seen that familiar frame? The solid mass of him, his chest with its smattering of dark curled hair, his feet, second toe longer than the big toe. I knew his body as well as my own. Then I thought of his foot last night, thought of his body on the floor next to our sofa. I shook my head. I couldn't think about that: he was back. He was here.

Dan disappeared and I moved into the bathroom, saw again the orange dots in the sink. Flecks of powder from my bronzer. I touched a couple with a finger, the tip turning orange.

"Ouch." The shower came out way too hot and I dived away, pressing my body against the cold tiles as I turned it down.

Drying myself, my hand paused over the outfit on the chair: sensible white shirt, burgundy skirt. Heels? Not a chance.

Screw that, I thought, moving to the wardrobe and sliding back the door.

"Now let's see . . ."

I headed downstairs. Ping ping ping.

Logging on to Instagram I saw a hammock, a bright red cocktail. I paused for only a second before typing *OH MY GOD WRITE YOUR FUCKING BOOK* in the comments. *Send.* Hahahahaha.

I was laughing on the bottom stair as Dan returned from the shop. He squeezed past the bike. "God, this bike." Then he stopped, staring at me, eyes traveling down my outfit.

"I know. And do you know what?" I said marching forward and seizing the handlebars. "It needs . . ." I said, pushing it backward past him as he pressed up against the wall, "to . . ." I huffed as the chilly air blew in and I could see the street outside. "Fuck . . ." and I pushed it clattering down the pathway to our house so it banged against the low front wall and fell on its side with an almighty crash, "Off . . ."

I cackled and then, brushing my hands together like a cartoon villain, I passed Dan staring at me slack-jawed.

"Where's my cinnamon swirl then?" I called over my shoulder, moving back down the corridor, feeling wonderfully, marvelously out of control.

Fuck today. Fuck whatever this thing was, fuck it all.

"What was that noise?" Poppy asked from the landing. "Where's my blazer?"

"Who knows, who cares," I sing-songed, watching her come down the stairs.

"Oh my God, Mum, what are you wearing? So embarrassing."

Dan stepped past me. "Not sure, Pops. Er . . . Emma," he lowered his voice, "um . . . are you . . . ?""

"You're wearing mascara," I said to Poppy, stepping in front of her.

"No, I'm not," she said, a hand moving self-consciously to her face.

I shrugged, "Doesn't matter. Nothing matters."

"Why are you dressed like a fairy?" she asked, taking in my large-netted skirt, my gold sequined sweater, my red DM boots.

"A really weird one." She stepped past me slowly, giving me a sideways glance, and joined Miles at the table.

I shrugged, "Just felt like it."

Dan followed me without a word, placing the milk in the center of the table. As they ate cereal and eyed me curiously I stood staring round at the cupboards.

"What do you want for breakfast? I want the cinnamon swirl and then I want ice cream. Who wants to join me?"

Miles paused to look over at me, milk dripping from his spoon.

"Um . . . I'm all right on ice cream. Sit down, OK," Dan said, steering me to a chair at the table. "Let me get you a coffee. Decaf maybe."

Poppy and Miles were openly staring at me as I smiled at them. I reached over and seized Poppy's arm. "Isn't this nice? We are a happy family, aren't we? And you and Miles get on, don't you? It's all good?" I said, watching Miles squirm in his seat, Poppy bite her lip.

"Here's your coffee, Ems," Dan said, placing it down gently on a coaster.

I sat back. "I don't think I'm going to work today."

"Mum's joking," Dan smiled at the kids.

"I'm really not. A joke would be something like "Why did the mum go to the loo?" I looked round at my family. "Because she lost her shit! Ha!"

"Emma," Dan's face twisted and he glanced at the kids.

"I think they've heard the word shit before, Dan."

Miles looked as if he was stuck on a very complicated math equation and Poppy's mouth was now hanging open.

"I'm being serious. There are so many better things I, *we*," I added loudly, "could all be doing."

"But the kids have school," Dan reminded me.

"SCHOOL SCHMOOL," I shouted, making all three of

them jump. And then I was laughing loudly, and then tears came into my eyes and I got up, away from the table and the coffee and my family.

"Emma?" Dan called as I drifted to the door.

I looked back at him.

He stepped across to me, drawing me to one side as the kids watched him. "Are you OK? Are you feeling OK?"

I felt a stab of sadness at the genuine concern on his face. Where to even start to explain? I felt like I'd been awake for a week, snatching at sleep, the worry and intensity of each day taking me to this mad breaking point.

Last night, that terrible, terrifying moment when I'd realized he was dead. I thought I'd saved him, I'd *heard* the crash, knew he'd been nowhere near it. But he'd been lying there, still. I hadn't known what to do as his skin gradually lost its heat, as I'd panicked that the kids might come down, find him there. So I'd stayed, curled into a ball by his side, not wanting to leave him alone either.

"Ems?"

I couldn't respond, blinking the film of unshed tears away.

Behind him the kids looked uncomfortable and pain stabbed my side. I shouldn't be here, around them, around him. I was out of body, my mind fuzzy and disjointed.

I smiled slowly, tried to make my voice normal, "Sorry. I am. I'm fine." I picked up my bag, avoided looking at Poppy and Miles. I was no good to them in this state. "Just tired. I'll call you later, OK?" I reached up and kissed him.

He snatched up my hand as I stepped back.

"I love you, OK," he said earnestly.

I stared at his hand on mine, his neatly clipped fingernails. This time my smile was genuine. "I love you too."

And then I was definitely going to cry so I turned and walked out.

"Mum's gone mental," Poppy announced.

"Why's Mum gone mental?" Miles asked.

"She is . . . she's under a bit of work stress," I could hear Dan saying as I left the house, skirted round the bike on its side, out into the pale winter sun.

Denise @CommitteeChat 6:30pm tonight. Please don't be late.

Catrin @Emma Denise is totally referencing you.

Denise @CommitteeChat The rota states that Emma will be taking the minutes this evening.

Catrin @Emma God forbid you fuck up the rota. Lol.

Emma @CommitteeChat The rota doesn't know yet but I'm not coming and I'm quitting too. Byyyyyyeeeeeeeeeeeee.

Catrin @Emma OMG. I am dying.

Denise @CommitteeChat We have bylaws for procedures such as these. We do not accept.

Emma @CommitteeChat OK! Arrest me Denise. Over and out babe.

AuthorLou @Emma Sorry it's early. And you so don't need to reply quickly. I don't want to be *that* author. I've just been on Amazon and I've got 2 new reviews today! But one of them was a 1 star that said the binding is loose and I was wondering if I need to ask Amazon to take it down?

AuthorLou @Emma Sorry! Should have added it to my last message. So I've just been on Goodreads and someone has 1 starred it saying that they think Carl is a bit rapey. Do you think I should mark their review as offensive?

AuthorLou @Emma He's not rapey is he?

Emma @AuthorLou He is a bit rapey and I remember telling you precisely that on the edit notes that you studiously ignored.

AuthorLou @Emma Sorry! Last one I promise! Should I worry that I've got no reviews yet on the Waterstones site? I've checked other authors with books out in the same week as me and some have got over three so far. Does it matter?

Emma @AuthorLou Nothing matters.

Hattie @Emma Time for a catch-up at lunch?

Poppy @Mum Dad says he doesn't know where my blazer is.

Emma @Poppy Wear anything. Love you. X

Dan @Emma Love you OK, if you need me to pick you up from work I will. X X

37

"Right," I said aloud to myself, a woman with a red handbag glancing my way as I walked down the road.

Where am I headed? Should I go to work? The only thing I absolutely knew was I wanted to move, to get away. What I didn't want to do was keep thinking about my predicament. I needed to escape it.

My phone was pinging at me as ever and I felt a strange exhilaration at saying whatever I liked in response, ignoring the replies, switching off the sound notifications on the phone so the ping ping ping didn't bother me.

I went to cross the road to the tube, remembering the cyclist only at the last moment. His bell, me wobbling.

"Woah," I said.

"For fuck . . ."

"Sorry," I shouted after him before stepping into the road to the tube.

"Whoooop," I called out as I stood on the escalator, recognizing some of the faces. "Morning everyone, GOOD MORNING to you all."

The woman in the blue coat probably hadn't heard me over her music, the sad man in the padded coat looked up and then glanced away. Only the little boy, head peeking just above the escalator, stared at me curiously. I grinned at him and poked my tongue out. He laughed, the joyful noise traveling across the space and stopping me in my tracks.

My smile slipped, I watched the boy walk away, one look back at me as his dad steered him down a tunnel. Someone bumped into me from behind as I froze at the bottom looking around. Where was I going? I'd left my own house, my own kids, and was about to go to a meeting that I had been to already, twice, with a man I loathed and a boss I didn't respect.

My feet responded to this thought by taking me down another tunnel, on to another tube line, going in the other direction. Bumping along with the other commuters, I sleep-walked onto a tube carriage, pressing myself into the side as I realized the day was mine. None of it mattered. I got some glances as I found an empty seat, my netted skirt spilling over the suited man on my left, the cargo pants of a student on my right.

I'd always liked the tube. Maybe because I could read on it and I could never read in a car. Maybe because I met the love of my life on one. His horrified expression on that platform as I pulled away clutching his phone number, that glow in my stomach knowing something special had just happened. Thinking of Dan caused a horrible mess of feeling, one I didn't want to face. I pushed down those thoughts and focused on the adverts overhead promising me cheap flights, better broad-band speed, and a meal supplement that would make me look like the toned silhouette in the picture.

*

"We should go to the zoo," I said the moment I had exited the tube at Green Park and Hattie answered. "Do you want to go to the zoo?"

"The zoo?"

"No one will be there on a Monday in December, right? Let's do it."

"But . . . the zoo? Really?"

"There'll be penguins! Probably baby ones."

"I'm not really in a zoo mood," Hattie said, her voice low. Oh shit, I shouldn't have mentioned baby penguins. I thought back to the last time I saw Hattie, her rounded shoulders, her untouched food. Was that it? Had she got news? I'd drunk the wine—had she? I knew she'd been seeing a doctor privately, knew it was causing tension with her and Ed; he was finding it so hard, she'd said. I'd sympathized with him but had been more concerned with how she was finding it. Or was it something else entirely?

"Well, I definitely want to see you so what shall we do?" I said, walking along the pavement as people passed me.

"Are you not working today?"

"I've taken the day off!" I sing-songed.

Hattie sounded brighter then, "You never take the day off!"

"Well, I have," I said, stung a little by the words, said in jest but uncomfortably true. My meetings with Hattie recently were always squeezed between work meetings or a lunch break I invariably cut short. I loved seeing her with Dan too but there'd always been something special about seeing her on our own. Although in the last few weeks she had been the one to cancel on me.

"I could come over to yours?" Hattie suggested.

I hadn't heard her, too busy staring upward. "I've got a much better idea. Get a taxi to Green Park, I'll pay."

"I can get the bu—"

"Get a taxi now," I interrupted firmly. "And wear some nice shoes," I added, looking down at my boots. They just wouldn't do.

"Now?"

"Now," I said.

"Well, I could move a few things, could probably leave in just under an ho—"

"Green Park, Hattie. As soon as you can," I said, marching on and hanging up the phone like I was in a movie.

I entered the first absurdly fancy shoe shop I could find, the air leather-scented, and spent £480 on the most gorgeous gray soft suede heeled boots. I never normally bought things in suede, too easy to scuff and ruin in bad weather, and I'd never spent more than two figures on a shoe. I handed over my card without a thought.

Missed Calls: Linda (6)

Jas @Emma Emma are you coming? Linda is losing her nut.

Lena @Emma Denise has asked me to confirm your attendance this evening.

AuthorLou @Emma I think we should meet, I'm in town. Call me.

Dan @Emma Hey, still a bit worried about you. Just let me know if you need me OK? I love you X

38

Just over an hour later I was back outside the Ritz wearing the new suede boots. I'd kept the netted skirt and had upgraded my sweater to the softest black cashmere. A stunning fitted single-breasted jacket with satin lapels, silk crepe lining, and cropped cuffs completed the look. Hattie emerged from a taxi, wearing plain black bootcut trousers and a thick green woolen three-quarter-length coat.

Beside me Hattie looked shrunken and I noticed the gray bags under her eyes, her whitish pallor.

"My treat," I said, smiling and tucking her arm in mine, her hand freezing to the touch.

She gave me a disbelieving look and allowed herself to be pushed through the revolving doors of the Ritz into a lobby that shimmered gold, warm air enveloping us. A dazzling glass chandelier overhead threw light in intricate patterns across every surface.

My new boots made a satisfying clack as we walked across a polished marble floor, an enormous Christmas tree dominating the corner, beautifully decorated in red and gold ribbons and baubles, which filled the air with the scent of pine.

I approached a large mahogany desk. "We have a reservation to dine in your restaurant," I said, tilting my chin. Say it with confidence, I thought, channeling my best Linda vibe.

The receptionist, a young man with impossibly flawless skin, smiled. "Of course, ma'am, if you would be so kind Jerome can show you the way. Please let me take your coats."

He had either pressed a bell or done something magical as Jerome appeared, an actual pencil moustache like he was a cartoon sketch of a Ritz concierge. We handed over our coats and I noticed Hattie's sweater, baggy on her frame. We followed dutifully behind Jerome, feet sinking into rich, patterned blankets as we passed statues in enclaves and soaring marble columns.

"This isn't very us?" Hattie whispered, tugging self-consciously on her striped sweater as we entered the dining room.

"Roll with it," I murmured back, sweeping through the room like a queen in my fancy new clothes.

It was the most stunning, high-ceilinged room, with intricate plasterwork and one wall made up of a hundred square mirrors, exaggerating the space that spilled out onto a spotless stone terrace, the view of Green Park beyond. We both sucked in our breath.

"I've always wanted to come here," Hattie admitted as Jerome pulled out a plush pink padded chair for her to sit on, quick to make a flourish with a bright white, beautifully pressed napkin.

"I do recall," I said, realizing that was where the idea had come from.

"Might I suggest a beverage before you order food?" Jerome handed us beautiful gold-embossed cream card menus and melted away as we perused them, the room filled with the gentle chatter of other diners.

"It's £14 for an orange juice, Emma!" Hattie said, eyes rounding.

I smiled and batted a hand. "Honestly, it's on me. Order whatever you like, I'm going to."

A pianist we hadn't even noticed began to play on a shiny grand piano in the corner of the room, the sound filling the space. His hands raced across the keys as the playful melody provided a welcome distraction from the madness in my head. I started dancing along in my chair, body swaying, other restaurant-goers glancing over. But literally who the fuck cares? I thought suddenly as I scraped my chair back and stood, moving to the music.

"Emma, oh my God, Emma, sit down."

This was a dream. Me dressed in absurdly expensive clothes, in this insanely stunning place about to spend eye-watering amounts of money (beluga caviar for £700, anyone?), dancing to the best pianist ever with my most wonderful friend.

"No chopsticks for you," I called out to him.

And I laughed and the waiter had taken a step in my direction and I turned to drag Hattie up to dance with me but when I reached my hand out I saw her, horrified expression, body curled into her chair—her face still gray despite the soft lighting in the wall brackets, her mouth pursed, sat on her hands. An inch of dark blonde hair at her roots. Hattie was always religious about keeping up her hair coloring. How had I missed all this the other day?

"Hattie," I sat down abruptly and reached across for her. "Sorry. Just . . ." I coughed, tried to get a handle on myself.

"Shall we go? We don't have to spend £42 on an omelette, Emma."

"No, I want to stay. Sorry. I want to see you, to talk to you."

Studying her face, I realized that she was in her own world of pain and I wanted to forget my own problems and fears and worries as I was thrown back to all the times she'd supported me. "What is it? What's wrong?"

She bit her lip, "I don't want to tell you. This is special, a treat. I don't want to ruin it. And you're being strange," she added with a ghost of a smile.

"I'm sorry. I won't be strange anymore. And you can't ruin it—it is wonderful to be here, seeing you. We don't do things like this enough," I said, squeezing her hand, and realizing it was true. "Please tell me, Hatts."

I could see the internal battle but I waited, swallowing down my natural impulse to dive in.

"I had a miscarriage," she admitted, her voice almost drowned by the voices, tink of cutlery, the piano. "At seven weeks."

I felt the sharp pain in my chest, knowing this wasn't the first, that this was part of a struggle to get pregnant. "Oh Hattie. I'm sorry."

"I know I should be grateful we can get pregnant but I just, I really thought . . ."

"Can I take your order?"

I drew back in my chair, dazedly looking up at the waiter who had interrupted us.

Taking control, I ordered quickly for us both, wanting to get back to the conversation, wanting to get rid of the perfectly starched waiter. "Let's get some alcohol too," I said aloud. "A bottle of white Pinot, please." The waiter nodded and left.

Hattie stared. "It's not even midday on a Monday."

"Exactly. It's almost the afternoon," I said firmly.

I felt a wave of guilt ripple through me that I hadn't discovered this sooner. I'd known something was wrong but had been too selfish to push it at the time. I hadn't noticed the extent of how crumpled and weary she looked. How had I missed her haggard face, her hollowed-out cheeks, her dull eyes? I had been going through something huge and crazy but I felt terrible for being so self-centered. This was Hattie; Hattie was such a huge part of my life. I should have done better.

"I'm sorry, Hattie, and I'm sorry for not knowing what you were going through."

"How could you?" she said in a small voice, clearly trying to get a handle on herself. I could count on one hand how often I'd seen Hattie cry.

The waiter returned with a rattling ice bucket and a bottle of wine wrapped in a tissue. We both watched him pour. The first sip was exquisite and I closed my eyes and really focused on the flavors. Hattie was scrutinizing me over the rim of her glass as I opened them again.

"OK. What's going on? Have you sold a book for a million pounds? What's all this about?" she said, waving her hand around the room.

"No, I just . . . It's nice to indulge," I said, not quite meeting her eye.

There was no way I was going to tell her. She was already drained from sharing her pain and there was no way I would heap more on her. And what could she do to help me? The hideousness of the last few days had eased a fraction. Sitting opposite her, focusing on her life, remembering she was someone I loved, felt good. I didn't want to mar the moment.

And I'd missed Hattie; seeing her now reminded me how much. We'd always looked out for each other. I'd visited with emergency care packages, wine, chocolate, at the end of relationships, or work frustrations. She'd done the same. Once, after I'd told her my parents had taken away my very favorite childhood toy on the eve of starting school, as being too babyish, she'd tracked down a replica on American eBay and paid a fortune in shipping to have it sent over. I hated seeing her brought so low now.

"Today is about you," I said firmly, taking another mouthful of wine. "How has Ed reacted?"

It was Hattie's turn to look away; she pulled on the sleeves of her sweater. "Well, you know Ed, not one for sharing too much of what he's feeling. But that's from his childhood, you know, his dad . . ." She licked her lips, took another sip of wine. "He finds it hard; he hasn't mentioned it since I told him but I mean, he's quiet, you know?"

I tried to rearrange my face in time. "Have you tried to talk to him about it?"

Another strained silence as Hattie played with the fork in front of her. "He thinks I should get more tests. That it's probably something wrong with me . . ."

"Well, that's a ridiculous way to put it," I said, affronted on her behalf.

"He thinks I should quit my job completely. Focus on getting pregnant."

"And do you think that?"

Hattie looked up desperately. "I don't think it makes a difference. In fact, I think I might go mad without something to do. The company have been great about me taking time out when I've needed it."

"Well then."

"Ed doesn't agree," she said, whisper quiet. "We fought about me quitting."

"Well, he needs to listen to you: it's your decision."

"I hate making him angry," she said, not meeting my eye. "If I do he shuts down completely, doesn't speak to me for days."

I couldn't help my mouth gaping at that. "Doesn't speak to you? Hattie, you *live* together—how is that even possible?"

Hattie looked away, her hands nervously plaiting her napkin. Worry niggled at me, Dan's comments over the years about Ed solidifying in my mind: that he had a dark side, that he seemed overbearing. I'd often accused Dan of being paranoid, I thought, with a guilty flush.

"That's not good, Hattie," I said gently. I didn't want to intrude on their relationship. But when did being silent and supportive cross over into being a bad friend?

"Well, he's still talking to me for now," her laugh sounded hollow. "But you know Ed."

"Do I?" I said, meeting her eye and suddenly feeling horribly sober.

Dan had always said Ed was punching above his weight. Certainly he could be grumpy—that whole thing at Sunday lunch about Hattie getting under his feet had made Dan so cross; his face had really twisted with disgust. But that lunch hadn't been the first time he'd rubbed Dan up the wrong way. Sometimes I'd dismissed it as Dan being an overprotective elder brother, seeing things that weren't there.

Ed had always been so nice to me, charming, and Hattie said she loved him, always told me how hard Ed had had it, growing up with an aggressive, dominating father. How he struggled emotionally, that Dan didn't understand because they'd had such supportive parents. That had rung true for me, quicker to accept this than Dan.

Ed's reaction to her loss though seemed cruel. And the knowledge that he could ignore her, sometimes for days, was unsettling.

The waiter sidled over, silently refilling my glass, his face bland even if he did think two glasses before an omelette was an extravagance. If I said something would I ruin this time with Hattie?

We ate. We tried to talk about other things around the solid shape of Ed between us: Dan, work, Poppy and Miles. I told her they'd had a row. She frowned, "A bad one?"

"I'm not sure," I mused, thinking back over the last few days. "I think so, maybe . . ."

"I'll message Pops," Hattie offered as I drank more wine. Hattie had always been close to Poppy: living with us in those early days when Dan had left had given them a special bond. Hattie had always been her greatest supporter, as proud as Dan or I when Poppy showed us drawings or school reports, coming to dance recitals and school plays.

I finished the bottle. Hattie had barely touched her first glass, eyeing me as I continued to make her laugh, gesturing wildly as I moved on to work, wanting to cheer her up, take her away from her sadness. Telling her about the time Linda had learned how to leave Amazon reviews and one-starred all our rival clients' books, but under her own name so the whole industry found out.

"She's awful! Ems, you have to leave there."

"I know," I admitted, blinking as Hattie swam in front of me. "There was a meeting booked. I was going to ask for more freedom over my list, for Jas to be made an agent in her own right, for lots of things. But now . . . I know I need to go."

The pianist was back, playing something jaunty and playful. The wine was going to my head as I looked across at my friend. "Maybe you need to go too, Hatts?"

The words hung in the air between us for a beat before Hattie removed the napkin from her lap.

"I need to get back, Ems, I've got a work call." She signaled to the waiter for the bill.

"No, don't go," I protested, loudly enough for the man at the table next door to frown at me. "Ssssshhh," I said quickly, holding a wobbly finger up to my face.

"Ems," Hattie hissed, looking at me aghast. "People are looking."

I woozily looked around me, the setting spinning, faces indistinct.

"Let's get the bill and get out of here," Hattie said.

"I'm gonna pay for this," I said quickly, twisting to rummage in my handbag for my wallet. The movement made me blink and clutch the back of my chair.

"Are you OK?" Hattie asked.

Locating my bank card, I turned back to her. "I'm fine," I insisted, slapping the card onto the table and missing so it bounced onto the floor. "Oops," I giggled.

Everything felt fuzzy, but the alcohol gave me renewed confidence to get back on track, find out more. "I don't want to talk about me, I want to talk more about you. About what's going on with you. You and Ed," I said, keeping my voice steady.

It was the wrong thing to say, Hattie pushing out her chair as she spoke, "I'll get your card. And I really do need to get going," she said, sliding my bank card back to me. "Thanks so much though, for this," she said, gesturing at our empty plates. "That omelette was amazing."

My stomach lurched as I stood, moved around the table for a hug, "Hattie you know we're here for you, OK. You're family," I finished, arms wide.

"You're drunk," she commented.

"You're still family," I wagged my finger. "I'm just shaying we love you and you always have somewhere to stay if you need."

Hattie tucked her hair behind her ears. Was it the wine or was she not meeting my eyes?

The waiter sidled over with our bill on the small silver tray.

"This was a real treat, Ems," Hattie said, quickly giving me a kiss. "I'm going to get off . . . that call, you know . . ."

"But . . ."

By the time I'd paid she'd gone, no sign of her as I moved through the corridors and foyer, the patterned blankets blurring, the columns multiplying. My stomach churned uneasily as I pushed through the revolving doors, the shock of the wintry day hitting me immediately.

I vomited on the pavement outside. Salmon pieces, black caviar, frothy wine-based bile. A passerby watched me curiously as I leaned over, hands on my knees, a light sheen of sweat on my face. All that waste. All pointless. I straightened, wiping my mouth and stumbling away into the rabbit warren of Soho.

It was hours later and miles away when I realized I'd left my new £1,160 coat behind.

Missed Calls: AuthorLou (7)

AuthorLou @Emma Please phone me.

AuthorLou @Emma And Carl isn't rapey. He is misunderstood.

CharterHayley @Emma Are you coming to this meeting?

Denise @Emma This is utterly unacceptable.

Amelia @Emma I think your account has been hacked! Someone left a really rude comment on my Instagram post.

39

3rd December 2016

Dear Emma,
I'd been really good at keeping it a secret—I wanted to surprise you so much because I'm always the avid planner, the slow decision-maker. But I was actually surprised you were surprised. I mean, how did you not guess on the train there? I was SO NERVOUS. Yes, it was basically the hottest day of the year but I don't normally sweat so much. And you didn't even seem suspicious when I was really weird about my bag, territorial. I thought you'd guessed when I wouldn't lend you my pen from it and made you ask a stranger for one, but you just thought I was being a dick. Like I really cared about my pen. It was a four-color ballpoint but still, I'm normally happy to share.

You seemed distracted because Pangbourne was so lovely—all cutesy chocolate box cottages and quaint artisan shops selling things made of wicker, and then panicked because you thought I'd brought you there to persuade you to leave London. Freaking out over the fowl (I had not anticipated the substantial number of geese) also helped move the spotlight from my jumpy behavior.

Then I was nervous because you looked particularly amazing, even in the insane sandals with all the ribbony bits up the leg, like a sexy gladiator, and your bright white cotton sundress really showed off your tan. When I told you that Pangbourne had inspired Wind in the Willows *I thought my throat would close up with nerves. I love that book, you said. I know, I squeaked.*

I still think the boat was a good idea and if I hadn't knelt I don't think I would have gone overboard. It had all been going so well too! I'd literally just pointed out the "beautiful weeping willows" and you'd stopped googling goose-related injuries. I really thought the whole thing had been ruined when I saw the rucksack go under. But thank God for my habit of putting things in bags, inside bigger bags—it literally saved the day and I'm so pleased you loved the book. The kids loved helping me decorate the pages (I slightly wish I hadn't let Poppy draw quite so many Numberblocks on it) and it was brilliant to track down all those photos of us over the years (We were so young! And tanned!). Mum's ring survived intact too—and I'm so pleased you immediately recognized it. I know she would have LOVED that you wear it now.

I know we've signed a thirty-five-year mortgage and have two kids but I hope you really feel like this is something special. A chance to celebrate with everyone we love—I know I do.

And wedding planning has been fun, yes? Not just because I got to buy a special ring binder especially for it. We've agreed on so much of it (although miniature board games as favors was never going to make the cut, Emma). I love the evenings when we've got pissed and sung hymns vetoing the ones we can't have.

Do you know what one of my favorite moments was too? Telling Dad—his hug, his trip to the attic, emerging with the photos from their wedding. I'd never heard about their wedding—why had I never asked?—but I loved the story of the creepy mink stole his mum foisted on Mum to wear—I can totally picture her expression. Although FYI you need to be the one to break it to Dad that our wedding isn't a lunchtime affair—it's going to blow his mind when he finally hears our plans.

So wedding planning and a slightly calmer life now? The kids are that bit older, and I think surely it gets a bit easier when they can at least pee without us (scratch that, Miles just called me over to see his "massive poo").

Ten years, Emma. A whole decade of us. I'm so glad you let me stumble into your life. You've made me so happy, and I can't wait to be your husband.

Dan x

40

Life was so unfair, Hattie battling to get pregnant, her relationship rocky with the strain.

Dan. The overwhelming hopelessness of it all.

We worked and we hustled and we moved through our days at a frantic pace—for what? To pass each other like worker bees. "I got milk, I picked up bread, have we paid the TV license?" Swapping dull facts about the children, the house (I put a wash on/Miles needs new shoes/is their optician appointment due?/have you seen my red scarf/do we need a water softener though?) and never stopping, looking around, taking the time to appreciate any of it. I have a husband! Children! I found my red scarf! The water *does* taste better! I was always moving on to the next thing on the endless To Do List that would never fuck off.

These were the thoughts that chased around my head as I meandered around the streets of Soho: left, right, left, what did it matter? A pub, another drink. Left, right. Shivering hours later I hailed a cab, wanting to get home.

I wanted to *be*: wanted to see my children, I mean, I *have* children, how bloody lucky am I? Hattie had always wanted to become a mother. And I wanted to cuddle my husband and hold him close and appreciate how bloody lucky I was to live with my best friend, a really decent human.

An hour later though I was not cuddling my husband; I was being frog-marched to the bottom of the stairs by my husband who might generously be described as "displeased."

"Oh my God, you're hammered, Emma, what the hell? Don't let the kids see you like this." Then I listened to my children almost tear each other's hair out in the room next door to the one I was exiled in. I'd forgotten the desperate bad mood they'd returned from school in; they were next door in Miles's room now, screaming at each other.

I crept to the wall that separated our rooms, balancing precariously on my glass-topped dressing table that was a dumping ground for eighteen thousand products I never opened and a tower of books I never read. Three of the books tumbled to the floor as I wobbled on the glass top, straining to listen.

There was crying but I wasn't sure from whom.

"You need to tell Mum and Dad."

"No way.

"Well, I will."

"Don't, please Miles—they'll kill me."

"They're going to find out anyway."

"I didn't . . . I don't . . ."

"Everyone's talking about it, saying stuff. Liam said you were going to be expelled . . ."

I swayed from my position on the table, room spinning, unsure if it was shock, alcohol or kneeling awkwardly on a narrow dressing table.

Why was Poppy in danger of being expelled? Oh God. I needed to know what had happened but I knew Dan would be furious if I went through in this state.

As I clambered unsteadily down from the dressing table I could see why. The woman in the tri-mirror was in disarray, a legitimate mess of a human. My makeup had run, my hair was sticking in every direction, my netted skirt had somehow torn and my beautiful new cashmere sweater had a stain down the front which I thought, smelling it, might be vomit. Shame threatened to swallow me whole as I stared back at her.

I took the sweater off, standing in the room now in just my bra and the crazy netted skirt.

And I was so tired all of a sudden, my body heavy, my brain overloaded. Thoughts wouldn't stick. Thinking about Miles and Poppy and then Dan made me want to clamp my hands to the side of my head and scream.

I almost fell backward onto our bed, leaning sideways to pull at the corner of the duvet, clambering beneath the soft cotton.

And maybe I could just lie there for a second. The pillow felt so nice and my head had stopped pounding quite so much. My stomach gurgled manically, insides uncomfortable, but when I rolled on to my side, legs curled up tight like a fetus, it felt better. And the distant sound of voices faded away and it was fine, really. I would only be here for a few moments and then I would need to go downstairs and see my family and unravel this mess that I was stuck in. For how long I didn't know. And that thought made the pounding worse so I squeezed my eyes tighter and I disappeared to another place: away from this room, this house, somewhere safe where I didn't need to think anymore.

Jas @Emma Bit worried about you after your no-show this morning. Hope all OK?

AuthorLou @Emma I am still waiting for your call.

Missed Calls: Denise (2)

Missed Calls: CharterHayley (5)

Missed Calls: Linda (4)

41

"What is wrong with you?"

Dan's voice was low and tight, his fists flexing at his sides as he loomed over the side of the bed.

In my dreams he was angry, telling me the kids were worried, telling me to get up and join them for dinner. I ignored them.

It was dark outside when I came to, groggy and confused, roused by a call on my mobile. School Office on the screen. How many hours had passed? God, I needed water. Clambering out of bed, I answered the phone without thinking—maybe something had happened to the kids? Then I remembered the kids were home, they'd been shouting at each other moments—hours?—before. Had Dan been in the room?

Clutching the doorframe to the bathroom to steady myself, I blinked in the stark light.

"Hello," I whispered into the receiver.

"Mrs. Jacobs, this is Yvonne Sweeting, Head of Year."

"Oh right," I coughed, looking up to see my reflection in the bathroom mirror opposite—just in my bra, hair and face disheveled. "Hi."

"I'm sorry I am having to phone with disappointing news but, as you can imagine, we take this kind of thing very seriously."

"Right." I absentmindedly wiped the orange dots stuck to the sink. "Sorry, what kind of thing?" I asked.

"Posting abusive comments on the internet," Yvonne continued.

Abusive. I felt my stomach drop. "Who's being abused?" Oh my God, was Miles or Poppy being internet bullied? "How horrible."

"The girls in Year Six came forward today and showed us the messages Poppy has posted. They are, of course, very upset."

"What?" It came out as barely a whisper. I gripped the edge of the sink. Poppy was . . . doing what? My ten-year-old daughter. My firstborn, my ten-year-old girl was . . . an internet troll? "I'm sorry, there must be a mistake. There is no way. I mean . . ." A small laugh hiccuped out of me.

"Has Poppy not told you what happened today?"

My eyes stung. I swallowed, "No . . . no, she hasn't. I . . ."

There was no excuse. I'd had literally numerous opportunities to discover it for myself. I'd known something was going on. My head drooped as she carried on.

"Poppy has been found to be behind an account sending a number of unpleasant comments on the TikTok accounts of some pupils in her year."

Oh good, a swell of relief in my body. Some mistake. An anonymous account—someone must have hacked her or stolen her photo or catfished her or whatever it was called. There was just no way. "But Poppy isn't even on TikTok."

Was she? I thought back to Miles and Poppy earlier; if there was no way then why was Poppy so frightened of our reaction?

"She's not on social media at all," I insisted. "We discussed it. Just WhatsApp," I said, staring at the sink, at the one stray orange dot. I wiped it with the tip of my finger and held it up to the light. Oh God. More details were slotting into place in my fuzzy brain. This was my bronzer. She'd been wearing mascara. That strange repetitive music I'd been hearing. Was it possible?

"We will need you to come into school first thing with Poppy."

TikTok. Abuse?

"She will not be permitted to attend classes until this matter is resolved."

No classes? This wasn't real. Not Poppy. We'd only got her the phone a year ago. She'd been pestering us forever and we'd installed all the security checks they advise, lectured her endlessly. And we checked, the endless threads on WhatsApp, the inane back and forth, most of it emojis or acronyms we didn't understand. It was bland, dull, mind-numbingly so. But we checked. Well, we used to check.

And it was Poppy. It was fine. The messages had always been so boring and there were literally thousands of them. Who had the time to monitor every comment, every . . .

A troll?

"I have to . . . I'm sorry, I have to go," I said, ending the call mid-sentence.

Setting the phone down I stared at my red-veined, exhausted reflection. I ran the tap, bent down, and splashed handfuls of cold water on my face so that I gasped with the shock of it.

I was confused, aching, my head woolly as I moved back to the bedroom to step out of the torn netted skirt. Finding a fresh top and pulling on black cotton harem pants, I left the room, clutching the banisters as I moved down the stairs.

"Poppy," I called, peering into the kitchen, the windows to

the street beyond dark; someone had put their Christmas lights on in the house opposite and I stared for a few seconds at the cheering colors.

Miles was in his green striped pajamas on the sofa with Dan. I realized pretty quickly that Dan was quietly furious. He could barely meet my eye as I stepped inside the room. Miles's face was blotched and sad.

"Where's Poppy?"

"I made you dinner, it's on the side, you can heat it up."

"Where's Poppy?" I asked.

"Did you hear me, Emma? I made you dinner."

"Thanks," I said, drifting over to Miles. "Why didn't you tell us?"

Dan frowned. "Miles has just told me a little of what's going on . . . you weren't around," he said, a muscle flickering in his cheek, his eyes averted.

"Is it true then?" I asked, aghast. "Is Poppy sending messages to people at school?"

Miles was frozen stiff.

"Let's discuss it when Miles is in bed. You were going up now, weren't you, buddy?" Dan gave me a knowing look. "Miles?" he said softly and he leaned into him and gave him a one-armed hug. "Thanks for talking to me. We'll get it sorted."

"What will happen, Dad?" Miles whispered.

Dan put on a sympathetic smile. "We'll work it out. But you did the right thing, OK? I'm proud of you."

He steered Miles out of the room, me twitching to know more. Dan returned, rubbing his face.

"What happened? What did he tell you?"

"Holly's brother Liam was teasing him today. Calling Poppy . . . names," he cringed at the memory. "He couldn't sleep, he's worried she'll be expelled."

"It's got to be a mistake," I said, the room blurring as I tried to arrange my thoughts.

"Look, Emma, you came back drunk, you passed out on our bed, you freaked out the kids. We need to talk about you, about what the hell is going on with you."

"No, no, I want to talk to Poppy."

"Do you even know it's our anniversary by the way?" he added. "Do you even care?"

"I do know. Of course I do, it's just . . ." I clutched my head and sank into the armchair. What was happening? Why did everything feel as if it was collapsing around me? A whining sound from the kitchen.

"I need to take Gus out," Dan said. "We can talk to her when I'm back. Together, OK?"

My mouth felt dry, limbs heavy, a delay as I realized Dan had left the room already. Gus barked. "I'll talk to her, sort this out . . ." I said to the air. I could fix this, surely? It couldn't be as bad as it sounded.

Then I heard it—the front door close. Then the significance of the moment crashed over me.

Oh God. My head snapped up and I raced out of the room, scrabbling to pull on mismatched shoes over bare feet.

"Dan," my voice was loud in our hallway. "Dan!"

Shit.

It was definitely around now. I had to stop it. Not tonight. We needed to talk. Not tonight.

"Mum?"

I ignored my daughter's voice behind me, intent on only one thing as I streaked out of the house. The bike had been moved to the side by our bin as I raced past and in the direction of the scene.

A faint voice behind me. "Mum! Come back!"

"Dan," I shouted, hoping he hadn't got far, hoping he could hear me. "DAN."

A deafening screech, a sickening crash, so loud it made me jump.

"No, no, no," I said, breathlessly turning into the road, the scene ahead so horribly familiar.

Oh God. The car. The headlight. The crumpled metal.

And Dan.

He was there, broken in the road, Gus already edging toward him, unscathed. A bark. Another bark. Nudging at him as I kept moving toward them both, pieces of glass spat across the scene.

I looked up and the truth struck me in the chest. I knew why something had felt familiar that first night. It wasn't because I was going to be back here. It *had* been familiar.

I stared at the car for a second time, at the make, at the model, at the part of the number plate not buried in the parked car.

Oh my God.

The woman behind the wheel was lost to the airbag, just a hint of her hair, an arm.

I knew that car. I knew that woman.

42

3rd December 2017

Dear Wife,
We did it. 2017—the year we tied the knot, became hitched, sealed the deal. Got me the old ball and chain, the trouble and strife, her indoors, didn't I?

Highlights from the wedding: YOU. The dress you chose with those lace panel things—you looked amazing. I couldn't stop sneaking glances through the service.

MY SURPRISE—I knew how much you'd love it if Miles and Poppy were involved somehow and, yes, it took forever to get them all to learn it but it was SO worth it. I'll never forget your face when Pharrell Williams began and Miles appeared in those oversized sunglasses, all our friends screaming when they realized what was happening. And who knew Dad could body pop? Every time I hear the first strains of that song, I'm transported back to a sandy dance floor in Ibiza with everyone I love in a tight circle around you and me. I think of Mum, somewhere above us, laughing about Dad moaning about getting sand on his posh wedding suit. Why did the man wear a three-piece suit in such hot weather in the first place?

We played it endlessly for weeks afterward and it still makes me smile months later.

Being married to you feels absolutely right. Also I feel like a trendsetter too now that Ed has taken the plunge and proposed. And I KNOW you are going to try and persuade Hattie to get mini Connect 4's at theirs—and I will support you in that. Haha.

But that day, that week in Ibiza on our honeymoon, just the two of us, has brought other things into sharper focus. Wedding planning, parenting, work, committees, sporting fixtures, book launches—we lead such busy, full lives and I like that we do separate things—that we used to come together and tell each other about the people we work with or saw that day. But in the last couple of years we barely do things as a couple. And if we're together inevitably one or both of the kids is there too. Making those vows reminded me that all this starts and ends with us.

We need to keep carving out time for each other—it's so easy to just collapse next door to each other and not really talk. Or swap endless details about the kids and forget to ask anything else. I know I'm guilty of that. But in the past, when we've set aside time out together to do things we both love, it has always brought us closer. Because we haven't always acted like a couple, we've shared the same space but we've been focused on different things. Sometimes I convince myself it's healthy, it's good to have separate lives, but not when one person is unhappy, or struggling. So, even though I didn't think two rings would really change things for us, it's a reminder that we should be sharing our lives together. Now, don't panic, I'm not going to start tagging along to all your book launches and asking your authors how they all write good, but I am going to make you sit down with me and the wall calendar and ensure we are putting ourselves front and center.

This year has been a reminder that I love you so much, that we have drifted apart at times but that we are best together.

So here's hoping we can keep making that effort. I love you, gorgeous wife.

Dan x

43

"Hattie," I screamed, running across the road. "Hattie."

I watched as she blundered out from the crumpled, steaming vehicle, heard the sound she made when she looked in the road. Her terrible scream. Then guttural noises as she lurched backward. She hadn't heard me calling. She only had eyes for Dan, inert, in the road, Gus whining and nudging him.

She was staggering backward when someone appeared from the darkness, a man in a dressing gown hushing her, steering her gently to the pavement with soothing words. A woman joined them, others opened doors and windows, footsteps, urgent words.

It was only when I was standing a meter away from her that she took in my presence.

"Emma . . . Emma!" Her voice was strangled, choked.

The two strangers looked at me as I stared down at her, my chest heaving up and down, up and down, my breath a cloud in the air as I shouted, "You killed him, you fucking killed him!"

The words streamed from my mouth, ugly, accusatory, spittle flying, eyes rolling. Every awful thing vomited her way, intended to hurt. I hadn't realized I'd advanced on her, clawing at the air as I furiously shouted. "You. You . . . oh my God."

She looked numb as the man in the dressing gown moved, clamped onto my arms, wrenched me back from her.

"Get off," I screeched, "What the fuck, Hattie, what the—" I didn't recognize the voice I was shouting in, high, frantic, furious.

"Stop, stop this."

Voices, other hands, someone was kneeling in the street, someone else was shouting instructions into a mobile phone. In the distance a siren could already be heard as I strained and bucked against the people restraining me.

She was barely registering it, repeating phrases, words, her eyes fixed on the road, hugging her body tight. "I . . . oh my God. Emma. I . . ."

I realized she was only wearing a T-shirt, thin cotton pajama bottoms. Her teeth were chattering, her eyes wild as she struggled to get any words out.

"I left, I left him. The baby—he said—next time—next time it would be . . ." She broke at that point. Disjointed and rambling. "I drove here but there was ice, the car . . . then the dog—I didn't want to hit the dog, but the man, I felt him . . . I felt . . ."

I wasn't listening to her, just staring, my face screwed up in fury. Hattie. The driver being comforted on that first night by these people was Hattie. Hattie had been the one to kill him. Without her, that first night, this whole thing would never have begun. It was her fault—all of this, every time I lived through this day, it was her fault. If she'd never been here, Dan would never have died the first time and set this never-ending day in motion.

"And it was Dan, I saw him, Emma. Oh my God. It was Dan." Her face filling with the agony of it.

Hattie had killed Dan. Hattie. Hattie who we loved and trusted and left in charge of our children. Hattie, the first to phone in a crisis, the first to come over with ice cream and wine, the first to offer to babysit if we were ill. Hattie. His own sister. None of this would have happened if she hadn't run him down, none of it.

Then another sound broke into my head, a voice I knew too well. Shrill, terrified. And then a scream.

"Mum. MUM!"

Hattie struggled to her feet too, both of us reacting to the voice.

Something twisted in my gut as I turned and saw my young daughter, oversized unicorn slippers absurd in this moment. Her face was a terrible mask of pain as she rushed forward, took in her father, the grotesque angle of his limbs, the blood that had leaked farther, a lake of it, the glaze of his eyes. Gus sitting dolefully at his head, still waiting for his master to get up.

Oh my God.

Hattie was moaning as she saw her too. "Poppy, I . . . oh God, *Poppy*."

"Don't touch her!" I screamed as Hattie stepped forward, Poppy tumbling into my arms.

Hattie froze beyond and I stared at her over Poppy's shoulder, soothing, circling. "I've got you, I've got you," I repeated.

The ambulance arrived, paramedics spilling out of the side door, jumping into the road with their bags of equipment and serious faces, lit by blue flashes as they bent over Dan in the road. Poppy shuddered as she watched them check Dan, their movements becoming less urgent when they realized he was dead. Wailing, she squirmed out of my arms, a paramedic intercepting her and drawing her to one side.

I should go to her but I was still staring at Hattie, the woman I loved who had ruined our lives.

The police were seconds behind, the street slowly filling with different emergency vehicles stopped at angles, squeezed into the narrow street. I saw neighbors pointing at Hattie. A policeman moved toward her, handcuffs swinging on his belt, his hat obscuring part of his face. They would arrest her. She deserved it, I thought, fists curling. She deserves whatever happens.

She seemed somewhere else, her eyes fixed on Dan's body, her arms hugging her own. She was barely aware of the policeman now standing in front of her as she turned to me slowly. "Emma, he can't be dead, he can't be . . ."

I couldn't respond, taking two steps backward, anger filling me up as I looked at her wretched face.

I had to go to my daughter, now held by the paramedic. She was snot and whimpers and fear. I had to go. I had to get her away from this scene.

"This is the driver who killed him," I said to the policeman, voice shaking. I lifted a finger, anger making my hand tremble as I pointed it at her. "This is the woman who killed my husband."

I bent and picked up Gus, his body heavy, a whine: not wanting to leave Dan's side.

Hattie's legs gave way and she sank to the pavement as I moved away. As Poppy called out for her dad.

I walked in the opposite direction, back to my ten-year-old baby, to hold her, comfort her, knowing that nothing would ever be the same again. I didn't think my heart could fracture any further.

Hattie.

Missed Call: Unknown number.

121: One answerphone message.

I'm sorry, Emma. I'm so sorry. I, please . . . I have to speak to you, to explain. Not explain, but Emma please. Will you tell Dad? I'm in Acton police station. I need to talk to you though, I think they'll keep me here. Emma, I didn't mean . . . I would never . . . Emma, I loved him too. Emma . . .

44

I was on my side, facing the window.

The sound of a bicycle bell.

I opened my eyes and winced. A slight crack in the curtains, a shaft of sunlight crossing my face.

I turned over.

Dan.

It was Hattie. It was Hattie. All this time it was Hattie.

The days passed and I didn't get out of bed. Although outwardly everything seemed the same, a repeat of the last twenty-four hours, inside I was aging rapidly, months and years passing on my face, on my skin, in my bones. I was so tired. And no matter what I did, Dan died. He died when he went out, he died when he stayed home. He died every day, at 10:17 p.m. He died because of Hattie. She had started it all, she'd stuck us in this day and ruined all our lives.

Some nights stood out. The night where I'd screamed at him not to go out, not to be run down. Watching his face contort mid-argument, his hand clawing at his chest as he fell to the floor in front of me. Both children stood in the doorway behind, drawn by our shouts. Their screams as he fell.

The night Poppy and I had rowed, the moment she left the house, flying out into the street, Dan running after her. The fear that had flooded my body as I shouted and shouted for her to come back, slipping in the street as I searched for her. What if I found her? What if she was lying in that road? She witnessed the crash that night, screaming as her dad cartwheeled through the air, screaming as I wrapped myself around her, tried to press her to me, to force her not to look.

The nights I spent next to him, lying where he'd fallen, one hand holding his. Feeling the gradual chill of his flesh, the unnatural color of his skin, closing his eyes. He wasn't Dan anymore; the energy, soul, whatever it was that made him *him* had left.

The nights when I asked others to come round, begged them to be there, to save him. The retired GP who'd pitied me, his disbelieving face when he watched Dan die in front of him. His desperate attempts to resuscitate him: all useless. Nothing mattered. Nothing made any difference. He always died. I couldn't stop it. He always died.

The darkness swallowed me whole.

The days became a blur. I wasted them. I didn't get out of bed. I was barely present. When I bothered to leave our bedroom I didn't make meals, just ate Twix bars, Pot Noodles, marshmallows, and whatever else I could see. I didn't bother to wash or dress or do my hair or wear my makeup.

Some days I didn't even get out of bed or talk. Some days I was angry with everyone and everything, lashing out, screaming abuse: at Dan. At the world. Those days sent me spiraling, head screeching with pain as I cried and Dan paced. Was I having a breakdown? He didn't know what to do. That night he died in our bed, holding me while I raged at the world.

I was on my side, facing the window.

The sound of a bicycle bell.

I opened my eyes and winced. A slight crack in the curtains, a shaft of sunlight crossing my face.

I turned over.

Other days I got angry in different places. In the supermarket, steered out by security, the crazy bag lady. I got angry at Poppy's school, humiliating her and Miles as I swore at Holly and Liam in the playground. The teachers threatening to call the police. I got angry on Facebook, writing long, incendiary posts, insulting strangers I'd never met. I messaged the bike lady that I would melt down the fucking bike unless she picked it up NOW. That night he died in the conservatory where he'd miserably retreated after another row with me.

Sometimes I channeled it into my WhatsApp messages and Denise felt the full wrath of my mood.

Other days I got angry on Twitter. It was the perfect forum for my bile.

I tweeted celebrities who I loathed, big brand names for past poor customer service. I tweeted an editor who once turned one of my books down by curtly telling me, "I was offended you thought to send me this book." That one went viral.

I tweeted the patronizing male Senior Commissioning Editor asking why he only ever commissioned books from male agents he played in a squash league with.

I tweeted the awful big-name author who never quoted on anyone's books and when asked in interviews to give book recommendations only ever gave the names of dead authors. That one caused a flurry of direct messages, mad-eyed emojis, people doing the dancing emoji, the cry-laughing emoji, and one or two asking me if I was OK and actively trying to get fired.

By the end of the day I couldn't keep up with the notifications and direct messages and I was totally drunk on the power, and, by that time, also totally drunk.

And it was in this post-Twitter/alcohol frenzy that Dan found me and got really angry. And that night he died, alone, downstairs, while I sobbed in our bed, too self-pitying to go to him.

None of it made a lasting difference: none of it helped me stuff the black hole that was gaping within me.

Denise @Emma I do not appreciate being called a “Playgroup Nazi’

AuthorLou @Emma I am not needy!

Amelia @Emma Oh my God. I’ve written like 3,500 words! What am I meant to do with them? Throw them away? Oh my God. This is sooooo not cool. Answer your phone.

45

I was on my side, facing the window.

The sound of a bicycle bell.

I opened my eyes and winced. A slight crack in the curtains, a shaft of sunlight crossing my face.

I turned over.

On other days I deleted Lou's messages and I dumped Amelia over Instagram, imagining her crying into a large, oversized cocktail. And dumping her solidified the thoughts that had been building inside me for months. The reason I'd wanted the meeting with Linda. That night Dan died in the kitchen ignoring me as I simmered with rage, sploshing red wine around as I ranted.

The next morning I headed straight into work, bursting in on them in Linda's filthy office after they'd sent Jas out for the bloody pods.

"Gemma," Arthur said, his voice oily with condescension.

"It's Emma," I rounded on him. "Which you should know being that I've worked here for seven years. Seven fucking years, Arthur."

Linda made a strange squawking noise, fluttering already to appease her client. "Emma, this is unacceptable!"

"No, Linda." I rounded on her, "No, do you know what's unacceptable? You sitting there listening to this hideous misogynist! How can you represent this guy? He's disgusting. We should have got rid of him after that bullying claim, someone who was *finally* brave enough to break the silence about him. And we swept it all away. We're a joke for keeping him on, worse, because it's not actually funny."

Linda was so shocked she simply sat there and stared at me as I warmed to my theme. "I was going to ask for a pay rise, a role for Jas, who by the way you barely notice unless she hasn't replaced the handwash or fixed your fucking printer, but who has worked tirelessly to discover new ways of making *you* money. But I don't want a pay rise, or a new role for Jas, or freedom over my own list. I want out. I want to leave and take my clients with me. And because your filing system is a joke and you don't believe in paper I've checked and I can. So I will."

Linda was spluttering now; Arthur had stood to defend her honor. "This is the tragedy of hiring women, Linda. So emotional." The office was cramped; books looked to be teetering over us all, ready to bury us.

"It's not being emotional, it's being a decent human being, you selfish, corduroy-wearing prick. And do you know what," I added, spinning around, "we have to be nice to you because we're professionals. But there is no justice in the world when your shitty, lazy books full of bad tropes and clunky exposition that you refuse to edit 'because the work is done' are still selling."

"Emma, apologize to Mr. Chumley!"

"Absolutely no way. I quit. And also," I said, "you better start to learn how to use your printer because I will be taking

Jas with me." I finished, leaving them both, mouths gaping. Jas stood frozen in the doorway, eyes round, a box of coffee pods hanging loosely by her side.

"My books do not have clunky exposition . . ."

Jas followed me out without a sound. That night I don't know how Dan died because I stayed out by myself, ignoring his increasingly frantic calls and messages.

I was on my side, facing the window.

The sound of a bicycle bell.

I opened my eyes and winced. A slight crack in the curtains, a shaft of sunlight crossing my face.

I turned over.

On one of the very worst days when messaging my parents was not enough, because they never gave me the satisfaction of replying, I phoned them.

Mum answered the call with a puzzled expression on her face as she squinted at the screen from their balcony in Valencia.

"Emma," she spoke over her shoulder, "it's Emma." Turning back to the screen she said, "Your father is doing the crossword."

Apparently enough of a reason not to walk the few steps to the phone and speak to his only child. "Could you put me on speaker, please?"

"And I can't be too long," she added, just to remind me she'd rather not be on the call either.

"This won't take long."

"Is this about Christmas?" my mother continued, oblivious to my dangerous tone. "We'll be out here. Did we not say?"

"You didn't," I said, my nails biting into my skin. Years of trying to act nonchalantly, enacting Dan's advice, in the hope that that approach might work, a hard habit to break. I broke it.

"You didn't say." I took a breath, "You never say. You don't even think about it, Mum."

"There's no need to be so difficult about it, Emma, it's only one day in the year."

"It's not, Mum, for some people it's not just another day. Some people want to see their grandchildren over Christmas, think it's sad if they don't—"

"Well, if we could be in two places at once," Mum bristled.

"Then I'd imagine you'd choose Spain and somewhere else. Anywhere else. Because you never choose us." I could feel my throat thicken but pushed on, needing to say this stuff, to tell them. "You know you have two grandchildren? They're growing up so quickly and they barely know you, and maybe one day they'll never want to know you. You don't know Dan."

Mum's mouth had puckered as I ranted.

I gripped the phone in my hand. "You don't know me. You show no fucking interest in my life, my family, my work, my friends."

"Emma," Mum finally seemed to react. "This is not called for!"

"It *is* called for. I'm done, Mum. I'm done, done, done."

A noise behind her. "Emma, this is your father," seeing his face appear over Mum's shoulders, his bifocals pushed up on his forehead. "This is no way to speak to your mother."

"I wish I wasn't speaking to either of you like this," I shouted, finally breaking down, finally allowing the tears to flow. "Do you think I want to feel like this? That the two people who were meant to love me never noticed me? I've spent so much of my life trying to be needed because ultimately I thought no one ever would. Well, I am needed and loved and liked and I need you both to know that is not because of anything you two did for me. Happy bloody Christmas," I finished, and I pressed "End call," leaving them both gaping at the screen. That night Dan died next to me in our bed, my hand over his heart as he took his last breath.

It was on days like that one that I missed Hattie the most. Sometimes I wrote messages to her: long, rambling messages I then deleted. I missed her, I hated her, I hated this. I couldn't even tell her the hell I was living in. When my missing her overwhelmed the rest I cried. I felt like I'd lost both of them that night, the two people I loved best. But no matter how much I missed her, I couldn't forgive her, couldn't forget that without her recklessness I wouldn't be stuck in this endless loop where the very worst thing happened to Dan, to my children, to me, again and again and again.

Missed Calls: Hattie (2)

46

I was on my side, facing the window.

The sound of a bicycle bell.

I opened my eyes and winced. A slight crack in the curtains, a shaft of sunlight crossing my face.

I turned over.

Some days, when I had no energy for confrontations, or even thoughts, I watched every streaming service. I sat through hours and hours of shows I'd always wanted to watch and had never found the time to. I watched the kids leave for school, still in my pajamas, Dan's worried face as he left for work, and me sloping out of the house in slippers loading up on chocolate Christmas tree decorations, Skips, Coca-Cola, and Haribo Strawbs for another session. I watched the whole of *Gray's Anatomy*, all fifteen seasons, which took a while. I found Meredith Gray so irritating in the first four seasons that I almost bailed but then I found my mojo and stuck it out. I didn't remember some of the shows afterward. Mouths and bodies moving but the stories weren't going in.

Dan returned on those days, surprised, concerned, a little bit pissed off if I decided to pick a fight but mostly just worried.

Was I feeling OK? Was I ill? The row between Poppy and Miles often distracted him and it felt as if the whole house went to bed crying on those nights. More often than not, Dan died alone, in the kitchen, in the sitting room, once keeling over while brushing his teeth as I miserably listened for the tell-tale thump.

On other days I roamed.

I bought stuff (Tiffany bracelets, silk scarves, Chanel perfume, a sapphire brooch, a ruby ring) and then discarded them nearby. I once got a taxi to Brighton because I wanted to see the sea. It was overcast, the sea churning gray, and when I breathed in the salty air wanting to be brought to life, I didn't feel anything. I got in the taxi and told him to drive me home.

I went to Nobu and ordered sushi and champagne and stared at the chair opposite and I remembered Hattie in the Ritz and the things she told me. I wondered again why she'd driven at that time of night to our house. I thought of Ed. Of her rambling words that night, trying to piece together the fragments of what she'd said. Why she'd been dressed in her pajamas. Then I pushed those thoughts deeper inside me, and when the night came round it wasn't difficult to reignite the anger every time I heard the bang. On those nights, Dan died with me by his side, always with me.

Some days I felt full of energy, a crazy fizzing energy, and those were the days when Netflix wouldn't do, when I would go out in search of adventure or trouble. Shout at people in the street, stand in the road, cars swerving, ambulances, helicopters. I was arrested three times.

Other days I felt the bone-aching weariness of it all. I didn't want to talk to anyone. I stayed in our room and watched the light fade from the windows as the clouds came, watched as it got dark, as the sleet fell in tiny, slushy flakes, listened to

Miles and Poppy fighting in the next room, heard Dan intervene in that calm voice, simmering it down. He would bring me lemon and honey and I would let him believe I was ill, that I would feel better in the morning.

He would wish me a Happy Anniversary, stroke me on my head, leave pills by a cup of water for me to take, leave my Kindle fully charged in case I wanted to read.

I would curl away from him on some days. He would bring me his letter, not even in an envelope. He wanted to talk about us. Once I told him to just fuck off. Fuck off and leave me alone and what was the fucking point.

Some nights I read his letter, felt his pain. *"Sometimes I lie here and even when you're next to me I feel alone."* I let his hurt words seep inside me and do their worst. I was no good to him. I couldn't help him.

Sometimes I let him leave the house. Sometimes I left the room. 10:17 p.m. Sometimes I watched him die. It was very quick, as if he had bent down to reach for something and then just kept going, hitting the floor with a strange thud that always made my flesh prickle. Sometimes I would cover him in a blanket and lie next to him and on other nights I slept alone.

I avoided spending time with Dan. He would try his best, the frustration growing on days where I wouldn't engage. He would leave the letter on my plate, on my pillow. I wouldn't give him one back. He felt forgotten, he felt alone. So did I. We moved around each other like islands of anger.

There was one night when both children watched Dan die. Both screamed for me to do something. Poppy frantically summoning an ambulance, Miles wordlessly clutching Tigger as he stared at his father on the floor, stared at me, wondering at my inaction.

I walked past them both and went upstairs to start the day again.

As I got under the covers, Miles and Poppy frantic downstairs, Poppy screaming my name, Miles crying for his father, I stuffed the pillow over my head, muffling their agony.

It was the first time I thought it. That *I* wanted to die. I wanted to be dead.

I couldn't do this anymore.

Missed Call: Unknown number

47

3rd December 2018

Dear Emma,
I can't believe this is my twelfth letter to you. But I really love that we still do them. Sometimes when life speeds up, and recently it does feel like it's getting faster, it forces me to stop and look around and see where we're at. I mean, it seems two seconds ago Miles was chewing on his crib, now the guy is playing chess (I mean, INCREDIBLY BADLY but STILL).

Miles now being at school means life is a tiny bit less complicated. I love the half-days we take when we drop them both off and sit in our kitchen, drinking coffee, Gus at our feet begging for some more cinnamon swirl. A chance for us to be Emma and Dan, not Emma and Dan the parents: just us.

And yes, I have to hide your phone some days. And yes, I know sometimes that annoys you, but my job is also important and I manage it—OK, not quite a book sold at auction for six figures and in twelve countries and counting (show off) BUT we were nominated in The Drum Awards AND Matt finally got us a coffee machine that froths the milk. Just sayin'.

A big highlight of this year was Hattie's wedding. Seeing Miles and Poppy walk down that aisle scattering petals for Hattie was one of the cutest things EVER, although Miles breaking away because he wanted to show you "THERE'S A MAN STUCK ON A CROSS" definitely pissed off Ed. And yes, maybe it's because he doesn't have kids yet, or maybe it was me laughing that annoyed him, or he was cross the attention shifted from Hattie (who totally found it funny too). God, I don't know with Ed. I know you like him but you should have seen the look on his face. I felt something cold slice into me—like a mask slipped and only I saw it. But I know I was wrong to say something to Hattie on her wedding day, and of course I trust her, I do, but actually she hasn't always had the best taste in boyfriends (ugh, remember Ian?) and this is NOT just me being an overprotective big brother. It really isn't.

I'll drop it now because I don't want to fall out with you about it again. And I'll always be there for Hattie. I just want him to be the person she deserves. Anyway, talking about Hattie's wedding has reminded me that we need to sort out Christmas with them. Hattie wants to host and Poppy and Miles will be fine as long as we ASSURE them Father Christmas will get the memo. Did I tell you Dad's going to the Seychelles with Irene? I mean, they do say you meet people at weddings but Dad was quite the sly dog. Irene the bell ringer rung his bell (sorrrryyyyy, I promised I'd stop making that joke). It'll be weird without him but I'm relieved he's met someone who enjoys history and culture as much as he does so I can stop traipsing around the National Portrait Gallery after him learning about the Tudors (apparently they wore those puffy shorts during the Irish campaign because the terrain was so boggy!).

*I think for you this year has been a bit strange. Turning *whispers* forty seems to have made you a little quiet at times. And I can say this because I am a youthful thirty-nine but it does seem like a proper Grown-Up age, like we should know when to change a hoover bag and be able to name all the Prime Ministers since the Fifties. You said that sometimes it's like someone clicked and your thirties were gone. That you wanted to have done more by now. Sometimes it's like you can't see what we all see—like you're still trying to impress someone that doesn't exist. And I know you hate me saying it, but I do think you should say something to your parents—tell them how you feel—it might help, or at least allow you to let go of the hurt. The fact is they are just two people and loads of other people are paying attention.*

I'm glad we celebrated it. Forty is huge. And, despite almost dying together on a Vespa, I'm so glad we went to Florence. You were right about the place—it was romantic with all those courtyard cafés and cobbled side streets. The best thing? Being alone for a few days, lying in, mooching around side streets, holding hands without embarrassing two children. We must make sure we don't wait for your fiftieth to tick off another destination on your bucket list.

I love you, Emma. Here's to plenty more times together. Here's to slowing down a bit in your forties and taking time out to soak it all in.

Dan x x

PART 3

48

I'd forgotten to stop him again last night. He'd left, the same bang and I was sitting on the sofa staring dejectedly around. Was this it? I'd thought as my husband lay broken in a nearby road.

Poppy had emerged. She'd heard the sirens. She heard me answer the door with a weary sigh to the policeman. She heard what he told me.

I'd barely reacted to the news, almost closing the door on the poor man's surprised face. He must have put it down to shock but there was Poppy pale as a ghost in the hallway behind me, listening to the brand-new information.

They were the most terrible, anguished sounds. I wished I'd remembered to stop him.

Those sounds were still with me the following morning. As I lay on my side, still staring at the now-familiar sight of the crack in the curtains, the shaft of sunlight on my face, the briefest hope that something would be different, then scratching that thought when I turned over to see Dan still there. In this world Dan was still here.

As I snuggled close to him, my whole body feeling weighty and aged, I wished for a day of normality. For me not to be hearing the wails of my beautiful daughter in my head. For my son to not be miserable. For my husband not to be living the last day of his life. For this to just be any other day.

"The kids aren't even up yet. You've got time."

I stayed in bed, enjoying the simple pleasure of being held by my husband as he placed a hand on my hair, an action he had done a thousand times before. Every touch bittersweet.

"Hey," he said, studying my face, "are you all right?"

I hadn't noticed the single tear tracking my cheek until it dripped from my chin. "I'm fine," I said, but I couldn't settle back, the moment had gone.

"Emma?"

"Just tired," I said, twisting round to reassure him with a smile. "Happy anniversary," I added.

His features lifted at the words and I reached across and kissed him on the lips. He had always been a brilliant kisser.

Our first kiss had been at the end of our third date. He had dropped me back at my flat in Ealing which I'd shared with a girl who I'd met on Gumtree and who, I was fairly sure, was a witch—but not one of the good ones—despite the fact it was the opposite end of the Central Line to his house share in Stratford. It had been our third date and the conversation came easily, the shared smiles, the wonderful moments where we agreed, the way he made me laugh. But we had yet to kiss.

I'd lingered on the doorstep, fumbling with my house keys and wondering what had come over me. I wasn't normally this shy but I knew that if I kissed Dan it would be important. That it would be the start of something. So I'd continued to fumble and then I'd felt him move closer, his breath hot on my forehead as I stayed bent over in the dark. The anticipation was killing me, the moment stretching for infinity as he reached a hand out to cup my face. The touch of his fingers, his skin chilly in the January air, sent a shiver through my whole body.

I looked up slowly and his face was inches away, head dipped down, a question in his eyes. Our lips met then and I breathed him in, his hand moving on to my back, drawing me closer. Heat flickered in my stomach at the intensity of it. My legs trembled as I wrapped my arms around him, wanting to drag him through our grotty front door and straight upstairs to my bedroom. When we pulled away we were both breathless, staring at each other, and then he grinned at me, a smile so perfect it made me burst into laughter.

The kiss this morning was a kiss we'd done a thousand times, our lips fitting together, the same frisson as I knew he still wanted me.

"Happy Anniversary to you too," he whispered.

It was all so easy, so straightforward. Our relationship had always just felt right. I'd never needed to hide things from him or lie to him. He wasn't judgmental, he didn't store things up to produce in some argument, some row. But living with the pain of losing him every night and then waking tormented by the fact I couldn't share that with him, that he wouldn't believe it, or if he did that it would frighten him. It had exhausted me.

I didn't want that today. I wanted normality. I wanted to pretend.

So I got up and I got dressed and I greeted my children. I didn't pretend to understand what the knowing looks between Miles and Poppy meant; I squeezed past the bike in the hallway, even finding it in me to complain about the woman not collecting it. I let my phone ping, ping, ping and I left the house to go to work.

Because it's Monday. It's normal. If I could just pretend it was maybe it would become so.

Jurek was wiping the surfaces of the café when I stepped inside. I felt as if I'd been away for months, years. I supposed I had. Blinking, I stepped across to the counter.

I ordered my hazelnut latte, accepted my free blueberry muffin which Jurek immediately popped in a takeaway bag and then, as I was about to walk out, I stopped and chose to perch on a bar stool in the window.

The glass was steaming up with the warm air as I watched passersby in woolen hats and winter coats going about their day. Sipping my coffee, I tried to relax. Be normal. A woman dropped her newspaper, bent to pick it up. I imagined her doing that again the next day, and the next, into perpetuity.

Normal, I internally screamed at myself. *Normal.*

I was grateful when Jurek appeared nearby with his cloth, forcing me out of my thoughts.

"You stay today," he said, the smile with the gap in his teeth. "Normally you whizz," he motioned with his hand and little droplets sprayed from the cloth. "Sorry," he said, quickly rubbing them away.

"I just wanted to . . . feel normal."

"It's good."

"I'll go soon, I work round the corner."

"I know, I know. You are book lady. You always have book."

I smiled at that. "I do. I always have," I added.

"My mother is same. Always book, although her eyes are, how you say, the cataracts, she is not so good now."

"I'm sorry," I said, this glimpse of Jurek's life adding more weight to my sadness. I hadn't even known Jurek's name before and he'd always been so kind. "That must be tough. Are you close?"

He nodded, a sort of amused eye roll too. "She lives in flat in Tulse Hill, she wants me to marry my girlfriend, all the time she asks. She is a romantic. I visit often, since my father . . ." He trailed away, his expression morphing, and I felt another pang in my chest.

"He's not here?"

Jurek shook his head sadly. "He's not here. We bury him back in Poland."

Another customer appeared in the doorway and the gloom lifted from Jurek's face as he threw a greeting their way and moved back behind the counter.

I slid off my bar stool, wrapped up against the cold, and stepped outside, giving Jurek a small wave goodbye.

The taxi was purring outside the agency as I rounded the corner. Stepping back quickly I watched Linda and Arthur get inside and leave, turning away so they couldn't see I was there, relief I had the office to myself.

My hazelnut latte, my blueberry muffin, my untidy desk. It really did feel like it could have been one of any number of Mondays.

I opened up the twenty-seven new emails and ignored the ones that weren't submissions. I didn't want to deal with angry editors, feckless Amelias, and the three from Lou, all increasingly hysterical.

I wanted to lose myself in my work.

So I read. I read the synopsis of a meaty historical crime based in Georgian England, a nonfiction proposal about the importance of the introduction of mink to Scotland, the first few chapters of a romantic comedy, and the new book idea from Scarlet which made me feel fizzy inside. She'd nailed it. A quirky love story set in the London Library between two shy loners. Their voices were perfect even in the short pitch document—such a heart-warming, sweet idea. Would this idea help convince editors to take a chance? I thought then of that enthusiastic call with the US agent, I could mention this book too.

The smallest flicker of the old me reignited for a second. Before I remembered and it was dashed out.

Leaning back in my chair, I stared up at the floating shelf above my desk, at the row of books that lined it, all books that I had helped bring into being. From the first: a crime series set in South Wales with the most fabulous female protagonist, the film option constantly being renewed but the TV show yet to be made; to the latest—a historical saga about a kitchen maid who served in a manor house only to inherit the estate when the lady of the house died. Would I ever be able to add to that shelf again?

The thought broke another little piece of me. Sitting in my office chair, the air smelling of books and coffee, pretending everything was normal. But it wasn't. Nothing was normal.

I knew I had to go soon, had to give myself some purpose because this wasn't it. But it had helped perhaps, a fraction. Helped pull me one step back from the edge. I felt breathless as I remembered the mad anguish of recent nights.

I barely noticed Jas appearing in the doorway in her woolen teal coat, staring intensely at her phone.

"Emma, what the—!" She almost dropped it when she saw me sitting there.

Then she obviously caught sight of my face, my haggard face. I'd never been very good at disguising my feelings and she quickly moved to my side. "Did the meeting go terribly? Are we fired?" she began.

I shook my head. "I didn't go."

Jas put two hands to her face. "Oh God, has she fired you? What's happened?"

"No one's been fired," I said. "I didn't go, I . . ."

And then I told her. Everything. And she hadn't even taken off her coat.

When I'd finished, I was hunched over myself, wrung out of tears, Jas's hand circling my back in total silence.

"I don't know what to do anymore. It hurts too much, it's so tiring. To live it again and again and fuck it up and watch it fail and . . ." I could barely get the words out.

Jas patted me as I wiped fruitlessly at my eyes.

"Every morning I see my son is sad, my daughter is about to blow up her life, and my husband has no idea it's his last day on this planet because his own sister recklessly runs him down with her car."

A noise from Jas, a small whimper at the magnitude of it all.

"And the dog's ill. And I don't even know what with," I added, a bubble of snot making an unedifying appearance as I turned to Jas.

Her face was stricken. Staring at me for a good few seconds, she was clearly completely at a loss for a response. Then she tucked a strand of my hair behind my ear.

"Fuck," she said simply.

And the word made the sides of my mouth lift. "Fuck," I agreed.

"Well . . ." she paused, straightening her shoulders. "Maybe you've been given, like, a chance to save him?" she suggested.

"No," I said, quickly shaking my head. "No, you said that last time. And he still died. He dies every time, Jas."

"I said it last time—you mean we've talked like this before?"

I nodded miserably. "We spoke . . . probably four months ago? Five? Maybe more, I don't know. I haven't kept track."

Jas's face drained. "Five months." Then she sat down slowly.

"That's . . . that's . . . God, Emma, you've watched Dan die every night for five months?" She gulped as she looked at me, her eyes wide. "I'm so sorry."

We sat there glumly. Despite the fact there were no answers, my chest lightened that I'd shared. We even talked about Ernestina's book; Jas thought it was ready to go out, wanted it to be her first submission. It sounded interesting and I encouraged her: she was ready to start her own list.

I knew I was hiding there, avoiding engaging with this day. Nothing was normal and I shouldn't keep pretending it was. And I didn't want to be here when Linda and Arthur returned from screwing up their meeting.

I looked at Jas and took a breath, "Would you ever consider leaving the agency? In the future?"

Jas tipped her head to one side. "I was probably never going to stay forever. But I like it here, I like working with you, I've learned an insane amount."

"But would you come with me if I left? Would you work with me somewhere else?"

Jas barely paused. "Yes," she said, decisively.

"Because I'm going to leave," I said, knowing as I announced it that it was true. That it was definitely what I wanted. No more Linda. No more being tainted by this agency. A new, fresh place where I could build a list I was really proud of, represent people with something to say about the world. Jas at my side, growing her own client base. Then my shoulders slumped. "Not that it matters. I can't hold you to it, you won't remember this tomorrow," I said. For the first time the idea seemed comic and Jas looked at me in surprise as I laughed, my face twisting so it became a sob.

"Oh Emma." Jas scooted over to me and took my hand. "Do you know what I think?"

I wiped at my eyes with the sleeve of my sweater.

"I think if I was going to be stuck in the same day forever I'd be glad that I had a husband like Dan, two kids who I adore DESPITE one being an internet troll . . ." Jas smiled. "I think what I'm saying is maybe this could be, like, a wonderful thing? An opportunity to really get to know them, to reconnect?"

I tilted my head to one side, really listening as she continued. "We always say we never have any time but you do, you now have limitless time with your children and the man you love. It's not all bad. It could be a sort of gift."

"A gift," I repeated. I thought of their faces over the last few months: the hurt, the confusion, the anguish. I didn't want to be the cause of any of that pain anymore. Jas was right, this time could be viewed in a different way. It was an opportunity to cherish them in the moment. Something shifted inside me, a little beam pushing the shadows back.

"Oh, but Emma?" Jas said, letting go of my hand.

"Hmm . . ." I was still lost in thought, making tentative plans, my chest lighter.

"Promise me you'll take Gus to the vet stat, yeah?"

Dan @Emma You seemed a bit quiet this morning, hope you're OK? Love you x x

Jas @Emma Here if you want to talk, or I can travel over. Remember Emma, it could be a gift. Much love, Jas x

49

I was on my side, facing the window.

The sound of a bicycle bell.

I opened my eyes and winced. A slight crack in the curtains, a shaft of sunlight crossing my face.

I turned over.

"Hey," he said.

"Hey," I smiled, actively recalling the things I had gone to sleep promising myself.

A gift.

I reached over and surprised Dan with a kiss. "Happy Anniversary."

He scooted down, his whole body lying warm next to mine, his arms pulling me close. He kissed the side of my neck. "Happy *Date*versary."

I laughed, well sort of honked a bit, then hid my face in his chest and waited there. His hand circled my lower back and I arched against him as I felt his fingers move across my skin.

"The kids aren't up yet," Dan said, a hopeful note to his voice. "You've got time."

"You're right," I said and I sat up slowly, peeling off my pajama top.

Dan's eyes darkened as he took in my naked chest, hurriedly removing his own pajama bottoms before I could change my mind. "Do you want me to clean my teeth?" he asked, voice muffled from our duvet.

Miles thundered past our room and Dan's gaze darted to the door, past experience suggesting that this would put an end to what we were about to do.

Then he looked back at me, encouraged when I met his eye and wiggled out of my own pajama bottoms.

He smiled widely as I moved to straddle him, his eyes traveling my naked body.

"Motion to start every Dateversary like this," he said, cupping my breast in one hand.

"Motion to stop calling it a Dateversary."

Dan laughed, his finger stroking my nipple. "I would literally agree to do anything you say right now."

It was great sex and it felt like a much better way to start the day, reminding me that I loved him, the solid feel of him, the smell of his skin, the way he knew where to stroke, to tease, when to make me shiver and tremble.

"That. Was. Amazing," he said, lying starfished and sweaty.

My limbs relaxed as a genuine laugh erupted out of me.

By the time we both appeared in the kitchen Poppy was downstairs too.

"We've run out of milk," Miles accused, his face rather pitiful.

"Dad's going to get some," I said confidently, flicking on the kettle as I heard the front door click. "Let's have breakfast all together this morning," I said.

A gift.

"And I'll walk you both to school," I said.

Poppy shot Miles a look. We had started letting them walk the three residential streets at the start of the school year and in four months I had probably walked with them once, right at the start, to check it really was safe and Dan and I weren't being irresponsible parents.

Dan returned with milk and cinnamon swirls and I sat back in my chair in the kitchen and looked round at my family. The pastry was still warm and a burst of cinnamon filled my mouth as I watched them all. The winter sun sliced across our kitchen, dust motes dancing in the yellow stripes that lit up Dan's face as he smiled across at me. I chucked the paper bag in our kitchen bin, seeing ripped-up paper with Dan's handwriting. The disappointed letter that had broken my heart so many times. I smiled as I stared at it now, torn up into tiny pieces.

"Won't you be late?" he asked, because of course as far as he knew, I had stayed up long into last night to prep for a meeting I now had zero intention of attending.

"They moved the meeting," I lied, "so I have time."

We squeezed down the hallway, out of the house, and I breathed in the chilly winter morning. The blue sky above stretched ahead, colors still hazy in the morning light, clouds wispy. Seeing the kids in their winter hats and coats, cheeks flushed, reminded me of Bonfire Nights and woodland walks. Miles was quiet as he fell into step beside me and Poppy seemed filled with a nervous energy.

"Are you all right, Miles?" I asked, voice gentle.

"I'm fine, it's not me that . . ."

Poppy flashed him a look and he bit his lip and tailed away. Today, I thought madly, she would send abusive messages to her friends. I looked across at her, at her smooth skin, a smattering of freckles crossing her nose, the gap in her teeth when she spoke—it seemed impossible that she would do anything so unpleasant.

Miles sloped inside but before Poppy left I took hold of her hand. Her eyes rounded in alarm—this was "soooo embarrassing"—and I released her when I realized she was worried people were looking. When had she stopped holding my hand?

"Poppy, can I ask you something?"

She still looked jumpy, her focus not really on me as her eyes darted about the railings of the school. How had I not picked up on this nervous energy?

She shrugged, mumbling, "Sure."

"Whatever happens today can you promise me something?"

Her forehead puckered as she listened.

"Just . . . just promise me you won't post anything on your phone on any social media sites."

Her head snapped up at that. I didn't want to cause a row, tell her how much I knew, and I was still unsure about how it happened. But maybe this would help avoid it. I supposed I'd find out later.

"Can you do that for me?"

She nodded slowly and I leaned forward and hugged her tight. "Can we talk later? Properly. I feel like I hardly know what's going on with you these days."

Something on her face shifted a fraction, the wariness thawing slightly. "Yeah, yeah, all right . . ." And then she gave me the briefest of smiles, the gap in the middle of her top row of teeth a reminder I hadn't seen her smile much lately. It made my chest feel a fraction lighter.

"Love you," I said, quickly, as she adjusted the rucksack on her back.

"Love you too."

The brief walk home was pleasant. I noticed Christmas

wreaths in golds, reds, and greens, green bushy trees silhouetted in windows. Smoke curled from chimneys, ice frosted the low walls and the wrought iron of the gates, twinkling when the sun hit them. We should put up our tree, I should get the decorations down, I loved seeing it in the living room, filling the space with that comforting smell of pine.

I tried not to think about whether I'd ever know Christmas, how long this thing would last. I lifted my chin a little higher, focused on the path ahead. They were thoughts for another time, not when I was trying to see things in a more positive light. Not when I was trying to see it as a gift.

My phone pinged, Hattie asking me for lunch. I quickly deleted the message and kept walking. That wasn't for today either: nothing would blight today.

Now, what could I affect next?

Missed Call: Linda (8)

Jas @Emma Emma are you coming? Linda is losing her nut.

CharterHayley @Emma Emma, where are you?

Dan @Emma Keep thinking about this morning. X X X

50

"Jas," I called as I arrived in the office. "Jas, are you back?"

"Yup, in here slaving," came the reply.

I didn't remove my coat but barreled down the narrow corridor and into our office. Jas was sat, the familiar mustard-yellow sweater, a pencil stuck in her hair.

"You," I said, as I reached across and removed it, "are a publishing stereotype. Do you even use it to write?

"Ha. And also," she glanced at the clock, "how are you back this quickly? How did it go?" She lowered her voice, "Are you alone?"

For a moment I wondered what she was referring to and then realized somewhere in London, Linda and Arthur were blowing up a meeting.

"Oh," I waved a hand dismissively, "I didn't go."

"What the—!" The panic was real and sudden and I held up a hand to stop her.

"It's OK, it's OK, I'll explain another time. I wanted to ask you about that book."

Jas was still all rounded eyes and flapping hands. "Which

book, Emma, there are a lot of books," she said, indicating the eighteen thousand piles of books stacked on every surface in our office alone.

"Ha, ha, very funny. I mean the book you keep asking me to read, by Ernestina, that book."

"Oh," she said, her eyes lighting. "Yes, what about it?"

"Oh my God, I want to read it, obviously—can you send it over?"

"Of course." Jas looked startled as she turned to tap on her keyboard.

"Actually could you print out the synopsis and first three chapters."

"All right, Linda."

"Ha ha."

She clicked on the mouse, and another ancient printer that Linda had never learned how to work whirred as it spat out the pages.

"Amazing," I said. "I'm going to take them to the café, I don't want to be back here when Arthur and Linda return. I would advise you do the same."

"Oh my God, Emma, how are you not more worried? If we lose Arthur we a) probably lose some serious money coming into the agency and b) have to deal with a neurotic Linda, like a turbo neurotic Linda, Linda on speed. And why are you not there anyway?" She narrowed her eyes. "You don't look ill. Are you ill?" She threw her hands up to her face. "Oh God, you haven't got something serious, have you? Invisible but deadly?"

"No," I said, "I haven't. Look, I can't be bothered to explain today—just trust me, OK? Now, hand those over." I held out my hand for them.

Jas paused for a second, the A4 sheets in her fist. "I'm suddenly nervous," she admitted, "like, I really love this book but like what if you don't? What will that mean? What if you don't love it?"

"Jas, oh my God, you're worse than Lou. I'm sure I'll like it."

"No," she said, still not handing the pages over, "you need to *love* it, like, they need to blow you away and you should want to beg me for the rest."

I waggled my fingers impatiently.

Jas bit her lip and relented, placing them in my hand. "If you don't like them what will that say about my judgment, our friendship?" she said dramatically.

"I'm leaving," I said, folding the pages and putting them in my bag as I left the office. Exiting down the darkened corridor I sent an enormous pile of Arthur Chumley thrillers flying. "Oops." I didn't bother to put them back.

The café was almost empty, two women leaning across the narrow table lost in conversation, a pram idling by the side. Jurek greeted me warmly as I approached the counter. I noticed the red tinsel he'd pinned along the countertop, the sprayed Father Christmas silhouettes on the mirrored menu board behind him. The sight vivid, cheering.

"Hazelnut latte. Blueberry muffin?" He was already reaching for the tongs.

"Thank you. I love the decorations," I said at the same time as he spoke.

"Muffin on the house."

I took my coffee and plate over to the window, admiring a small Christmas tree in the corner of the room, baubles golden, fairy lights flashing in the soft light. I settled myself down with the pages.

I was used to reading submissions; you could tell something might have potential from a synopsis, even a cover letter sometimes. But the book was always an unknown. You wanted to be hooked from the first page. Sometimes a first paragraph had given me a thrill. Those books where you felt nervous phoning the author, praying they couldn't hear the tremble in your voice, worrying someone else had got in first because you *needed* to represent the book.

I recalled my first phone call with Lou. How overwhelmed and self-deprecating she'd been on the phone. Her quiet intake of breath as I'd told her I'd loved her writing. That exploring the darker side of motherhood was fascinating, and her setting in the Lake District—the descriptions never slowing the pace—was perfect. "It's a stunning book. I'd love to work with you on it if you would like that?"

Her explosion of excitement. "I'd love that, oh my God, I was so nervous when I hadn't heard anything but, oh my God, you're like my dream agent."

Poor Lou. I needed to set boundaries with her and try to remind her of the excitement rather than the anxiety of it all, manage her expectations better, give her a clearer insight into the world of publishing. It had been partly my fault—I'd assumed she knew what to expect, and I hadn't spent the time I might have done preparing her properly. But how can you truly explain the mad ride of publishing to a writer?

As a heady first-time author you really don't have a clue—imagining when you get an agent, a publishing deal is a cert. Then when you get a publishing deal you have visions of walking into a Waterstones, of immediately seeing your book on the table, possibly a poster of your face on a tube station wall, or a TV advert. A promotion in WHSmith's. A review in *The Times* (glowing, obviously, something about "the defining book of the decade"). Marketing departments talk in jargon that all sounds so thrilling. So when publication day comes, for some it can be an enormous anticlimax. There's no tube poster, no book on a table. In fact, when you ask the bored assistant why it is not on the shelf, he taps his computer and tells you they don't stock it. There is no *Times* review, but three people on Goodreads with names like UnicornGirl67 have told you your writing is lousy, the plot predictable, and they skim-read most of it. Even your own friends and family haven't noticed. One random aunt has bought six copies, two friends you barely remember from primary school leave notes on your Facebook wall. And other than that: radio silence. Lou was experiencing all of this and I needed to support her through it. She was just scared her efforts had been for nothing.

I picked up my mobile and tapped out a message to her. "Let's meet later this week and come up with an action plan!"

Then I settled back to read.

It was obvious from the first page that I was in assured hands. If Jas hadn't told me the author was a mere twenty-six years old I'd have assumed they were older. The premise was great, and the protagonist seemed really interesting—I could see why Jas was excited. It had that great mix of the dark alongside the humorous and, despite the subject matter being pretty devastating, it contained wonderfully poignant moments.

When I went to take a sip of my latte I almost spat it out. It had moved beyond tepid to cold. The women and the pram had left without me noticing and I had finished the twenty-four pages. Outside clouds had gathered, time had moved on while I'd been lost in Glasgow's merchant city. Jurek was grinning at me as I placed the cup down, my face twisted in disgust.

"I'll bring you fresh one," he laughed, "you were off dreaming."

I was disappointed the pages had ended so abruptly: a great sign. It was clear from the synopsis that the book would absolutely deliver. Excitement fizzed in my stomach for Jas and this excellent book.

Jurek replaced the latte and I smiled at him, enjoying the knowledge that I could now sit in this quiet café in London, a city I'd always adored, drinking the best coffee as I ran through potential editors in my head. Jas had been spot on; this was an exhilarating submission, current, fresh, dark, funny. The list of editors who might be interested was already forming in my mind. This would be an ideal first book for Jas—she could really make her mark as an agent in her own right.

"Today you are happy," Jurek commented.

"Today," I tilted my head, "I *am* happy."

I watched him move away, thinking of the tiny exchanges we've always had, and realized that part of the reason I liked coming to the café was seeing him, something joyful in the small moments of his being. A ready smile, a lighthearted comment, something solid and contented in the way he moved. I thought of what I now knew about his life, as complicated as many others—the loss of a father, the worries he had about his mother—and then a simple idea struck me forcibly and I downed the last dregs of the coffee.

"Hold on," I said, flinging on my coat and collecting up my things to return to the office, "I'll be back in a second."

Missed Calls: Linda (3)

Missed Calls: CharterHayley (3)

CharterHayley @Emma Where are you?

Jas @Emma I didn't listen to you and am now trapped in the bathroom waiting for them to leave. Do you like the pages? Say you like the pages.

AuthorLou @Emma I'd really love that! Thank you so much! X

51

3rd December 2019

Dear Emma,

*A fountain pen! I know. I'm forty now so this is how I roll. No mere ballpoint pens for me. I sneer at a ballpoint pen. This velvety smooth pen is all I shall be writing with from now on in. And yes, I know you laugh that I keep it in its own special super-soft suede box but that is how you do not lose things, Emma Jacobs *coughs RIP so many sunglasses.**

I am old. We are both old. Middle-aged if you will. I am prepping for the midlife crisis. I have never been that fussed about cars, I'm not keen on a younger woman so I think I'm just going to go all out weird and start collecting something like bicycle parts or rocks from a specific part of Scotland. We'll see! I'm certainly excited to discover how it'll manifest.

So, of course after more than a year or so of me harping on about Florence and what a great and thoughtful husband

I am you pulled out the stops too. Hattie and you arranging the secret Grease fancy party in the vintage bowling alley with all my friends—er tick—brunch in bed with the kids and then lunch out with you handing me the list. Forty Reasons You Love Me, aka Forty Things to Stroke My Ego.

OK, so admittedly I think you struggled a little with the last five ("The way you nibble on your bread rather than take a bite'? 😂) but it was so bloody cute. And how did I know you loved me? Because you'd printed it off, hole-punched it so I could put it in my "Memories" folder and remembered to put the stickers around the holes because you knew I would love that. (I did. Thank you.)

You are always thinking of someone else. You've got me into vitamins after telling me to get into vitamins for like twenty months. And I've been less ill and you don't even rub it in that it's the vitamins, you're just happy I get less sick. You remember what our kids' friends like to eat, and you send brownies when a friend is sad, flowers when someone is ill, frozen COOK meals to anyone who has given birth, you phone authors late at night when you've just finished their manuscript and are buzzing, you send cards to people for literally anything. Sometimes you send a card to thank them for their card. You are insanely big-hearted.

BUT—can I say something honestly now? You might not like it. But sometimes, because you are trying to do everything, for everyone, sometimes you're exhausted for us. You disappear on us. Not physically, not like your own parents, and not like I did. I know I can't ever take back what I did when Poppy was born but I've made up for it now, so *deep breath* you need to stop throwing it back in my face when we argue, because it hurts. I'm here, I'm present: I'm not going anywhere.

Mentally you disappear—you wander away. Miles or Poppy will be telling you something, or I'll ask you a question and . . . you're just not with us—you're somewhere else. In a conference room at a publisher's, or in a manuscript that has kept you up or in an author meeting, or worrying about a friend's divorce or dreaming up a letter to force the council to reinstate the lollipop man.

I've taken things off you, only to find you doing them anyway, and yes, doubling up on jobs makes me cross—but it's like you don't trust me to get it right. I know you worry about play dates and socialization and what size shoes the kids now take, and their optician appointments and if the dog has been walked long enough (he always has, Gus is literally the laziest dog I know) but it's too much for one human person. So when I offer to do something, you just need to say thanks, and let me do it. I think you need to realize you don't have to agree to everything, you can't please everyone. The kids pull you in a million directions too and you can't run this committee, or set up that online petition, or host every time.

You worry about Hattie like she is your own younger sister too, and she opens up to you in a different way. About the baby stuff. I can't imagine losing two babies, it makes my guts wrench. I try to talk to Ed about it but he just shuts down the conversation. Maybe he's embarrassed or I'm not who he wants to talk to about it. He's never really forgiven me for that comment at the wedding.

I love the way you love my family and how you're always there for people. But you can't shoulder it all. You can't just checklist the day away. We said we would find time together: once the kids were both at school, once our jobs calmed down, once the house got sorted, but there is always something else sucking our time, so we need to be better at prioritizing time off.

Because there is nothing better than those quiet hours together. There is nothing better than the movie afternoons as a family, or bundling the kids into the car for a weekend on some rain-soaked British beach, sand in our toes and mugs of coffee in our hands. And there is absolutely nothing better than us sat opposite each other at a table eating and talking and laughing. Being with you makes me feel completely content.

I love you so much, Emma Jacobs. Happy Thirteenth Anniversary. Not unlucky for me.

Dan xx

52

Jurek didn't speak for the first few minutes when I reappeared with a small box of cases. I slid them across the counter to him. "I wasn't sure which genre she'd like but perhaps your mum could try a few of these," I said, as, perplexed, he picked up one of the CDs. "Audiobooks," I explained.

He looked up at me, his Adam's apple moving up and down.

"I remember you telling me once that your mother was having trouble with her eyes . . ."

He frowned, clearly not recalling the conversation. "Cataracts."

"Well," I said, "maybe these are the answer." I leaned over and pointed. "I can highly recommend the C.D. Major one—she is one of my authors and *The Other Girl* is great if your mum likes her books creepy. I also put a few of our Polish translations in. I'm not sure about the Rosie Blake ones—they might be a bit young—but her last one, *The Gin O'Clock Club*, has a wonderful older character, Teddy, actually based on the author's real granddad—it's cute."

A silence stretched on as Jurek took in the box and I worried

I'd somehow offended him. Did he not want me knowing so much about his mum? Did he think I was forcing my reading tastes on her?

I realized then it wasn't an uncomfortable silence as he pushed back his shoulders, his expression wobbling. "This is . . . you are very thoughtful."

"I'm not," I said, batting away the suggestion. Christ, I mean I had literally only learned his name "today."

"I give you another muffin?" he said, reaching for the tongs.

"No," I laughed, feeling my chest lighten. "Honestly, it was nothing, I'm just pleased your mum might enjoy them."

Jurek closed the lid of the box and gently carried it into a backroom. "She will be so happy, you will make her day."

"Well, I'm really pleased," I said, turning to leave.

"I'll see you tomorrow," he said on his return.

I wavered, my back to him, and then I pivoted to face him. "I think you will," I agreed. And I left the café, my steps light as I returned to the office, as I scooped up my bag and my mobile and told a desperate Jas, waiting to hear my thoughts on the pages, I'd be back in touch soon.

"The book's complete, isn't it?" I checked.

"Yes, it's ready to go. If you think it's good enough?" She bit her lip, hope filling her voice.

"Keep your mobile on today," I called cryptically before slamming the door.

I was still feeling refreshed and brighter when I walked down the street back to our house, the sky a little cloudier, the temperature dropping. I opened the door, squeezed past the bike that today didn't make me want to kick it. In fact, later I might even cycle it. My heart lifted as I took in the bright orange roses on the kitchen island, stopped to bury my nose in them, the sweet scent filling me up.

I had plans for this afternoon and one of them was lying in the basket next to the fridge.

"Oh Gussie, I'm sorry, how are you doing?"

I stroked him and he gave me a pitiful look as if to say it's taken you long enough to notice.

Finding his leash, I carried him out to the car. The vet had moved an appointment to see him and I drove the short distance and coaxed him out.

Gus had been rescued with the intention of being the children's dog. To teach them responsibility, empathy, and care. The kids turned out to be pretty fair-weather dog owners, happy to chase after him, cause chaos in the house (RIP ceramic coasters/glass fruit bowl/most of my shoes), happy to roam after him on sunny days in the park, less keen when it was cloudy and cold or raining. Gus loved us both but became Dan's dog, accompanying him to the office some days where clients would fuss over him, chucking him tennis balls and feeding him treats. He'd pine for him if he went away and spin on the spot when he returned.

The vet emerged in blue scrubs, crinkled eyes over a face mask that he pulled down when he greeted me. Inside the small, square consultation room I gently laid Gus on the table.

"He's lethargic, he's off his food," I explained to the vet, the stethoscope round his neck, the mask back up as he felt gently around Gus's body.

Gus lay perfectly still. He'd always been playful and easy-going—I should have noticed the change in him. Relaxed wasn't struggling, laid-back wasn't lethargic. Shame stabbed me once more.

I wanted the vet to reassure me he'd be OK, that he'd be back to being the idiot we loved. I thought fondly of all the times he hadn't wanted me to leave the house. He would steal one of my socks, race to the sofa, his bottom wiggling feverishly until he had got underneath it and, when I went to rescue said sock, would poke it out of his mouth like a comedy tongue. It never failed to make me laugh. He loved having his belly rubbed and would flagrantly roll about on the floor in front of visitors to see if they would oblige and, if their biscuit just happened to be in reach, they would lose their custard cream to his innocent face.

The vet took his bloods and asked if I could wait in Reception with Gus for the results. I bundled Gus out of the room, his expression bruised after the big needle.

The wait took a while and, with Gus nestled at my feet, I could have started phoning or emailing the people I planned to, I could have scrolled social media. Instead I reached down and stroked him behind his ears, feeling him lean into my hand as we waited together.

When the vet emerged I stood, my palms slippery as he walked the few steps toward me. What was the verdict? How badly ill was our beloved dog?

"Thank you for waiting, Mrs. Jacobs. We ran the bloods and found Gus here does have a raised white blood cell count."

I felt my stomach plummet.

"Fortunately," the vet continued, "none of the major organs appear to be affected. He's fighting an infection. We'll inject him today with Synulox, an antibiotic, and send you home with some tablets. I'd also like to give him something to bring his temperature down and you can administer more of that at home."

I was nodding as he spoke, desperate to fix him.

"He should hopefully start feeling better within twenty-four to forty-eight hours."

My body sagged with the relief that Gus was going to be all right, that this was fixable. I clung to that thought. Gus's problems were fixable.

It's a gift, I repeated. It's a gift.

We left the vet with me professing my thanks, medication in a bag. Even in the car I felt that something inside Gus had been ignited. Maybe that wasn't possible. I placed a hand on his head, my fingers lost to the curls. "Good boy, you're such a gorgeous boy." I was rewarded with a wag of his tail.

The kids were almost home as I let us both in and settled Gus in his bed. I made myself a frothy coffee and sat by the window as the sky grew more overcast. Today had already beaten the endless angry days, the spewing hate, the terrible loneliness. Perhaps Jas was right and I could make something of this time. This weird broken world. I knew one thing: I had to try. I had been so close to giving up, so close to losing everything I loved. This was a chance to get things right.

That thought filled me with hope as I sat back, hands cupped around the warm mug, the enticing smell of coffee in the air. I'd been missing so many of these small, precious moments, not just in this loop but before too, leaping ahead on the To Do List in my head rather than pausing to look around, to feel, to taste, to smell: to live.

Better yet, I could bring joy to other people too. I thought of the pages I'd read earlier, the fact that Jas was waiting on a call. I drew out my phone and scrolled down the names feeling a frisson of possibility, a spark in my belly. Something I hadn't felt in ages.

A gift.

The phone rang and a woman greeted me. "Charlie," I said, launching in, "this isn't totally normal but I'm sending you over a few chapters and a synopsis and I need you to read them today, now really, and get back to me, tonight if you're interested to read more . . . I know . . . I know it's fast but it's important, I think you're going to love them."

Emma @Dan Looking forward to dinner with you tonight. I love you x x

Dan @Emma Happy Dateversary!

Emma @Dan Seriously stop calling it that.

53

It wasn't long before I had a list of four editors crying out for the full manuscript, desperate for Jas to contact them about it, and I was certain that this book would be the making of her.

I rang Jas, holding the phone away from my ear as she squealed in excitement.

"I've got some ideas too of who might want to see it . . . you need to send it out."

"You think I'm ready?"

"You're more than ready."

Jas was quiet for a second. "Thanks so much, Emma."

I was still smiling when Miles returned from school. Rather than sloping past the door he came into the kitchen. Heading to Gus's bed, he nestled down close to him, Gus responding with a thumping tail and a hopeful lick on his hand: always quick to find the treats.

"Be a bit gentle with him, Miles, he's not very well."

Miles looked up at me sharply, worry flashing across his features. "Is he going to die?"

"No. No, it's just an infection. The vet gave him some medicine to make him feel better," I said.

Miles relaxed back into him. "I don't want him to die."

The words threatened to knock me off course but I blinked and distracted myself with questions about Miles's day. Taking a seat, sneaking Miles one half of my Twix, I reveled in his cheerier mood. "We made . . . planetary system . . . Mr. Wilks . . . so stupid anyway because everyone knows you can't . . . English so boring . . ." Was it me or did he still seem slightly less buoyant than normal? He had always been so easy, so calm in the face of Poppy's dramas, that it wasn't hard to assume life was sunny. I studied his face as he spoke. His serious expression as he relayed his day, his face more angular, less the little boy these days, growing up to look increasingly like his dad.

"Mum," he stopped halfway through a story about adverbs. "Why are you looking at me like that?"

"Like what?"

He shrugged and went back to cuddling Gus.

"Is everything all right, Miles? At school?"

There it was, the tiniest bite of a lip, before he answered. "It's OK."

I frowned. Stopping Poppy posting anything online meant that Miles wouldn't have been teased, which meant him and Poppy didn't fall out, so why hadn't that fixed everything? And then I remembered what he'd told me, what had also been worrying him.

"You know," I said, taking a bite of my Twix before picking my words, "when I was at school I was always a bit worried that other people seemed to have a best friend, and I didn't."

Miles was quiet, burying his face in Gus's curls.

"But do you know what?" I said, looking at them both,

surprised how big Miles seemed next to Gus, no longer able to fit in the basket with him, curl his body round him as he'd once done. "I liked being friends with lots of people, moving between groups."

Miles sat up, peeking at me under his eyelashes. "Albie won't even play with me anymore and we used to be friends."

I swallowed my instant reaction to start ranting about Albie and instead listened to my son.

"I think Liam told him not to because he's his best friend."

"Well," I said carefully, "that's not really what being a best friend is. It doesn't mean you should leave out other people."

Miles nodded miserably.

"You'll find your best friend one day, Miles, or have a few of them," I said, leaning down to be more at his eye level. "You will meet so many people and some of them will be your people. OK?"

He looked up at me then, at the same moment we heard keys in the front door.

"Aunt Hattie's your best friend, isn't she?"

"Well, um," I hesitated. "Yes, she is," I said carefully, feeling my throat thicken at the words. In the months after Dan had left me, she'd become the most important person in my life. She had been there all the time, helping with Poppy, cooking meals, making me smile. She had become my sister too, insisting on sleeping on the sofa some nights when she knew I was wobbly. I know she thought of me as her best friend too. The pressure on my chest was building as I thought of her face, suddenly not seeing the woman behind the wheel of a car but Hattie, fleeing Ed for a reason she hadn't been brave enough to share. Something tiny shifted inside me.

Glancing at my phone I remembered every message I'd deleted in anger, my fingers tingling. Should I?

"And Dad," Miles added.

"Dad?"

"He's your best friend."

I smiled as Dan appeared in the doorway to the kitchen, cheeks flushed from the cold, tugging off his scarf.

"He is," I agreed, warmth filling me up.

Dan appeared and I wordlessly got up to make him a tea, handing him the mug and his own Twix.

"I love the roses," I said, leaning to kiss him.

I left Miles and him together and went up to the office to write my anniversary letter. I took care with my words, knowing what they would mean to him. Forcing back the darker thoughts that swirled at the edges, I recalled Jas's words to me. It was about living in the present, making *this* day count.

The floor above my office was pounding as I was working on an analogy about my love for Dan being like an orange rose, and the more I noticed, the less the analogy made sense. "You smell good, like a rose, and are bright like an orange" was not my best work. Rolling my eyes, I stood up and left the room, ascending the stairs rather than texting Poppy to turn it down. I was growing, I smiled to myself. And for some reason I totally forgot to knock and appeared right in the middle of seeing my ten-year-old daughter, fully made up, scarlet lipstick, and school shirt knotted over her stomach, talking at her mobile phone, which was attached to a professional-looking tripod in front of a circular light.

"What the . . ."

Her eyes widened, her hands flew to her bare stomach, and I backed out as if I had stumbled into something horrifying.

As I reversed onto the landing my brain caught up with me. Hold on a second. This is my ten-year-old! She'll be practicing dance, right? She'll be . . . Everything was muddled. I remembered the orange dots in my sink, my bronzer. She had been using my makeup. Why would she wear makeup to practice dance? She was filming herself, to check her moves, but then why the light . . . ? And the comments, on TikTok. I needed to face up to this.

I stepped back inside her room. She had hurriedly unknotted her shirt so it hung, crumpled and loose. The phone was now off and in her hand, the tripod and light still there, making her skin glow.

"What are you doing? You better tell me now."

I bit down the urge to end "young lady."

The fact she wasn't getting cross with me for bursting in told me everything. Jas's "it's a gift' slipped from my mind as, without waiting for an answer, I launched into a tirade.

"Is this TikTok? You're too young! Why would you film this? Who are you sending things to? How long have you been doing this?" I didn't wait for answers and my voice was shrill and high. "You don't know who's watching! We trusted you. We said just WhatsApp. Take that makeup off now."

Then Dan was in the room, taking in the scene, and he was asking his own questions and the atmosphere was fraught and then Miles was there and he was saying "Tell them Poppy" and Poppy had started to cry. And the pleasant evening was definitely ruined. And I knew I could do it a lot better . . .

The next day I did better. I'd remembered to warn her in the morning not to write anything online and then I intercepted Poppy after school, knocked on the door of her room to change her bedding, folded sheets in my arms.

She drew back the door to her space slowly. There was no tripod, no circular light on—although it was propped up on her desk. And there was the tripod folded in the corner. How had I never noticed it before?

"What's that for?" I inquired politely, perching on the end of her bed still clutching the sheets.

"Oh, like . . ." Her eyes shifted from left to right as she obviously ran through a story. I felt a stab of sadness that she felt she needed to lie.

"Is it to put your phone on? How clever," I said, my mouth a little dry. Be cool, Emma, take your time, wait it out.

"Um . . . yeah, yeah, it is."

"So do you record yourself doing dancing and things. For social media?"

She looked utterly miserable as she nodded. "For TikTok," she admitted.

"Do you have an account?"

"Yes," she whispered, tingeing as though bracing for a lecture about trust. "Are you going to tell me to stop?"

I had been. That was precisely why I was there. *Obviously* I was going to tell her to stop. But . . .

"Do you like doing them?" I found myself asking.

She pressed her lips together and nodded once more.

"Well." I took a breath, "Are you any good?"

She looked up, smiling tentatively, then flicked her phone screen open to show me one of her latest clips on her mobile.

She was good. Her moves were slick and totally in time to the song. And the makeup looked less shocking on the video. Her face bright.

"You know you don't need that makeup," I said, gently. "You're so beautiful already. Go on," I said, pointing at the phone. "Show me the rest."

She lingered before doing it and then bowed her head. Guilt washed over me. She looked genuinely sad. And the videos obviously brought her joy. "They've got a WhatsApp group," she said quietly so I almost missed it.

"Who's got a WhatsApp group?"

"Holly and the girls from school. Even Gee's in it."

"Well, what's wrong with that?"

"No, Mum, you don't get it, *everyone's* in it. *Everyone* . . . except me."

I watched a tear drop into her lap, darkening her school trousers. "Gee didn't even tell me, Miles did."

"Miles!" My head snapped round. "How does Miles know about any of it?"

Poppy fiddled with the fabric of her trousers. "Liam was laughing about me, telling him I was a slut."

I winced at the adult word.

"Said Holly set up a group two weeks ago with all the other girls in my class and sends my videos round to everyone."

"That's not kind," I said, wanting to rip down the walls of Holly's home, pull her out into the street, and get her to apologize.

"Every time I do a new one they share it, laugh about it . . . and Gee's in the group." Poppy twisted the cotton in her hand. "She *knew* and she never even told me."

"Oh," I said, realizing why she must have sent those vile messages. Retaliation for this nasty group. The girls targeted—Holly, who had set it up, and Gee, her best friend who had betrayed her—those were the accounts she'd written nasty comments on. I felt sadness pool in the pit of my stomach for all of it.

How had I not realized all this was happening? How had Dan and I missed that she was uploading endless hours on TikTok? I'd always assumed she was dancing, an innocent nineties idea of a hairbrush, a mirror. But I'd heard the strange beats, the voices—why hadn't I checked her room on the countless occasions something had sounded off? I really didn't know my daughter at all. This was a world I needed to understand.

"You know lashing out yourself isn't the answer," I said, realizing as I did who I sounded like. Reasonable, calm, not the woman encouraging her daughter to burn it all down . . . I sounded like Dan. "I can help if you like. We can tell someone at school, get them to stop," I said.

She shook her head from side to side, "No, Mum, I don't want them to get in trouble. I told Miles that. He wanted me to tell you. That's why he's been so . . ."

I thought then of Miles's downturned mouth, the covert looks at his beloved older sister who was being bullied in a way that even he could see was wrenching her apart. He was so open and honest it would have killed him to have kept a secret like that, but he had always adored her, would have obeyed whatever she asked him to do.

It took me a few days of questions and answers, of asking Dan for advice. I learned more, I watched more videos. I was there to support her in her sadness about Gee, realizing the group upset her but it was Gee's betrayal that hurt her the most. That her best friend not only hadn't told her about the group but hadn't left it and allowed the videos to keep circulating.

I had time to practice my speech, the words that really empowered her. Sometimes I failed, overwhelmed her, or made her cross, but the next day I would tweak things and I'd get it spot on. Some days I was exhausted, wanting to speed up the conversation, admit I knew more than I did (I'd learned the light was a ring light, she'd told Dan it was for an art project, he'd got it off Amazon), but other days I just relished the fact that I knew her better, that she was opening up and we could find a way through this weird pre-teen world I needed to admit to myself she was in.

I'd always been determined to show my children they were loved and cherished in a way I had never felt. But my quick and fierce reactions had made Poppy feel she had to hide things from me. And my need for everyone else to like me, to feel that I was doing a great job, meant I hadn't always been focused on them. Pretending to be present, as my mind flitted over the thousand jobs in my head. In this reality I forced myself to really listen, to engage with what they were telling me.

So I nailed down a sort of routine, a kind of checklist. Most mornings began in bed, a lot of mornings began with sex, savoring Dan's enjoyment, our closeness, the smell of him, his hands on my skin, his eyes darkening. I'd get ready, book the vet appointment for first thing, walk the kids to school, warn Poppy off messaging anyone. I headed to the vet's after that, insisting on an injection of Synulox and something to bring down his temperature, the vet often complimenting me on my thorough research, bemusedly agreeing to administer them because the symptoms made sense.

I often went to the office, told Jas she was right about the pages, she should absolutely submit the book, and gave her a list of editors to contact, watched her face break into a smile. I messaged Lou arranging to meet up to discuss an action plan, phoned Scarlet about how much I adored her fourth book idea and that I'd be pitching both books to our co-agent in the US—delighting in giving her hope. I left a note for Linda resigning my job and telling her I'd be in touch but I couldn't work for an agency that didn't see that Arthur was wrong, among a myriad of other things. Then I'd get a coffee with Jurek, my arms always filled with a box of audiobooks for his mum. My good deeds of the day made me feel so light and happy. Sometimes I'd persuade Dan back for lunch, or I'd cycle through Wandsworth Common to meet him, the winter weather biting at my skin as my legs burned with the exercise, head clearing.

A gift.

I would get back and write my letter to Dan, picking out different memories from the last fifteen years. Us in a sweaty upper room of a pub in Clapham, crammed into too small seats watching bad one-woman shows and drinking sticky cider at the bar afterward. Traveling in Australia, walking along a deserted beach on Fraser Island at dusk, a whale turning elegantly in the water only fifty feet from the shore: a performance just for us. The camping holiday Dan dragged me on when we were saving money for the house, woken at an insane hour by Miles who was already desperate to go crabbing. The honeymoon in Ibiza, his arms around me in the infinity pool that looked out over the olive grove that tumbled down the hillside, the air smelling of oranges. I'd draw these memories out slowly, twisting them this way and that, relishing the chance to relive them all and share them with him.

I'd see the kids and some days I'd force them to play games I'd dusted off from the attic. Shrieking over Pictionary, Monopoly, once Twister, everyone a wonderful mess of limbs on the floor. Gus would be brighter, work was on hold, my phone on silent. No more pings that made my chest hurt, reminding me that Hattie was phoning or messaging.

Dan and I would have dinner, I'd enjoy his face as he read the contents of that day's letter, swap idle chat as we settled together on the sofa, my head on his chest, the soft cashmere against my cheek. I'd suggest we go to bed early. So that Dan was comfortable.

I never told him. How could I tell him? He wouldn't believe me. Or he would and it would frighten him.

I ignored the desire to share it, telling myself firmly, as I stretched out next to him, as I held my husband in my arms and heard him take a final breath: this was all that mattered. This moment.

Missed Calls: Hattie (2)

Missed Call: Unknown number

54

3rd December 2020

Dear Emma,
What a year. We're almost there, maybe. Or not. It's really hard to tell what the next few months will bring. I think it's official that global pandemics suck balls. And we should all definitely be awarded some kind of medal. We're still together. I mean, we sort of have to be because as I write this we are in the second lockdown. Neither of us can leave the building—but would you even have the energy to leave me? I am definitely running on about 15 percent these days. Leaving sounds like Very Hard Work. Remember how long it takes to build flatpack furniture? And I wouldn't lend you my electric drill if you left me.

I joke but it has been tough, hasn't it? After the clapping/sunshine/whoop/furlough first lockdown the year has dragged on. It's not as sunny and warm and we're all definitely wearier and less let's-make-a-viral-video-in-our-downtime. Even that Les Mis family have gone quiet.

And I've convinced myself it's the lockdown, it's COVID, it's all the added stresses on you but . . . it still hasn't really forced you to slow down.

In fact, what with back-to-back Zooms, endless reading in the evenings and weekends to catch up because of home-school hell it feels like although I see you all the time, it is rarely in any meaningful way. I feel like we are flatmates sometimes. You're on a committee or dropping a sack of toddler clothes to a neighbor or comforting a friend over the phone on her marital breakup or an author over a rejected book. And it is one of the things I love about you—that you are so generous, loving, kind—but sometimes I feel like we're so far down your list, or we need to be hurting or sad for you to notice us.

Poppy is changing so quickly it throws me off, and although I am trying to be a great dad, a cool dad, I know it is you she often needs to go to for advice or reassurance and sometimes she asks me where you are, when you'll be finished with the meeting or that chat, and I realize it's the fourth evening you're talking to someone on a screen in the office and Poppy has barely spoken to you since the weekend.

I'm sorry if this makes you feel guilty—I don't want you to feel bad for being busy and kind. I just think sometimes you need to ask whether everything is as important. Whether you could drop something to make more space for us. I know you'll laugh and say, "I wish," and make it up to me by having sex, but I'm serious. It's not good for you, or us, if things keep going like this.

Sorry, I don't want to be an arsehole for the whole letter, but I know from past experience that when we write stuff like this down it can prompt us to talk more. I can quote parts of your letters to me from years ago. They've jolted me; they've acted as a reminder of what I could lose. I want to do that for you.

Maybe I'm feeling frustrated because when we've done things together this year it's reminded me how much I love you, love our family. I thought I'd hate homeschooling the kids but—it was, AT TIMES *(let's not go too far) a little bit fun. You googling what a fronted adverbial was (I totally saw you) and then pretending to just know, was a highlight. You laughing with me because* I LITERALLY COULD NOT DO POPPY'S LONG DIVISION *(math has definitely got harder). Obviously where I excelled (and I'm glad to see at least* ONE *of our children might take after me) was presentation—getting them their own little box file, upgrading our home printer, having the excuse to buy myself an industrial-sized hole puncher was the dream.*

We played homeschool relay as best we could. Sometimes I did drop the baton (I am still very sorry about appearing in the back of that marketing meeting asking you whether it was a mole on my bum cheek or a bit of chocolate) and sometimes nailing it—two kids educated, our jobs done, wine opened, nowhere to go, just us moaning about it but feeling like we were doing it together. But God, those crunch times were nuts—the crisis over tickets for Cheltenham, that 200-page presentation for the RFU (it became your turn to remind me that I'd barely spoken a word to the kids for a week), the production company canceling the option on Scarlet's book, trying to be the kids' parent/friend/teacher/counselor—it felt impossible for us both to juggle it all. So no wonder we've had some nights with tense backs to each other, clipped words before bed. "You again'—a morning greeting from you a definite low point.

Although this lockdown has a very Winter Is Coming vibe, it's made me cherish you all even more knowing that families have faced far worse challenges. That we've been lucky—I've felt lucky. Despite the work being almost nonexistent right now, despite the panic in our industry, I'm lucky that, so far, the family and friends we love are OK, that we are not grieving like so many others.

And fun? Well, instead of comedy nights or trips to the West End or jazz in Soho, we've improvised. Some of my best memories have been those evenings—fine dining from precooked boxes, Zoom Coronavision with Hattie and Ed, our living room decked out in the flags of Europe, games nights just the two of us when we had watched the whole of Netflix (who knew you were so good at chess!) and that one risqué Strip Chess Night. (I'm not sure Poppy will ever live down bursting in on me triumphantly shouting I SHALL TAKE YOUR QUEEN. *Therapy cures everything.) The outdoor cinema for my birthday, all of us crammed together on beanbags and blankets in the garden. The renting of a hot tub was a particular stroke of genius.*

I'm so glad Dad has had Irene—I can't believe we haven't seen him for months. And sod your parents—if they want to stay in Spain it's their loss. I'm not sure I'll ever get over watching you faking Miles's birthday card from them. God, it made me want to get on a plane, virus or no virus, and tell them how much they've missed out on. I am sorry they are so shit. And I'm sorry I hadn't realized how much it can affect you. It is NOTHING *to do with you. It is them. And you have us. Not just the kids but Dad and Hattie too—she adopted you years ago. Her evenings, blanket round her shoulders, on a deckchair on our tiny path with her flask of tea as you chat really brought home who loves us.*

So I know this year has been hard, I know we still need to navigate the rest of this pandemic but I am grateful that if they were going to lock me in a house, then at least it was with you.

I love you Emma,

Dan x x

55

There was no doubt I had rediscovered the joys in my day. But there was someone who always cast a shadow. Despite barely looking at my mobile I couldn't help glancing at the messages and missed calls. Any mention of her name from the kids, or Dan, sent a stab of pain through my stomach that never lessened. The questions didn't go away either; in fact, they seemed to multiply over time.

When had she got in her car? Why was she coming to our house? How had she not seen him?

The dreaded bang in the street still marked the moment Dan died and some days I would feel a red-hot anger fire through me at the sound. She had done this. She had killed him. She had run him down repeatedly. On other nights the urge to leave the house, to go to her, to check on her, snuck in and I forced those thoughts away.

I never let Dan leave with Gus, which meant I never had to comfort Poppy again. The memory of what she'd seen shot through me and I was grateful that I could protect her from that at least. Sometimes I left the house with Gus myself, intending to walk that short distance, drawn to that scene. The bang and crunch would send me home, checking on Dan, ensuring the kids didn't see him like that.

Over time, the desire to see Hattie grew stronger—but she was the one person I couldn't face, couldn't fix, couldn't forgive. I had turned to her for every important moment in my adult life; she'd been there with me when even Dan had walked away. I loved her kindness and her thoughtfulness and our shared memories. She'd been hurting, and I hadn't noticed. I'd excused things that I shouldn't have. And then she'd killed Dan and everything had fallen apart.

One evening, letters swapped, dinner eaten, it was too much. I'd looked down at my phone, her name there. So many missed calls. I kissed Dan goodbye, convincing him to wait for me in our bedroom—I wouldn't be long, I promised, not quite able to meet his eye. Pulling on Gus to come, I left the house, my fingers trembling slightly as I put on his leash. Would I turn back again tonight?

The medication I'd administered that morning had already had some effect on Gus and, rather than resist, he trotted out with me. I didn't turn left but set off in the direction of that street, knowing any second I would hear that noise. Sleet coated my face, Gus's fur, as I waited for it. When it came it still made the hairs on my arms stand up. I should get back to the house, to Dan.

But I didn't. I sped up.

Someone else needed me. The car was in the same position, the glass scattered on the glistening icy street. I thought of her words, all those nights ago now, the car losing control, her swerving Gus and Dan. The glass crunched beneath me as I stepped hesitatingly to the driver's side, staring down at her lost to the airbag. Reaching forward I pulled on the handle, wanting to release her, wanting to help her out.

She was shocked, shaky as I shouldered her weight. Confusion etched her features as she realized it was me, her forehead creasing. "Emma, I was . . ." She stared at the crumpled hood, the damage to the side of a parked car. As lights popped on behind curtains I guided her to the pavement. What was I doing here? The urge to see her, to achieve some resolution, weakened as I felt her thin frame.

"You're OK," I said, voice wobbling, wanting to reassure her.

It felt as if I hadn't seen her in months. Because I hadn't. And thinking of the endless loop I'd been living in, robbed me of breath. I stumbled too.

Heads peered from upstairs windows, bodies emerged from their homes as I let her arm go on the pavement, took a step backward, unable to stop thinking again about that first night.

The man in the dressing gown was there, he had his mobile out, others soon joined him, staring at the drama in their small street, "The police are on their way." His tone not as friendly this evening.

The alarm was piercing my skull, the sleet like icy prickles on my skin. My sympathy dissolved as I stared into the road. Dan had been lying there, because of her. Dan *would* be lying there if I didn't stop him. This had all started because of her.

She was pacing the pavement as I scooped up Gus, wanting him in my arms, his warm, still body a comfort.

"Thank God," she said, her voice wobbling. She placed her head in her hands. "Thank God no one was hurt."

I stared at her then, thinking of those words, imagining that first night with Dan in front of the car. Someone had been hurt. Dan had been hurt. Dan had been killed.

I looked away, the strange confusion of memories making my head pound, all the nights merging. The sirens were so close now, almost here. She *had* hurt someone. She'd caused the death of her own brother.

She turned to me, voice urgent. "Can I come home with you, Emma? Tonight? I need to come home with you, after the police."

I stood on wobbly legs, watched a police car pull in just behind us; the man who had broken the news about Dan stepped out.

"No," I said, backing away, clutching Gus to me. "No, I can't. I can't yet. Don't come." I stared at the devastation in the road. "You did this," I said, my throat tightening, unable to forget, not wanting to accept another reason for this nightmare, needing *someone* to blame for everything I'd lived through. "You did this."

I ran.

56

I went back to the same spot the next night, and the next. And the next. I was unable to stop scratching the itch that began every evening as the sleet started dotting the windows. The car would appear, slower than I'd imagined. I would watch as she seemed to inexplicably lose control, black ice, the car swerving helplessly, the terrible moment metal hit metal and the back wheels lifted off the ground, the jolt running through the whole vehicle. One moment I could see her face, the next a white cloud of airbag. I would lurk and stare. I wouldn't go over to her but slope back to the house, and see Dan.

He was always gone. 10:17 p.m. It never altered. And I knew he would always be gone at that time, wherever he was. So somehow, this strange penance, seeing Hattie but still not able to forgive her, was the start of a return to feeling something else. Every night that I stopped Dan leaving didn't just stop him dying in that street: it stopped Hattie running her own brother down, ruining her own life.

She was so close to Dan. I'd never forgotten the agony on her face when I'd rushed to the hospital after his fall from that balcony a decade ago. She'd been bent over him, white and trembling, clutching his hand as she urged him to open his eyes. His fall, his almost death, had frightened her to her core, the fear she might have lost him and their mum in such a short space of time. She had been frantic about the fact that she'd been angry with him that week, frustrated that he wasn't fixing things with me, being a better father.

Then the relief and happiness when that accident had been such a turning point for him, grateful he'd sought help, chosen life. Their relationship grew even closer. I'd find them sometimes gripping their sides over a shared joke from childhood, swapping memories of their mum, Dan casually slinging an arm across her shoulders on a walk. She loved him fiercely, would do anything for him, and had never let us down.

I returned to the scene again and again.

My heart ached as I forgot for a moment about my own pain and watched my friend, a faithful friend, stumble out of her car, staring at the wreckage around her, shocked and upset as she stood on the pavement. Later the owner of the parked car would emerge in a dressing gown, his swear words clear from my end of the street as she cowered, taking it all, before the policeman would draw him away.

She would go to the station. She would always call us from there. Every night. Missed Call: Unknown Number.

One night I answered, listening to her crying into the receiver.

"I had to come," she said. "I had to go somewhere safe."

Shame filled me as I soothed her over the phone. She had needed us. How often had we leaned on her?

The next night I was there. I was there to help her out of the car. I was there to take her home. She was so shocked she agreed to follow me, worrying that she should wait for the police to come.

"I've told them where to find you," I lied as I led her away. Not wanting the police to come tonight. What would it matter?

She followed me meekly as we walked back in the freezing cold, our breath cloudy in the icy air.

"I . . . had to leave . . . I had to get out, to get to you guys."

Her whole body was shivering as I let her quietly into the house, steered her to an armchair.

"Is Dan up?" she asked as I placed our waffle throw over her shoulders.

"He went to bed early," I said carefully. "You'll . . ." I swallowed, "you'll see him in the morning." Because of course he was dead. I didn't need to check tonight.

And in that second I accepted wholeheartedly that it was not Hattie's fault. He always died.

Months of fury dissolved as I looked across at her now, curled into herself in the oversized chair, her face a mask of pain, a red mark across one cheek. I'd wanted to cling to the anger, blame someone, focus all my energy on something tangible. Because it was so unfair, Dan's death felt so unfair. But Hattie hadn't begun any of this. It was always going to happen. The heaviness I'd been dragging around dissolved, the last of my anger left. There was only love and concern for my friend. I needed to be here for her now.

"I'll get you a pillow and duvet," I said, as I walked quietly up the stairs to our bedroom. Stepping inside I looked at him there on our bed, his face unlined as if he really was just sleeping. This was always going to happen, I thought sadly.

I returned to the sitting room with a duvet and pillow.

"I'll see you in the morning," I whispered to her. "I'm so tired."

"Can you wait up?"

"I . . ."

"I'm leaving him, Emma," she murmured. "I . . . I need somewhere to stay."

Instinctively I stepped across to her. "Stay here," I said, sinking to sit by her feet. "Of course." The words felt natural.

She squeezed her eyes closed as her voice shook, "Thank you."

I waited next to her. "What happened?" I asked.

She wrapped her arms around herself.

"Hatts?" I said, craning my neck to peer up at her.

"I lost a baby. A baby girl. Seven weeks."

"I'm sorry," I said, resting my head against her legs.

"It's not right. It hasn't been right for years. With Ed," she admitted. "He's different when we're alone. He's mean. He says things that . . . that hurt me. He refuses to talk to me, sometimes for days. He goes and stays away, never tells me when he'll be back. But tonight . . ." She started softly crying. "Tonight he talked about the baby, about her. He said it so plainly . . ."

She hiccuped as I waited, heart splintering for my friend.

"Said what?"

Then she looked down at me. "He said, 'At least next time it might be a boy,' and then," she swallowed, unable to hold my appalled gaze, "he kept eating his dinner. Just like that. His Dover sole. Like he hadn't just said the most devastating thing."

"Oh my God," I said, my own voice wobbling in the face of her pain.

She wiped a sleeve over her eyes. "It hit me then," she said, her voice stronger. "He'll do what he's always done to me to our child. He'll wear them down like he's worn me down. He'll say cruel things. If we had a girl he'll tell her she's ugly, fat, pathetic. If we have a boy he'll make him like him:

cruel. So I got up, got up to leave. And I can't go back, I won't . . ."

She tailed away. And then she cried again and I squeezed next to her in the armchair and circled her back and told her over and over again that it would be all right. It would. We would fix it together. Tomorrow. We would start again tomorrow.

I stayed with her until she fell asleep in my arms, exhausted. An owl screeched in the dark outside as I held her close, felt her breathing even out. She was safe, she would stay here with us. My best friend.

57

Hattie never crashed her car again because she was always with us.

It would begin with me agreeing to meet her for lunch. I would do my "jobs" that morning, my checklist that made people happy, that made me happy.

Then I'd take Hattie to a different restaurant in London. The South Bank, Mayfair, Fulham; a discreet table, good food. She would tell me about the baby and I would listen and tell her I loved her. Ask her to talk to me about Ed, reveal the ugly truth of him. I always persuaded her to come home with me.

Sometimes Dan would join us. I would look at the two of them and thank every star they had both come into my life. My true family. Then I'd cycle or walk or sit in the window seat at home, warming my hands over frothy coffee as Dan moved around the kitchen, as Hattie stroked Gus, or reading on days I couldn't quite keep the act up in front of them both. A talk with Miles, a pep talk with Poppy. Everyone feeling more at ease. Ready to face things the next day.

My phone on silent, bleeping away to nobody from people I didn't need in this new life.

I was sitting in the kitchen today, Gus nestled at my feet, hands wrapped around my mug, only the gentle tick of the gold sunflower filling the quiet. Dust motes danced in the shafts of winter sun as I closed my eyes and took a deep breath. I'd warmed up from walking the kids to school, a nip in the air that had made me sink lower into my scarf. I relished the feel of Miles's hand in mine as we ambled along. The warmth that infused me when I waved Poppy goodbye. Smiling as I listened to the shouts and giggles of the children in the playground as they bustled inside. I looked forward to my list of jobs, changing my routes some days to explore new London streets, appreciating the vivid red of an unseen wreath or a cheering Christmas tree hung with scrawled homemade decorations.

I returned from lunch with Hattie relaxed and happy. The kids would be home soon and today I didn't feel like another game of Pictionary. It had been painful enough the second or third time but now I knew all the answers and had to remind myself to stop shouting out IRONING and FISHING BOAT after they'd drawn the first line. None of the other games appealed either. I'd emptied the attic, dusting off games we hadn't played for years, or ever, rejected Christmas presents, trips to the charity shop.

Today I knew where we'd go.

"Let's go ice-skating," I said, beaming around the room, Hattie playing gin rummy with Miles. "I'll order a cab; you tell Dad to be ready in five. His scarf and gloves are in the tote bag in the hall with yours. Hattie, I've got stuff you can borrow."

"I should get back to Ed."

"Call him," I said, my voice tight, not wanting her to go through the pain of that day. Not if I could help her avoid it.

Miles leaned in to give her a hug, "Do come, Aunt Tattie," he said, his pet name for her. She relented within seconds.

The Natural History Museum looked beautiful silhouetted in the twilight; dramatic colored lights softened the grand walls as we approached in a babbling group, Hattie linking arms with Poppy and Miles, her face content, the kids smiling. The outdoor rink was stunning; fairy lights hung in the trees that surrounded it, a kiosk selling mulled cider scented the whole place in sweetness. Bundled up in layers we got our skates on and wobbled onto the ice. Dan's hand was firm in mine as we made our way around, growing in confidence with every circuit.

Miles was frightened at first, clinging to the sides or Hattie's hand, but once he realized he could get round slowly he let go and, eyes wide, was seen passing us, legs rigid as he called out a hello, or spinning round grabbing Hattie's waist until they ended up in a laughing heap on the ice. Poppy seemed completely comfortable; she really did have a talent for balance, dance, was able to control her limbs in a way I never could. As I watched her I vowed to encourage that side of her. The sounds of London faded to a blur as I listened to the scrape and sound of the rink, feeling Dan's hand in mine.

A gift.

"What are you thinking?" he asked.

"Just that, this is pretty great, isn't it? All this," I said, throwing out one arm and wobbling as I did so.

"And . . ." he said, knowing me, knowing my brain often flew in a hundred different directions.

And I laughed. "It's true. I really am just thinking that."

"Well, me too," he said, both of us moving in time together

over the smooth surface, watching our children. He reached to kiss me, pulling my head closer with a scarf, making my insides tingle.

The creperie in South Kensington was almost closed as we powered through the doors, filling the small space with noise. The smells—bacon, and cheese and apple and chocolate—clashed in the air as I squeezed into the booth next to Hattie. These days I seemed to notice subtle smells, details in places I'd walked past a hundred times. I felt like Miles and Poppy when they were small, stopping on a pavement to point to a bug on the stone, a yellow-speckled leaf, a disused red postbox buried in an ivy-covered wall. When had I lost that appreciation of the smaller things? I noticed them now.

We ordered savory pancakes, enormous ice cream sundaes, chocolate sauce dribbling down the sides. Miles's face lighter, a total contrast to the glum boy at breakfast. Hattie was making him laugh, two straws under her top lip, a walrus. Miles pretended to be too old, too mature to laugh at such things, and then couldn't help dissolving when she clapped like a seal.

The taxi took us back home, and we dropped Hattie on the way, Ed twitching at the living room curtain.

I took her hands in mine just as she left the cab. "Go and get a bag. Stay with us."

I didn't say anything else, I didn't have to. She paused, but only for a second, Dan tipping his head to one side in a question.

"All right," she agreed. And she was in and out in minutes. I felt the relief, the same relief I felt every day that she was safe and home with us. An image of a crumpled car a little more faded. Her terrible scream now just a whimper in my memory.

"Onesies on. I'll make popcorn," I called as we all squeezed past the bike in the hallway.

"Emma, when is that woman coming to get this bloody thing?"

"Actually," I said, "if it's OK, I think I'm going to keep it."

There was some vague debate over a film but I didn't care. I could have watched anything. Too busy enjoying the heat from Dan's body next to mine, our legs pressed together, Hattie curled in the armchair looking relaxed, Miles and Poppy cuddled into our sides. Blankets, cushions, the candles lit as the weather worsened outside. It was a haven of comfort.

Hattie yawned at the end, making her excuses to go to bed. The kids had stayed up way too late and she offered to take them up with her. Dan kissed them both good night, Poppy leaning in for a cuddle. Hattie almost had to carry Miles upstairs, his head dipping onto his chest with tiredness.

The room was quiet, a gurgle from a radiator, the gentle fizz of the candle.

"What a perfect day," Dan said, resting his head back on the sofa.

I couldn't speak for a second. A glow within me—it had been perfect, giving way to that bittersweet ache when I thought of what was about to happen. A few more droplets of sleet spattered the windows.

"What is it?" He smiled, opening one eye to assess me.

The temptation to tell him overcame me. I hadn't told him, not since those early days when he had dismissed it all as a dream. But I wanted to share this with him, this enormous thing; I could feel my body leaden with my secret.

I reached across and held his hand. "Do you trust me?"

He nodded and I squeezed his fingers.

I took a breath. "You die. Tonight. And there's nothing I can do to stop it. Believe me," I said, a tiny laugh I didn't feel, "I've tried to stop it."

His eyebrows shot toward the sky. “I . . . die,” he said slowly.

I nod miserably.

“How?”

He listened in perfect silence as I told him what had been happening. That he died every night, that he died in our bed at the exact same time.

“What time?” he asked quietly.

I bit my lip. “10:17.”

His eyes widened, his mouth half-opening and then snapping shut. He couldn’t stop the glance at the clock over the mantelpiece, the math making him pause. Neither could I.

“You always die,” I continued. “No matter what I try and do, no matter if there is a doctor here, or you’re in the street, or you’re in the living room. It always ends the same way.”

I didn’t tell him about Hattie, I didn’t need or want to. He wouldn’t be run over tonight; she was safely upstairs now. But he would die. And she hadn’t started this. It would happen wherever he was, during whatever he was doing. I knew that now.

“I used to think I could stop it; it literally made me lose my head. But eventually it made me realize how much time I’ve wasted on the wrong things, the wrong people, when all I wanted was more time with you.”

He squeezed my hand as I forced myself to continue, despite his quiet, shocked face. I needed him to understand.

“We’ve had wonderful days,” I said, trying to swallow down the catch in my throat. “We’ve played for hours with our children, you’ve taught me how to tackle them in their own way, you’ve shown me how to be patient and loving.”

“Like today,” he said, his own eyes now filming with tears as he gripped me. “Today was perfect,” he said simply.

I nodded wordlessly, biting back the words I couldn’t help

thinking: tomorrow someone will press the Reset button and I will need to find the energy to do it all over again. To live in the present, to live in a world where he is still alive.

I don't know whether he truly believed me but he was quiet for a long time. And then, without saying anything else, he took my hand and we walked upstairs together. As we lay down on our bed and he held me close to him, I felt myself relax, limbs loosening, thankful to have shared it all with him. I could feel his warm breath on my hair, his hands on my skin, and that was the last thing I remember before I fell asleep.

58

3rd December 2021

Dear Emma,
I'm in our bathroom writing this. You are asleep in our bed and, if what you've said is true, I am going to die in less than half an hour so I need to be quick.

You've just told me what you've been living through these last few months.

I believe you.

Maybe you'll never read this. And I hope I get to write it tomorrow too. But in case you do . . .

I love you.

Every year I was with you I'd convince myself no man could feel more love. Then when Poppy was born I really knew I couldn't love anyone more than I loved you in that moment. Yet every year my heart expands and expands. I've been so lucky. I've loved my life. I love my life.

Tell our children their father loved them more than they will ever understand. Poppy, our beautiful firstborn with her perma-frown and her impossibly small fingers. My memories of her are endless and wonderful. Her tiny body in that first white bodysuit, the way she'd nuzzle into my neck on dark nights, her warm, chubby toddler body starfishing when she snuck into our bed, trick or treating dressed as a ghost running around the streets on Halloween or curled up in my lap as we watched Frozen *for the billionth time. Now she is talented and funny and fiery and has her own secrets, her own opinions. We get flashes of the woman she'll become and it takes my breath away.*

And Miles, the gentlest soul, with a line of steel running through him. His countless childhood fears of grass and sand and buttons and balloons that would send him flying in our direction for a comforting cuddle, his hand reaching to squeeze ours. His love of jigsaws and building and watching me wield a wrench or saw, forcing me to speak to him in a solemn voice and pretend I knew what I was doing with them. His adoration of his older sister and his gentle approach with any baby or toddler who crosses his path. His rubber face when he impersonates us or his friends and teachers, his shaking laughter when he knows he's made us giggle. I will miss our muddy walks and our bike rides on Wandsworth Common that ended in hot chocolates and scraped knees (normally mine).

They are incredible and I hope they always feel me with them whatever they do and wherever they go. I am so proud to be their dad.

Tell Hattie I have written her a letter too, not long enough, but something. And tell her I am sorry. For what I've missed over the years, those tiny moments that might have meant she knew earlier that she could have told us what was going on. Tell her that she is the best aunt, the best friend, and she will survive it if she leaves him. She's such a warm, generous person and she shouldn't be with someone who takes advantage of that. Tell her I love her. Tell Dad I'm so sorry I left him too. But I'll be with Mum, and I know he'll cherish that.

And you, Emma. Where do I begin? I'm sharing this journey with you. I love you with my whole heart. You are my wonderful, vivacious, ambitious, gorgeous wife. I sometimes think back to that day on the tube. The woman in the scarlet lipstick and the black turtleneck, with the soft laugh. The look you gave me, that knowing half-smile, as if you knew we were already connected somehow. I wanted to be drawn into your world and I have been. I've loved being with you, married to you.

You've been my everything.

Thinking back to that trip in Australia, those weeks have a sort of golden glow—I thought I knew you already but I learned so much more on that trip. On that flight back, as I stared across the aisle at you, earphones on, tears streaking your face from the movie you were absorbed in, I knew I would never be without you. Your concern, your selflessness, your joy infected me and I wanted to be a better person because of you. And I did let you down once, but I hope I have done everything to fix that wrong.

However. I have held back one thing.

I never told you everything about that fall from the balcony, the fall that changed things for me.

But it seems I should tell you now. I felt like I struck a deal that night. I should have died then, Emma. They all said it. That fall from the second story of that house, Hattie finding me in the street below barely conscious, my fall miraculously broken by an old mattress. The bumpy race in the ambulance, Hattie holding my hand crying with shock and relief that I'd landed in that impossible way. You know I like rational things, explanations, but I remember the plea I made to whatever higher power might be listening as I fell.

Please let me live. Give me more time. I can't leave now, not like this. I can't leave Emma, can't leave our child. I want to be with them, want to cherish them. I want to see Emma happy again and living the life she deserves. Next time I'll get it right. Next time I'll make it mean something.

I fell at 10:17 p.m. Hattie phoned the ambulance the moment she saw it happen, they recorded the time, and for some reason when I read the notes that number stuck with me. I should have died at 10:17 p.m.

And yet, I didn't. I lived. And whether that was luck or chance or divine intervention, I'll never know. But I was gifted more time with you. And I took it. And I've been reminded on countless occasions over the years how bloody lucky I was to be returned to you, to be given a next time.

I loved being with you, loved making you laugh so hard you spat coffee, making you squeal in Wimbledon Park playing frisbee with the kids over your head as you pretended to read, glancing up with that enigmatic smile and pretending to be cross, loved snatching a hug in the kitchen and laughing as the kids wiggled in between our legs, loved when you raced home to tell me about a book deal, a film option—the passion in your voice when I listened to you on the phone to an editor or author. All those extra moments I might never have had.

So if what you say really is true, then maybe this was always written in the stars. Maybe somehow I made my deal—I had my chance to make things right with you, to fix all the things I'd broken and make you happy again. What if this was the universe granting you that same privilege? The chance to make things right—to remember us, find us again, love us again. Today was perfect, the absolute reminder that we are always best together. You clutching my hand on the ice, your cheeks flushed, your laugh infectious as we watched Hattie and the kids.

Maybe when any of us dies we will always say it isn't time, that we need another day, another hour, another minute. How lucky we two were then, to get this time.

What a gift.

And to stop me breaking down now, I want to leave you some practical instructions. I don't want this stuff to cause you stress, and you always teased me for being the organized one.

The details for my life insurance are in the top drawer of the desk in that purple A4 envelope folder, along with our passports, wills, marriage certificate, and the kids' birth certificates. All the info about the house, deeds, mortgage etc. is in the red box file in the attic. There's a couple of shoeboxes filled with old photos. Can you give copies of some to Hattie and Dad? I know they'd both really love them.

The furnace had a service last winter so it should be fine until next. And keep paying for furnace insurance because we've saved loads of money in call-out charges. You need to make your peace with the lightbulbs for the kitchen spotlights or get Dad over to do them because he will want to feel helpful. And that Chicken Tarragon recipe you go nuts for is p. 57 of the orange Gary Rhodes book.

Now for the hard bit, but you need to listen to me . . .

You aren't alone.

You have our children, our family, our friends. You have my dad, my sister. I know Matt will want to look in too, other friends of mine will emerge from the woodwork. They are there for you so please let them help you and be there for you. I know you find that hard, but you will be helping them as well as helping yourself.

And most importantly, Emma: you will always have me. I will live on in your memory, in our children, in my family. I know you will keep me alive in everything you do with them. I know you will tell them stories about me, raise them to share our values, mock me even when I'm not there to protest. I know you will keep me with them.

If this is really real, if this is really my goodbye and I don't get to be with you for the rest of our lives, promise me that you will be happy. Choose to live for the both of us. Know that no one could have loved you more or been prouder of you. If I really die tonight then I die knowing no one could have made me happier. Our love, our life together, has been the best thing that ever happened to me.

You are my best friend, my beautiful wife, the mother of my children, and I am going to go to sleep tonight holding you to me and believing that we will meet again, one day. Because who the hell knows anything. And maybe if I ask for that—that might come true too.

I love you. Forever.

Dan x

59

The sound of the alarm.

I am on my side, facing the window.

The hiss of a bus.

A child laughing in the street.

I open my eyes. A slight crack in the curtains, showing gray clouds.

I turn over.

Acknowledgments

This book was a passion project, an idea born a few years ago when I was mid-contract for other things, and a book I wrote during a pandemic as I was gripped with the desire to look more closely at my own life and how I was living it.

I've been incredibly lucky to have found such a passionate team to champion it. Thank you to my agent Alice Lutyens for her endless good humor, great editorial eye, and boundless enthusiasm (and for making me laugh often.) To Kristyn Keene Benton and her team at ICM for being so brilliant.

To Shanika Hyslop, and the wider Curtis Brown team, for such a warm welcome. To the foreign rights team at Curtis Brown—specifically Sarah Harvey, Liz Dennis, and Caoimhe White for shouting about this book far and wide. Thank you also to the literary scouts who have read and championed this novel. To Luke Speed and Anna Wegeulin for their tireless work in the Film and Television Department.

To Julia Stolz and Felicitas Lovenberg at Piper Verlag for their thoughtful and emotional response to the manuscript—I still think about the letter you wrote me.

To my editors at HarperCollins UK and US. To Martha Ashby who broke off her own maternity leave to read and phone me about this book (so Emma!). It has been such a pleasure to work with you and I hope I haven't been "too Lou." To Tessa Woodward for immediately loving Dan and Emma and their story and crying over every draft.

To the wider Harper Fiction team—I'm so lucky to have you all behind me. To Kate Elton, Izzy Coburn, Lynne Drew, Phoebe Morgan, Sarah Shea, Alice Gomer, Liz Dawson, and Abi Salter for writing such wonderful words about the book right at the start. To Chere Tricot in Editorial, to Sophie Raoufi in Marketing, Izzy, Alice, Sarah Munro, Gemma Raynor, Ben Hurd, and Fliss Porter in Sales. To Emilie Chambeyron in PR. And Ellie Game for the cover design. To Fionnuala Barrett and Charlotte Brown in audio and Grace Dent, Dean Russell, Melissa Okusanya, and Hannah Stamp in production. To Sarah Bance for her copyedit and Fran Fabriczki for the proofread.

I'd very much like to thank the whole team at William Morrow, HarperCollins. To Madelyn Blaney for her editorial eye, to DJ DeSmyter in marketing, Julie Paulauski in publicity, Jennifer Hart, and Liate Stehlik, who showed such enthusiasm for this book. To the sales team and all the booksellers, reviewers, and more in the US who work so hard to get the right book into the hands of the right reader. It's humbling to see how many people it takes to bring a good book to life.

To my writer friends who read early drafts or sections of the book: so many amazing, brilliant women and writers. Kirsty Greenwood, Isabelle Broom, Cathy Bramley, Sophie Cousens, Rachael Lucas, Jo West, and Pernille Hughes.

To Ginny Skinner, my screenwriter partner-in-crime, for the plot walks and the chats—I always leave you feeling energized. To Iris Skinner for her TikTok knowledge. Please don't tell me if

I've got it all wrong. To Cat Eastham for info about tech companies in Silicon Valley. To Lara Dearman for her snakes-in-the-grass story that I then edited out of subsequent drafts. Because I'm such a snake in the grass. To Tess Henderson and Ben Gardiner for allowing me to steal their meet-cute for this book; I will never bore of hearing it. Bens are the bestest. To the Jilly Cooper Book Club gang for their cute friendship stories—fabulous women all.

To the many agents and editors I interviewed or who answered publishing questions with such generosity and discretion. Thank you Julia Silk, Sam Copeland, Emily Kitchin, Anna Hogarty, Robert Caskie, Wayne Brookes, Gillian Stern, Diane Beaumont, Miranda Jewess, Louise Buckley, Lucy Irvine, Louise Cullen, Sam Humphreys, Jonathan Eyers, Ed Wood, Alice Sutherland-Hawes, Abi Fellows, George Morley, Gillian Green, Kate Burke, Juliet Mushens, Maddie West, Christina Demosthenous, and Isobel Akenhead. I know I will have left out someone but the long list just demonstrates how many publishing people were willing to give up their time and help a writer out.

To the wider writing community—the book reviewers, bloggers, booksellers who spend so much of their time spreading their love for stories. So many of you have been so supportive in the past. I love being a part of this world.

Lastly thank you to my family—to both my parents David and Basia Martin and my sister Naomi Billington for their brilliant notes on earlier drafts. To Amy, Dena, Rosie, Pangbourne Playgroup, and others that have helped take care of our children thus enabling Ben and me to (just about) stay sane.

This is Book Thirteen and has probably been the most personal book I've ever written—because I feel like I am Emma. This book was inspired by being a working mother pulled in a thousand different directions, trying and failing to focus on the right things and communicating with my (really rather lovely) husband by shouting child-related info at each other—"Where's the metanium?" "She's already done a poo." "We've run out of milk." Etc. Chuck in a global pandemic and it is quite frankly amazing that I got anything done at all and that we still like each other.

Maybe Next Time always had to be dedicated to my husband Ben who I also met in 2006. We barely celebrate our own anniversary because we're always too busy—so maybe this book might inspire us to slow down a bit! I love you lots.